"Those who enjoyed Harry Potter but who seek a feisty, determined female protagonist will find much to appreciate in the complexity and atmosphere of Dreadmarrow Thief."
-D. Donovan, Senior Reviewer, Midwest Book Review

"A novel that celebrates life and love the way only the best fantasy tales can."
-Kirkus Reviews

"A cracking adventure of discovery for all three of them... A book that could be read as a standalone but I am very fascinated to see where it will take me next."
-Susan Hampson, Books from Dusk till Dawn

"The quest narrative is exciting and compelling... a work of classic fantasy."
-The Booklife Prize

'A gripping fantasy adventure. A BRONZE MEDAL WINNER and highly recommended,'
- The Wishing Shelf Book Awards

"An epic quest takes three young people on an unforgettable adventure... this book is wonderful."
-Desert Rose Book Reviews

The Conjurer Fellstone Book One

Dreadmarrow Thief

Marjory Kaptanoglu

FIRST EDITION, OCTOBER 2017

Publisher: www.marjorykaptanoglu.com

Cover Design: www.ebooklaunch.com
Editor: www.bubblecow.com
Formatting: www.polgarusstudio.com

ISBN: 978-0-9994492-1-9 (softcover)
ISBN: 978-0-9994492-2-6 (hardcover)

Printed in the United States of America

For Mom & Pops

Life is a sea of vibrant color. Jump in.

- A.D. Posey

TESSA

Today, my fifth time as a russet sparrow, I felt as if I'd been flying all my life. I left caution behind, soaring over the town square, catching a beakful of rancid smoke rising from the shops and ramshackle homes. My wings flapped according to instinct and carried me toward Sorrenwood's outer edge, over rows of broken shelters. I continued across a field dotted with bent farmhands, past a thicket of trees that gave way to the swimming hole.

I flew lower to watch the three bare-chested boys who approached the water. I'd seen them before but they were younger than me and I could not remember their names. The dark one swung out on the rope and when he reached the highest point, he released with a shout and a splash. His friends followed in rapid succession, nearly landing on him. Their joy was infectious. I sailed up higher and dove down, letting myself fall until—an inch above the water's surface—I pulled up. The pale boy saw me and looked puzzled. He had probably never seen a bird play before.

I rose higher for my second dive. But as I shifted downward, a huge silhouette appeared above me… *a hawk*, its wings spread wide, a monstrous beast to sparrow-me. Shaking, I dodged left and then right and then back again, hoping to confuse it with my odd movements. I followed an erratic course and didn't realize until it was too late, that I'd crossed over the outer wall and now flew above the Cursed Wood. Gray mist seeped upwards like steam from a giant cauldron. The tips of black tangled branches reached toward me, but I knew better than to land on any of its foul trees.

The air whooshed as the hawk dove for me, and I felt a stinging sensation as it clipped off a wad of my feathers. I beat my wings in a panic, angling toward Fellstone Castle. It was a dreary, forbidding fortress but the only place I might find refuge. A shadow formed over me as the hawk prepared to dive again. My confidence shaken, I swore at myself for having so little practice flying. Whether to flap my wings or coast on the wind—I had no idea which would get me to the castle quicker. And so I flapped and coasted and flapped again, aiming to reach the nearest tower. The hawk's breath grazed my back as I flew over the moat, ducked under the edge of the roof, and hurled myself into a tight corner, where I crouched, trembling and desperately wondering what defense I could use if my attacker crawled in after me.

The hawk didn't come. Yet I feared it might still be out there, perched on the roof, waiting with uncanny stillness for me to emerge. That didn't sound like normal hawk behavior, but I knew so little about them. By now I should've been an expert on any animal that wished to make me its supper. I'd grown careless, caught up in the novelty and excitement of flying. My first time out, I only hopped across the yard and took a short flight up into the nearest tree, growing accustomed to the odd sensation of seeing things behind me. With each day I flew, I grew bolder. I'd half-believed, half-hoped the magic lent me a kind of protective shield, keeping other animals from perceiving me. I knew better now. In future, I would watch for shadows, and feel for subtle shifts in the air that flowed around me.

Movement below caught my eye. Down on the castle lawn, six

armed boarmen huddled together, speaking amongst themselves in snorts and grunts. Their pig heads with sharpened tusks were disturbing enough at the best of times, combined with the bodies of herculean men, broadened by thick padding covered in chain mail. Here, alone and unprotected at the castle, I shivered in dread, and shrank further into my corner. Their leader glanced upwards, revealing heavy scars across his eyes and snout. Even from this distance, or maybe because I knew the way they always looked at you, I felt the chill of his cold, black piggish eyes, devoid of feeling. Of course he wasn't looking at me, a little bird under the roof, but at an open window below me. Seconds later, a man extended his arm out the window and lowered it in signal.

The scarred boarman bellowed at another whose ear had been partly chewed off. The group opened up, revealing a frail man on his knees at their center, his hands tied behind his back. Pale and filthy with his clothing torn into strips, he looked as if they'd dragged him from the dungeon only moments earlier. Two of the boarmen lifted him to his feet and shoved him in the direction of the forest. His poor legs appeared weak and spindly from long disuse, but still he loped toward the trees, driven by a final, desperate hope that defied all logic. *If only I could help him.* But even if I flew down to lend him my wings, by the time I changed back, and before I could show the man what to do, the boarmen would surely have murdered us both.

Run, I silently urged. *Run as if the world were on fire beneath your feet.*

The boarmen salivated and raised their spears on their leader's command. The man stumbled just before reaching the trees, clawing his way up, fighting his way forward. *Faster! Don't give up!* The leader signaled for the boarmen to unleash their blood lust, and they pummeled each other to be first to their prey. They thundered across the field, hunched over and pig-like despite having the bodies of men.

Their high-pitched squeals formed a grating war cry as they crashed through the bramble into the woods. Seconds later came a heartrending shriek that froze my blood. The trees shook during the killing frenzy that must have followed.

I couldn't bear to watch any longer. I set out from my refuge, meaning to fly directly home, but instead, curiosity drew me to the window below. I had to see with my own eyes the devil who had ordered that brutal execution. Landing on the sill in the corner, I told myself there was no danger because I looked like nothing but a harmless little bird. At worst he might swish me away, and I would fly off before his hand could touch me.

The man was Lord Fellstone himself. Stripped to the waist, he sprawled in a chair by the window, his feet propped on a low table, and his hands overloaded with jeweled rings. He looked as he had when I last saw him at the Midsummer celebration, with a mane of auburn hair that, considering his age, ought to be showing some grey. His nose was sharp, his eyes shrewd, his manner bored.

But it was the tall young woman beside him who drew my eye with her extraordinary appearance. She was dressed like a man, in close-fitting apparel sewn of dark green leather. She wore a cloth cowl of the same color round her head and neck, hiding her hair. A thin leather mask covered her forehead, cheeks, and the top of her nose, leaving open her mouth and chin. This woman hunched over Lord Fellstone, holding a sturdy, intricately carved wand of black wood. Its tip caught a beam of sunlight from the window and diffused it into a wide circle over a pustulent boil on Lord Fellstone's shoulder. The infection gradually cleared until it was gone. She moved the wand over a second boil that sprawled in a circle of virulent red near his waist.

His lordship raised his head and gave me such a piercing look, it caused the contents of my stomach to flip. His eyes widened in astonishment, until a loud, "Ha!" burst from him.

The woman paused. "My lord?" She followed his gaze to sparrow-me. I tried to leap into the air and fly away, but somehow I couldn't get my claws to let go of the sill. I didn't know if I was frozen in panic or rooted in place by a silent spell Lord Fellstone cast on me.

"Oh, I do love sparrows," he said. He leaned forward, his face growing animated. "You know, this one would make a splendid appetizer for my supper tonight."

"Boiled or roasted?" said the woman.

"Cooked over an open flame on a skewer, I should say. Fetch me my sword."

I couldn't believe my ears. No sensible person would ever eat a sparrow. For two tiny bites of stringy meat, it would not be worth all the trouble of plucking. *Is his lordship mad?* I strained to pull my feet away, while they stubbornly clung to the sill.

The woman lay down the wand and retrieved a sword with jewels encrusted on its handle.

"There won't be anything left of it after we spear it with that," Lord Fellstone said, making me wonder if he'd been playing with me all along. "Why is this bird still here anyway?" His lips curled into a smile that was ripe with evil intent.

My claws released and I shot up into the sky. I raced across the Cursed Wood and over the castle wall with one goal driving me: *get home.* Once during the flight, a shadow moved over me, but it was only a crow. As I reached the house and swooped down toward my window, the crow circled above and turned back the way we'd come. *Did the bird follow me?* I dismissed the thought as quickly as it occurred. My nerves were frayed; soon I'd be imagining eyes peering out of every tree.

The instant I touched my bedroom floor, I scraped three times with my claw. The familiar tingling sensation shot through me as I changed back into myself, Tessa Skye, sixteen years old, wearing a plain wool gown that laced up the front over my white shift. My key pouch hung from a belt that cinched my waist. It was odd how anything I wore or held onto when I changed into a bird would still be with me when I changed back, but magic was a powerful force beyond my understanding, and sometimes one had to simply accept what was, without being able to explain it.

I remained frozen for a moment, struck by the memory of that terrible hunt on the castle grounds. The shrill cry of the wretched man echoed still inside my head.

"Tessa."

I jumped and spun around at the sound of Papa's voice. He stood just behind me, framed by the doorway.

"Papa?" I said, giving him a blank look, masking my fear of what he might have seen.

His form seemed more gaunt than usual, his features stern and angular, his cheeks darkened with the stubble of three days' growth. His eyes fixed on the sparrow amulet that hung from my neck. Normally I tucked it out of sight under my gown, but I hadn't had time.

"Where did you get that?" he said.

I felt my face flush red, but I rallied, affecting a light tone. "I thought you'd gone out."

"The windrider," he said. "Tell me where it came from."

"The what?"

"Your amulet."

I hesitated before answering. "I found it."

"Where?"

"I don't recall."

"Don't tell me a falsehood. I know it was your mother's."

I wanted to bolt but he filled the doorway and I would never make it past him. "I remember now. She gave it to me," I said.

"No, she didn't," he said.

"How do you know?" A tinge of defiance crept into my voice. "You were only four when she went away."

The old feelings of hurt and abandon rose. "I suppose she didn't love me enough to give me anything."

Papa scowled. "Don't talk nonsense. Tell me the truth. How did you get it?"

"I found it on her bedroom floor, the day she left," I said at last. "Was it so awful to take something that reminded me of her?"

"It's not a memento, it's a rare item of powerful magic. Give it to me."

I shrank back from him and clutched my throat. "No, Papa!" He had no idea what he was asking.

"You heard me. Magic is dangerous. Only the conjurers are allowed to use it. If it were up to me, it would be banished altogether."

"But you don't know... you've never felt... there's nothing else like it. Flying is pure and it makes me feel free, and.... How could anything be wrong with it?"

"You can be sure there's a price to be paid in using that magic. Not knowing what that price is makes it all the more troubling." He reached out his hand. "You're young yet. Be patient and good things will come, but not this way."

My eyes filled with tears as I lifted the necklace over my head and handed it to Papa. "I meant no harm."

He softened at the sight of my tears and clasped me to him. "Of course not. You didn't know the danger. Now you do. We'll speak no more of it." He held me for a moment. "Have you been to the Kettlemore's yet? We can't afford to scorn paid work."

I forced my gaze from the hand that clutched my sparrow. "Yes, Papa."

He had called it a windrider. The name suited my amulet; I would use it from now on. I would not despair of flying again, as I had my ways of bending Papa to my will over time. He simply didn't understand and I must find a way to convince him of the benefits. Perhaps he could be made to grasp its value by trying it himself. He would not want to, of course. And the truth was… I didn't want to let him use it. *It's mine and I should not have to share it.*

CALDER

Calder Osric was seated on a stone wall in the middle of the town square, pretending to push a metal straw into his nose and then pull it out of his ear. A small boy no older than six, with ginger hair and freckles on the bridge of his nose, watched in amazement.

His mother… not so amazed. "You said you were going to tell his fortune," she said.

"I'm getting to that," said Calder. "It's an art, you know. And all good art needs preparation. Let me see your palm, young man."

The boy held out his hand and Calder began to trace a line with his straw. The boy jerked his hand back. "Ew!" he said. "That was in your nose."

Calder looked at it. "Was it?" He tossed it aside and held up his finger. "I'm sure this has never been in there."

The boy seemed dubious, but nevertheless he allowed Calder to touch his palm.

"I see a long life full of adventure. Do you like pirates?" Calder said.

"Pirates?" the boy's mother said.

Calder squeezed his one good eye shut, the remnants of the other being covered by a brown leather eye patch. "I see swashbuckling. I hear the clanging of swords, the thump of a wooden leg." He paused to glance at the boy. "Not yours, of course. You'll keep your legs, and hands too. I see them reaching into a treasure chest filled with gold coins."

The boy brightened with excitement. "Were you a pirate once?" he said, pointing at Calder's eye patch.

"This is all nonsense," said his mother. "He's going to be a farmer just like his papa. When will he get married?"

Calder switched to another line on the boy's palm. "Women will throw themselves at him. They always do with pirates. But he'll be too busy commandeering ships to give much time to the ladies." Calder knew he should try harder to please the boy's mother. She had already paid his small fee, but if he gave the boy the future she wanted for him, her satisfaction might increase her generosity. At the very least, she could be inspired to recommend his services to her friends. But when he looked at the boy, who reminded him of so many of the other children growing up in miserable towns like Sorrenwood… he couldn't help himself. The child's eyes still shone with excitement, his soul had not yet been crushed and beaten down into dull acceptance of a lifetime of drudgery. *Let them have hope*, a voice inside him whispered. *Teach them to dream of wondrous lands and fascinating adventures.*

"Oh for goodness sake." The mother took her son's hand and tried to pull him away.

"Wait, Mama!" the lad said.

Calder, who was ever-vigilant, spied a stout constable flanked by two boarmen crossing the road towards him. Accusations of fraud were all too common within the fortunetelling community, forcing Calder to keep a constant lookout for law enforcement brigades and vigilante squads. He patted the boy. "Trick or retreat?" he said.

"Retreat!" the boy shouted without hesitation.

A child after my own heart, thought Calder. "I could tell you were a sharp one," he said, jumping up and tossing his leather bag over his shoulder. "WRAITHS!" he bellowed.

It had the intended effect. Faces transformed into expressions of dread. Women screamed and darted towards shelter, dragging their children. Men ducked behind buildings, reaching for weapons.

Calder bolted away and slipped into the nearest alley.

The constable shouted, "Stop, fortuneteller!" He sent the boarmen after him, their progress impeded by the panic that had enveloped the townsfolk.

Calder raced down the narrow way. A mastiff jumped in front of him and Calder stopped hard. Saliva dripped from the mastiff's jaw as it snarled and bared its teeth.

"Good doggie. Nice doggie." Calder turned sideways, held himself still, and averted his eyes. In fact, he was becoming far too accustomed to people setting their dogs on him. He knew from experience that running was fruitless; only a climbable tree within arm's reach offered any hope of escape from an attack animal.

The mastiff barked in a deep, intimidating tone, ready to pounce. Calder checked behind him to find the boarmen drawing nearer. Turning back to the mastiff, he discovered it had shifted its focus to them. "Smart doggie," he said, creeping past the animal, which maintained its aggressive stance against the boarmen. Just ahead Calder found a hole in the fence that the dog had most likely used. He dove for it and squeezed through, confident the bulky boarmen would never fit.

A whimper from the dog made Calder pause and turn back. The shorter and stouter of the two boarmen had raised his spear toward the mastiff.

"Leave him!" Calder shouted.

The boarman thrust his weapon but stopped just short of cutting the animal. He kept its deadly point pressed against the poor dog, now cowering at his feet.

"Wait!" Calder said, silently cursing himself. *Was there ever a scamp as pathetic as me?* It was just a dog, and not even a terribly nice one, and yet he couldn't bear to be the death of it. He was an idiot, a thorough blockhead, he told himself as he climbed back through the hole. The stout boarman released the mastiff with a kick, and the animal shot to safety with a yowl, but seemed undamaged for the most part. The taller boarman grabbed Calder with a giant hand that nearly crushed his shoulder.

To compound his defeat and humiliation, the boarmen carried Calder between them as if he were a rabbit snared for the slaughter, and brought him to the pillory where a wooden stand had to be placed beneath his feet, as he was somewhat below the average height. Under the constable's directions, they locked his head and hands into the stocks.

"What is the accusation against me?" Calder said.

"Inciting a married woman to adultery," the constable said.

"That's absurd. Do you even know who I am?"

"You're the fortuneteller."

"What, is there only one in this godforsaken place?"

"You're the only one with an eye patch." The constable started to turn away.

"So I'm being persecuted for my disability?" Calder said. "I would not have thought this was that sort of town. Who is my accuser?"

"Mr. Glenn. His wife ran away with the apothecary because you told her she would find romance with a man of science."

"Did she have black hair? I think I know who you mean. She told me she was a widow. I would never have predicted romance for her if I knew she was married."

“Then you admit you make these fortunes up.”

“Certainly not,” Calder said. “Though it may be a stretch to term the apothecary a man of science. Sir, you're blaming the messenger. I had nothing to do with it.”

The constable gestured for the boarmen to follow him.

“When will you let me out?” Calder said.

The constable left without answering. A tomato flew through the air and landed on Calder's forehead. Red juice dripped down over his face, set into lines of misery.

TESSA

I The familiar sound of wood clacking against wood met me as I approached the rear of the carpentry workshop where Ryland was apprenticed. His master took long naps every afternoon, allowing Ryland to sneak off and practice his fencing behind the building, using a sword of white oak he'd crafted himself. This time I found him paired against Ash Kemp, the sexton's son, an odd sort of boy who stole away whenever I showed up, never looking me in the eyes. Ryland glanced my way before leaping forward and going on the offensive. Ash seemed unable to put up much of a defense, to Ryland's annoyance as he did like to show off in front of me.

I didn't care for sword fighting—certainly not for watching it—but I indulged Ryland by leaning against the building and smiling my encouragement. He stepped up his attack, backing his poor opponent against a tree. Ash made a brief recovery before Ryland knocked his weapon out of his hand, leapt on him, and pressed his sword to his chest.

"I surrender," Ash said. He accepted a hand up from Ryland and retrieved his wooden sword, tucking it into his belt. His gaze shifted to the ground and he gave me a curt nod before scurrying away.

Ash wasn't bad to look at—tall and slender, with his light brown hair often tied into a neat ponytail—but he suffered by comparison to his friend. Ryland was broad-shouldered and narrow-hipped, with a fine sculpted face like that of a nobleman. People often asked if he was highborn, when in fact his father had been a potter before the disease that had crippled his hands. All told, Ryland was impossibly handsome, with hair that shone like gold in the sunlight, and a single dimple that was far more charming than if he'd had two. Among seventeen-year-old males, he might not be the sharpest, but he was hard-working, loyal, and rarely argued with me… everything a girl could wish for in a boy.

Ryland lowered his sword with a flourish and drew me into his arms. I sometimes asked myself why he'd picked me. I didn't think of myself as a beauty, though I supposed I looked well enough. Some people made fun of me for being more like a boy than a girl, but I saw no reason why a girl who spent little time fretting over her appearance and who worked as an apprentice and who loved adventure… why a girl like that must be considered more like a boy. Even Ryland often told me how he loved that I wasn't a "typical" girl, but I rejected the notion that girls were all of a type instead of each being unique.

Ryland led me to the bench. When I sat, he knelt before me. "What are you doing?" I said.

"What do you think?"

"Getting your knees dirty."

"Tessa Skye, will you marry me?" Ryland said.

"Don't joke about such things." He had proposed in jest before; I assumed this was more of the same.

"I mean it this time."

"Of course I'm going to marry you," I said. "In a few years."

"We should marry now. My brother and his wife just bought their own home… they'll be moving out from my parents' house soon. That will leave the spare room for us."

"We're to live with your family?" In addition to his parents, Ryland had three sisters at home, and I was not at all fond of two of them. I was used to a quiet house, just Papa and me, and I liked it that way.

"I thought you'd be pleased," he said.

I was pleased, and flattered as well. I fully intended to marry him someday; we only differed in our opinions on when the wedding should take place. If we married right away and moved in with his parents, no doubt they would expect me to give up my apprenticeship and join his mother in the kitchen. There we would prepare meals for the seven of us, or nine when his brother and sister-in-law came to dine. They would most likely begin to have children immediately, and then we would also have the little ones to feed and watch over. I'd been saving my money to avoid just this eventuality. If Ryland was doing the same, we could possibly afford a place of our own in two years.

"I'm only sixteen," I said. "Papa won't approve."

"Lots of girls marry at sixteen."

"Papa will say it's too young."

Ryland rose and turned away from me, annoyed.

Mr. Rees, the carpenter, stuck his head out the workshop door. "Why haven't you finished the table?" he shouted.

"It's my fault," I said before Ryland could speak. "I came to ask for his advice on repairing our door."

Mr. Rees grumbled what sounded like a curse before drawing back inside.

"Please just ask your father," Ryland said. He brushed his lips against mine, leaving me wishing he would linger for a longer kiss.

"If you wish," I said, though I knew what my father's answer would be. But at least then it would be Papa and not me who stood in the way of what Ryland wanted.

He returned to work, and I hurried to reach the Kettlemore's house before they hired someone else. I set a rapid pace across the town square, paying little attention to the activities of others around me, until a woman bumped me in passing. When I glanced up, I noticed a man languishing in the pillory. He was a stranger to me, a smallish fellow with an eye patch who looked near forty years of age. His skin was the color of acorns, and he was rather handsome, or would be if he wasn't splattered with mud and rotten food. Dead rats lay at the man's feet. Whatever his crimes, he didn't deserve this sort of treatment.

I would've moved on, but his leather wristband caught my eye. A cat's head made of pewter was set into it, but more importantly, its style bore a striking resemblance to a band owned by my mother, except hers was a fox. She'd been wearing it when she disappeared from our house. It was the only day I could recall her in every detail, down to the clothes and jewelry she wore, and the way her face was framed by several soft strands of hair that had fallen loose from her braid. My other memories of her floated like wispy clouds through my mind, often taking on new forms, so that I could never be sure what was true, and what imagined.

When I stopped to ask the man where he'd gotten the wristband, he stared down at me with a curious look in his one good eye. After a pause, he answered in a thick voice, his throat hoarse, no doubt, from the pressure of the stocks. "I don't know. I've had it a long time. Why?"

"My mother had a fox bracelet just like it."

His gaze sharpened. "Had? Did she lose it?"

"No, she… never mind. I'm sorry to bother you."

"Wait." He exploded into a fit of coughing and I waited for it to subside. "Does it look like I have better things to do than speak with you?" he said.

"No, but I'm in a hurry."

"What's your mother's name? Maybe she came from my village."

"Gillian Skye."

"I haven't heard of her. Where is she now? I'd like to speak with her."

"She... she isn't here."

A boy of about twelve leapt onto the raised platform and kicked the box out from under the man's feet, and since he was not very tall, he was left dangling from the pillory. Other boys laughed from the square as the man gagged and choked.

"I'll tell your mothers on you!" I shouted, and the boys dispersed, racing away to find some other victim to torment, no doubt. Seeing no one else coming to the man's aid, I pulled myself up onto the platform and slid the box back under his feet.

"Thank you... thank you so much," he croaked. "I'm Calder Osric."

"Why did they put you here?" I said.

"Fortunetelling is a dangerous business... if things don't come out as you predicted... sometimes more so when they do."

I glanced around to confirm no one was watching. Then I whisked out the ring of skeleton keys from my pouch and began to try them on the padlock that held the pillory together. It was a warded lock, which was not likely to require my picks or shims.

"Thank you, but I'm quite sure that isn't going to—" Calder said.

The fourth key turned and caused the latch to spring open.

"I'm Tessa Skye, the locksmith's daughter," I said. "Wait till I'm gone before you let yourself out."

"I owe you a palm reading, and I have a feeling your future will be bright."

I glanced back once as I hurried away, to see Calder lifting the top half of the pillory and slipping out of it. With surprising speed and agility, he jumped down from the platform, retrieved a bag at the bottom of it, and sprinted away.

I wondered if I might ever see him again. But I pushed the incident from my mind as I sped to the doorstep of the Kettlemore home, where Mrs. Kettlemore answered my knock with a sour look. "Don't need your services no more."

"I thought you had a chest that wanted opening," I said.

"Needed it sooner than later. When the collector came, he just told his boarmen to smash it. There weren't much inside, but they took it all anyway. Now we can't sell the chest neither."

"My apologies," I said.

Mrs. Kettlemore slammed the door in my face.

ASH

Today during their practice, Ash had decided not to hold back as he usually did. In the face of his attack, Ryland had become increasingly flustered, despite having greater physical strength. Ash had ignored Ryland's plea to take it easy on him, and kept coming in a flurry of lunges. It wasn't until Tessa approached, and Ryland quickly offered coins in exchange for a performance, that Ash finally let up. His aggression drained from him as he untied his hair and let it fall to his shoulders.

He had returned home directly, feeling dirty though not in the way he usually did after an afternoon of digging and filling in graves. It was his own fault for agreeing to accept sixpence in return for losing the fight. He didn't care about the money; it annoyed him Ryland had offered it. Ash had agreed because Ryland was his friend, and an honorable person always stood by his friends, no matter how difficult or unreasonable their requests. But when he considered his actions later, he had to wonder how honorable it was to do something dishonorable in support of your friends. He did not believe it mattered to Tessa whether he or Ryland were the better swordsman, yet it shamed him to have deceived her.

He enjoyed dueling with Ryland when no one was watching

them. Tying back his hair the way Lance used to do gave him a confidence he'd never felt in the past. If it hadn't been for his brother, he might never have tried using a sword at all. Unlike Lance, he wasn't aggressive as a child. He had liked reading when his work was done, or gazing at the stars after dark, finding the shapes he'd learned and sometimes imagining new ones. But these days he felt an obligation to keep up his skills and become the finest swordsman in these parts, if he could. His talent had improved every day, until he knew he could knock Ryland out of the fight in an instant whenever he chose. But he preferred to practice his moves, even if it must be against a weaker opponent.

In truth, throwing the fight would have meant nothing to him, if he hadn't suddenly felt the urge to impress Tessa himself. He had resisted the impulse, only to be left with a gnawing regret that she would judge him weak and ineffectual. *What does it matter what she thinks?* Generally he avoided girls, who often mocked him for the dirt that got in his pores and under his fingernails, no matter how hard he scrubbed. He'd be lucky to ever find anyone who would look deeper than his sun-darkened skin to see the person he was underneath. Tessa had never been one of those to taunt him, but he feared that was only because she never noticed him at all. The locksmith's daughter was a strange sort of girl—half bold, half skittish and unreliable—he didn't quite know what to make of her. But since she was Ryland's girlfriend, there was no point in thinking about her at all.

He sat in his favorite corner by the window with the sun streaming in and warming him, trying to read a worn volume of poems by Dayim Haru, though his thoughts kept interrupting. He hardly noticed when a rap sounded at the front door, until Father passed him on his way to answer it, throwing him a scowl for not getting up and seeing to it himself.

At the front step, the tax official announced he was taking

collection. Ash stiffened; they had been at the house just last week. He took the strip of leather from his pocket and bound his hair back, before rising and approaching his father.

Father wore his usual air of deference before the smarmy man, who stuck out his fat belly as if it were a source of pride. Most likely he was proud of his job shaking the last pennies out of people who could ill afford to feed their families, and serving the collection up to his greedy master. Two boarmen flanked the tax collector, their lips salivating in the hope of what might transpire in the case of non-payment. Ash felt like retching at the sight of them.

He leaned into his father's ear. "They came last week," he said.

Overhearing Ash, the official hardened his tone. "That's right. It's no longer once a fortnight. We sent a notice. It's every week now."

Father shot Ash a go-get-it nod, but he remained rooted in place.

"We could come inside, if that would help," the tax collector said with a leer.

"Go!" Father told Ash.

He thought of all the ways he would skewer the official and his bodyguards if only he had a real sword, as he fetched the tax money from the drawer in the kitchen. He heard the man tell his father he was supposed to have the money ready when they arrived, and his father's excuse of not having seen the notice. Father promised to have the money ready next time.

Ash returned with the coins and placed them in the tax collector's box. The man counted them and made a note in his ledger. Ash drew back and kept to the shadows, so no one would see the loathing in his face.

#

Ash's mood had not improved by the time he joined his parents for dinner in the kitchen. Two years ago, they had moved the table against the wall to pretend it had always been a table for three, as if that would somehow keep them from dwelling on the place where Lance would never sit again. As if it could possibly keep them from missing him every second of every day of their lives. Ash shoveled in his food, hoping to be excused quickly and avoid all conversation. He knew what his mother wanted to say, and he avoided her gaze so as not to encourage her.

"Mr. Ainsworth, the scribe, said you should come by early tomorrow and he'll give you a lesson," his mother said. "If you do well, he might take you on as apprentice."

"Told you I didn't want to do it," Ash grumbled. All day long, the scribe copied out official documents for the summoners, the bankers, the constable, bailiff, and bloody tax collectors. Documents that were used to rob, to cheat, to arrest, and sometimes, to kill. *Why would I ever want to be a part of that?*

Reading his mind, she said, "It's just writing what they tell you. It isn't as though you have to come up with the words yourself, is it? If you don't do it, someone else will."

"Your mother's right," Father said, his voice strained by the unaccustomed act of agreeing with her. "You're too smart to spend your life shoveling dirt. You want a job where your livelihood depends on the sorrow of everyone else?"

"It's been good enough for you," Ash said.

"I had no choice, it's all I ever knew. No more argument. You go there in the morning like your mother said."

Ash lowered his head and continued eating. His mother barely managed to stay silent for a minute before diving into another of her favorite topics. "We might see more girls come 'round if you cut your hair, don't you think?"

"Long hair, short hair, they don't care," Ash's father said. "They only want to know how much silver lines a man's pocket."

His mother turned on his father. “What do you know of a woman's mind?” Then back to Ash in her sweetest tone. “Remember how short you used to keep it? I liked it better than Lance's ponytail. Though I said nothing then, because how else would anyone have told you two apart?”

Ash couldn’t take any more on this, of all days. He rose, scraping the floor with his chair.

“Wait, stay a bit.” His mother jumped up, dashed into the kitchen, and returned with a plate holding a square of sugared cake. “Happy birthday, dear Ash,” she said.

There, she had done it. She just couldn’t let it go. He held back the anger surging inside him because he knew she meant well. She wanted to convey that just because his brother was gone, it didn’t mean his life was over too. Life goes on, birthdays must be celebrated, even if they would always remind him of the brother who entered the world seven minutes before he did, and whose loss thirteen years later felt exactly as if someone had cut away his arm or leg or half of his heart.

Ash took the piece of cake and rushed out with it, while behind him Father said to Mother, “You had to start with the hair?”

Beneath a silvery half-moon, Ash sat on Lance’s grave facing the oak cross that marked it. He touched the words engraved on the wood, "LANCE KEMP 13 Years of Age." He took a section of cake, then tore off a piece and dropped it on the grave. *A bite for me, a bite for you.* He and his brother had always celebrated birthdays together, and they always would.

Ash leaned his head against the post. Three years ago, they’d found the cursed ring no more than ten yards from here, near the top of old John Penworth’s plot. It was buried half a foot under the dirt and, from the look of it, had been there quite a few years. When they’d brushed it off and the sun had hit it, the precious emerald had sparkled green like nothing he'd ever seen before.

His life had changed in every way possible since then. It had left him with a single goal from which he would never waver. Nothing else mattered.

TESSA

By evening my mood had brightened and I found myself whistling as I assembled our supper. I fetched smoked pork, cheese, and bread from the pantry while Papa set out the plates. He was in excellent spirits, thanks to his good friend Mr. Oliver, who had visited late in the afternoon, and stayed long enough for my father to beat him soundly at backgammon.

"Did the Kettlemores pay you?" Papa said.

"They said they would tomorrow," I said, avoiding his gaze. I didn't like to lie, but I also didn't wish to turn Papa's mood sour. In the morning, I would find another small job to cover the amount they would have paid.

We took our seats. I was just about to launch into Ryland's marriage proposal, when Papa grew somber and announced there was something he must tell me. The seriousness in his tone took me by surprise. His shoulders stiffened, and he looked down instead of meeting my gaze. *So much for his mood.*

Curiosity overwhelmed me. "Of course," I said. "What is it?"

He was about to speak when his ears pricked up at the sound of a carriage and horses outside. Coaches almost never entered our road, which came to a dead end after three more houses down from ours.

Papa strode to the window and peered through the curtains, his face darkening at whatever he saw. I went to the smaller window closest to me and glanced out.

The royal carriage of Lord Fellstone had paused on the road just outside our house. Two knights flanked the driver, and two more sat outside in the back. I couldn't see into the dark interior of the carriage, so there was no way to tell for certain whether the lord himself might be seated inside.

"Put out the light," Papa hissed in a sharp whisper. He snuffed the lamp beside him.

I blew out the candles nearest me. Moonlight streaming into the back of the house provided dim illumination.

"Watch them," said Papa. "Tell me if anyone approaches." He hurried to his wall of master keys and selected one. Then he pulled aside the tapestry that hung in the back, revealing a hidden compartment I'd never seen before. He opened it with the key and took out a narrow sword. I stifled a gasp as Papa put his fingers to his lips to shush me. He drew the sword from its sheath, and stepped toward the door.

One moment I was watching Papa, and the next, my sight went black. Seconds later, I could see again, but I seemed to be transported to another place. Somewhere dark and full of shadows, with a ceiling of jagged stone. *A cave.* I was lying on a table, my back aching from its hard, flat surface. I tried to look to the sides, but straps held me in place… my head, my torso, my arms and legs, all bound with a tightness that nearly stopped the flow of my blood. Bile rose in the back of my throat from the putrid stench… like some animal's rotting corpse. Gravel scraped not far from where I lay. *A footstep?* I strained at my bindings, but they held me fast while panic welled up inside me.

And then it was over. My sight blurred and when it cleared again,

I was back inside my house, standing just as before. I rubbed my eyes, trying to wipe out the memory, feeling intense relief wash over me. It was such a vivid nightmare... though I had no clue how I had dreamed without first falling asleep. I wondered if it had anything to do with Lord Fellstone, or the strange woman I'd seen with him. I looked out the window to find the driver turning the carriage around. Papa joined me as the horses set off, and we watched together until the carriage disappeared from view. I said nothing to him about my brief vision, which would only have worried him for no good reason. His sword concerned me far more.

"You'll be arrested for that," I said, staring down at the weapon in his hand. Only his lordship's knights and boarmen were allowed to bear swords.

"In these times... given the tyrant who rules over us... we have to be prepared," Papa said.

"Not you. If there must be fighting, let it fall to the young men."

"It's ever the fate of the young to die for the old, but it really ought to be the other way around." Papa sheathed the sword and brought it back to its hiding place, locking it and restoring the tapestry over it. "Light the lamp, Tessa."

I did as he told me. "Do you think Lord Fellstone was inside the carriage?" I said.

"I doubt anyone else is allowed to ride under his crest," said Papa.

"What about the woman who wears a mask?" I said. He gave me a curious look, surprised I knew of her. "I heard talk of her in town the other day," I added.

"I don't know," he said.

"Why would they stop outside our home?"

"I have a bad feeling about it."

"I can't imagine it had anything to do with us," I said. "Maybe a horse stepped on a nail, or something fell out and they had to fetch it."

Papa returned to the table and sat down. His right hand trembled as he reached for his tankard. "I think we should leave Sorrenwood."

"What do you mean?"

"You know they've increased the collections?"

"I imagine it's the same everywhere."

"I've heard conditions are better in Blackgrove, under the Conjurer Lord Queshire's protection," Papa said.

"You can't mean we should go there. We would need permission to cross the border in any case." I could not believe what Papa was proposing. A carriage stopped outside our home, and suddenly we were planning to run away? He was making no sense tonight.

"There are ways," he said.

"This is our home."

"We'll make a new home for ourselves."

"You once said we should stay here always, in case Mama might return," I said.

"She would want me to protect you, above any other consideration."

"She left us. Who is she to have an opinion?" Cold anger swept through me, recalling the day Mama went away. She had an illness that made her fearful of open spaces. Papa did all the errands while she remained at home. She would not even come out of her room when neighbors came to call. I was told not to talk of her or her sickness to my friends. But I often saw her gazing out the window, and even at the age of four I recognized the longing in her eyes. Then, on one fine morning following weeks of thundershowers, she couldn't resist. She took my hand and led me to the backyard, where we planted spring flowers. Afterwards, when we came inside, she said she was tired and sent me to my room for a nap, but my excitement over Mama being "cured" kept me from sleeping for some time. At last I did drift off, and when I woke, Mama was gone.

Papa believed she was abducted, but I heard no noise that

afternoon, nor were there any physical signs of ruffians having entered our home. The neighbors thought she must have killed herself, because surely someone who never goes outside must be deeply unhappy. Yet I remembered how full of joy she was in the morning, and how she'd managed to conquer her illness by coming out into the garden with me. After months passed without her body turning up at the river's edge or at the bottom of a ravine, the rumors changed. They said she must have run away, most likely with a lover, because what woman would take the risk of setting out on a journey by herself? Especially a woman who was frightened by wide open spaces. Besides, only a powerful attachment to a man could've tempted a mother to abandon her young child. And the locksmith... people knew he had a kind heart, but his manner was gruff and he was believed to be much older than the young wife who had never been clearly seen by anyone. The few who claimed to have set eyes on her remarked on her great beauty. She *was* beautiful, but it was the sort of thing anyone would say to embellish a story, whether they'd known her or not. Still, when I was old enough to consider all the possibilities, the one that seemed least *unlikely* was that a man had fallen in love with her and enticed her to run away with him. I preferred this idea over the thought that she had so little joy in life—so little happiness in the company of her husband and daughter—that she chose one day to wander away and drown herself in a churning river.

Papa had long ago given up arguing with me about her. "It's not safe here," he said. "Boarmen lurking around every corner. Fellstone himself peering through our windows. We should go tonight."

"What? That's impossible. I have friends... You can't make me!"

"I vowed to protect you and I will."

"What do you mean, vowed? To whom did you vow?"

He pinned his arms against his stomach. "To myself. The day you were born."

"Well you've done your job. Look how healthy I am." My throat constricted at the prospect of leaving Sorrenwood. Perhaps there were better towns, ruled by less oppressive conjurers, who did not surround themselves with a ghastly array of beasts and wraiths... but none of those towns would have Ryland. *How can I make Papa understand my feelings?* He would tell me I was being childish, and that there would be plenty of boys wherever we might go, whom I would like at least as much as Ryland, and probably more.

I knelt beside him. "You're not feeling well. You should eat and get to bed. Let's decide tomorrow. Please, Papa?"

He gazed down at me, smoothed my hair, and sighed.

"What was it you wished to tell me earlier?" I said.

He hesitated before thrusting his hand into his pocket, and drawing out a lovely golden key attached to a plain necklace.

"It's beautiful." I touched the dangling key as he held out the chain for me. Its handle was decorated with a geometric pattern etched in delicate lines. "What does it unlock?"

Papa smiled. "Always the first question of a locksmith. But the answer is, I don't know. It belonged to your mother. I was going to give it to you on your eighteenth birthday. But... I think she would want you to have it now." He pressed it into my palm.

My eyes filled with tears. "Thank you, dearest Papa. I'll think of you and Mama both when I wear it." I kissed the key before putting the chain over my head, and then I kissed Papa's cheek. "But what was the thing you wished to say to me?"

"Not now, my child," he said. "We've had too much excitement already tonight. It shall have to wait."

CALDER

Calder sat on a hay bale munching on a carrot, watching Farmer Joshua loading crates filled with vegetables onto a cart.

"Years ago, when I was at the castle with my pa, I saw her in the kitchen, sorting out the meal plan with Mrs. Bailey, the cook," Joshua said. "She was a beautiful lady with a smile that could melt iron."

"Have you seen her since?" Calder said.

Joshua shook his head. "I hear things though. Maids twittering amongst themselves. They say the lord talks to her."

"Then why has no one seen her?"

Joshua secured a tarp over the cart. "There's some who say he turned her into a wraith."

Calder repressed a shudder. He would not allow his mind to wander there. Hope was the fuel that drove him, and therefore he needed to believe he would find her alive.

"How often do you deliver?" Calder said.

"Every evening. They've got an army to feed." Joshua took away the horses' feeding buckets and climbed onto his seat on the wagon.

"I could use your help, my friend," Calder said.

Farmer Joshua shook the reins and the two horses set off at an easy gait. As Calder watched the cart jounce over the uneven ground, he thought he must put the plan into action tomorrow, should Joshua be willing. Laying back on the hay bale, he lifted his arm to stare at the silver cat inlaid on his wristband. He picked out a piece of straw that had caught in its edges.

Calder was fourteen years old and still had two good eyes when Faline had given it to him. She was thirteen and of high birth, though she was just beginning to transition from a freckled urchin into the regal beauty she was destined to become. She had found him seated on a log at the edge of the woods, attempting to place sage leaves on his back to soothe the red welts. Faline sat beside him and adjusted the leaves on the spots he was unable to reach. He almost smiled to think how horrified her mother would be to see her daughter tending to the wounds of Cook's son.

"My brother's doing?" Faline asked.

"Why should Mace take the blame for breaking the stack of porcelain plates? Or for anything else, when I'm nearby?" Calder said. It meant a whipping for Calder, something that Joseph, the second footman, was all too happy to administer. Mace had watched, already a monster at the tender age of eleven, his eyes moist with excitement at the pain felt by another.

Faline lowered his shirt and gave the remaining leaves back to Calder, who stuffed them into a burlap sack. "I wish I could make him be kind to you," she said.

"He must have someone to torture. At least it isn't you." It was the only consolation that came of her brother's relentless persecution.

Faline reached into her pocket and took out two leather wristbands with a pewter fox on one and a cat on the other. "I want you to have the fox."

Calder touched his own long nose. "Because of this?"

"No, silly. Don't you know the fable of the Fox and the Cat? A fox boasts to a cat that he has a bag of tricks giving him hundreds of ways to escape his enemies, whereas the cat only has one. But then when a hunter chases them with a pack of hounds, the cat runs up a tree, while the fox is slaughtered before he can decide which trick to use."

"So the moral is… think faster?"

"I'm not sure that's what was meant. But the point is you remind me of a fox with your bag of tricks."

He pressed the fox wristband back into her hand. "I should prefer you to have it, so you'll think of me when you wear it."

She hesitated. "Then you must take the cat to think of me. Though I hope you'll always be near, so we won't require reminders in any case."

Even then, he did not need to be a fortuneteller to predict their futures would not follow the same path. Still, it had broken his heart when at sixteen her family sent her far away to be married, and it seemed he would never see her again. In the time since then, he had roamed the world, looking for distractions that would keep him from thinking of her.

ASH

Ash woke at first light in a brighter frame of mind, relieved to have a whole year ahead of him before the next birthday. He rose and ate bread covered in his mother's apricot preserves, before setting out for the scribe's chambers. During his walk there, he began to convince himself that some good might come of the lessons, despite his determination never to work in that trade. He was all for learning new skills, and was grateful to the young chaplain who had taught him to read when he was a boy. Unfortunately, the chaplain had moved on to another post before schooling him in the formation of his letters, but now Ash would get a second chance. He had a strong sense of the power of words and, in a kinder world, he might have wished to become a poet, or to write a work of epic fiction. But as things were, he expected to use his new skills to inspire mutinous thoughts in the good people of Sorrenwood, through a series of anonymous leaflets.

Ash turned down an alley from the high road to reach the entrance to Mr. Ainsworth's cramped chambers. The door was open and Mr. Crawford, a bailiff, lingered over the scribe. Ash slipped in behind Mr. Crawford and glanced down at the document on the desk between the two men. He saw to his astonishment that it was an arrest warrant for Tessa's father, Donal Skye, who was "wanted for questioning in official matters."

The bailiff snatched the document and threw a hard look in Ash's direction. He clasped the parchment close to his chest as he left the office.

Mr. Ainsworth glanced toward Ash with an utter lack of interest. The scribe—mostly bald save for several strands of wispy white hair—appeared older than his years. Leather-framed spectacles hung on his nose beneath drooping, bloodshot eyes, and the tips of his fingers had become black from the permanent stain of ink. Mr. Ainsworth nodded toward a tiny desk in the corner, where had been placed a quill and inkpot, a scroll displaying the handwritten alphabet, and a stack of blank, lined parchment.

"Begin your practice," he said in a nasally tone.

"What has the locksmith done?" Ash said.

Mr. Ainsworth paused and emitted a deep sigh. "This is your first lesson. All documents which are prepared in the scribe's chambers are of a confidential nature. The scribe never speaks of them under any circumstance. Those who have observed the documents in the scribe's chambers by reading what they were not given permission to read, are also bound by the code of confidentiality. Sit down, now. You won't learn penmanship by standing about."

Ash took his seat at the desk. He set his parchment in front of him, dipped his quill in the ink, and began to form the letter "A." He tried to concentrate but he could think of nothing other than "A for Arrest." *What could Tessa's father have done?* Probably nothing, but that wouldn't stop the authorities from persecuting him. *What if Tessa is implicated as well?* Ash knew better than most what passed for "justice" in Sorrenwood. He could not sit idly by and allow the man to be arrested without warning.

He shot to his feet. "Sir, I just remembered something. My

mother was feeling pain in her stomach this morning. I was supposed to fetch Mr. Evanson, the physician, but I completely forgot in my excitement to begin my first lesson here." He hurried to the door. "It won't take long." He ran out of the chamber before Mr. Ainsworth could protest, and continued running all the way to Ryland's house. He banged on the door with his fist and shouted Ryland's name.

After a minute, Ryland opened the door, looking as if he just rose from bed. "What is it?" he demanded.

"Donal Skye is about to be arrested. You have to warn Tessa," Ash said. He had thought about going to her himself, but that might have seemed as if he wanted to usurp Ryland's role as her protector.

"How do you know?" Ryland said.

Ash explained what he'd seen at the scribe's chambers.

"I didn't know you could read."

"Well, I can," Ash said, frustrated at Ryland focusing on the wrong thing. "You need to run; the bailiff will be there any minute."

"I doubt it's anything serious."

Ash could not suppress his impatience. "If you don't want to go, I will."

"No," Ryland said. "I'll handle it. Go back to your scribe."

Ash retraced his steps to Mr. Ainsworth's chamber, thinking how stupid and cowardly he'd been not to go to Tessa himself. Ryland didn't really understand what was at stake, and how a simple matter of questioning could escalate into an all-out accusation of treason. But it was out of Ash's hands now; he would have to trust Ryland to do the right thing. He shook off the thought which needled him the most: that his own motive was less to do with saving Donal Skye, and everything to do with being on hand to comfort Tessa when things went awry.

TESSA

I woke early to the crooning of songbirds outside my window. Without thinking, I reached under my pillow for the amulet I always kept there, and only then did I recall Papa had taken it. I felt a stab of loneliness; the windrider's presence had comforted me ever since the day Mama left, when I found it in her bedroom. Through the years I'd often taken it out and worn it for a bit, without having any idea of its power. I discovered its magic only recently, after blowing on it three times to polish it. It terrified me at first; I thought I would remain a bird forever. But eventually I had scraped my claws in frustration and discovered the way to turn back.

I lay in bed a while longer, listening to the birds' sweet trills, and feeling that nothing could make me happier than to be among them. I remembered the key my father had given me, and lifted it up to gaze at its burnished gold. *Sweet, kind Papa.* He could never bear to disappoint me for long. Over time, I hoped to make him understand that a key, however dear, was not a replacement for a windrider. I reminded myself of yesterday's events: the hawk attack, the need to take refuge at the castle, the prisoner's dreadful death… but nothing could quell my desire to be a bird once again, to spread my wings and glide through open air.

I sat up, rubbed my arms, and picked up "The Trials of Kallos" from my bedside. It had been a favorite of my mother's, a volume of epic poetry describing the adventures of the hero Jahn Kallos, who battled mythical beings in a time before conjurers even existed. She had read me passages from the book when I was too young to understand them, though I was stirred by the sound of her voice and the current of emotion that ran through it. I liked to believe she left the volume for me intentionally, because she so easily could've taken it with her. In time I grew to love its stories as much as she ever did, and I could recite many of its passages from memory.

Mama had written her name, Gillian Skye, inside the cover. It was my morning habit to open the book to her signature and trace its letters with my finger. This, the windrider, and now the key, were all that I had, the only physical remnants to prove she'd been in our house or had ever even existed at all. Without any explanation, Papa had burned everything else that had belonged to her. Once he even crept into my room late at night and tried to steal away with "The Trials of Kallos," but I woke and threw a terrible fit. In the end he had relented and promised never to touch the book again. Overall, his actions seemed like those of an angry, resentful husband, and yet he never uttered a word against her.

As I closed the book, my thoughts returned to the windrider, and I glanced toward the door. What would be the harm in a short flight taken and finished before Papa ever woke up? I rose from my bed, being careful not to make the wooden frame creak, and tiptoed out of my room. I paused outside Papa's bedchamber, looking in to find him sleeping on his back, snoring in his usual style of an explosive wheeze followed by a gap of pure silence. Unfortunately, my necklace was nowhere to be seen. I stole across his room, avoiding the planks that creaked, thinking wistfully that my intimate knowledge of his floorboards reflected poorly on me and my habit of sneaking about.

Seconds later, I regretted not knowing his dresser as well. The wood scraped loudly as I pulled open the top drawer, and Papa stopped breathing in mid-snort. I froze in place, my mind forming a blank as I tried to think of what excuse I could possibly give for getting into his things.

But Papa breathed in and drifted back to sleep. I felt inside the drawer without finding my necklace, then closed it carefully and reached for the next. I paused as the thought occurred that Papa often left items in his pockets. Whenever I washed his trousers, I was sure to find a key or sometimes several. Chances were high that he'd forgotten to put the windrider away. I darted to the chair where Papa had lain his clothing, and reached under his shirt, into his trouser pockets. The first was empty, but the next held the object of my desire.

I raced back to my own room, nearly broke the chain in pulling it over my head, and blew on the windrider three times. The familiar feeling of elation ripped through my body from head to toe—or claw—as I became a russet sparrow. Delighted chirps emerged from somewhere deep inside me. I wasted no time in hopping up to the window sill and flying out into the open air. When I'd cleared the trees, I leveled off and began a joyous acrobatic dance, full of swoops and dives and somersaults. I sang a song which did not seem anything like what a real sparrow might sing, but it felt like laughing to me.

In the midst of my celebration, my sharp sparrow eyes caught movement below: the shapes of men approaching our house from the road. What bad luck to have visitors when I most wished Papa not to be disturbed. All I wanted was for him to sleep until I was ready to fly back and replace the windrider in his pocket. I cursed the rudeness of the visitors for calling so early in the morning. They'd probably been careless and locked themselves out of some building or other, and they were too selfish and impatient to wait for normal working hours before summoning a locksmith.

I dipped down to get a closer look, and what I saw alarmed me. These men were knights. *What are they doing?* As far as I knew, no knight had ever had business on our street before. At least, not until last night when they had arrived in Lord Fellstone's carriage. Now there were three of them regaled in chain mail and carrying broadswords. The largest looked as solid as a tree trunk, though the one beside him appeared more dangerous, with a grim set to his eyes. The third wore a blank expression as if whatever they were about to do was all in a day's work. The tree trunk moved ahead of the others, approached our door, and without pausing to knock, threw himself against it. The frame splintered and our flimsy door fell open. Panic surged through me, as there could be no further question that they'd come with foul purpose. As they rushed into the house, I thrashed my wings and dove toward my window. In the last second, when it was too late to turn back, it flashed into my tiny brain that I should've flown to my father's friend, Mr. Oliver. He had brought us meals during the dark times just after Mama went away, and his advice was always sound. What could I do against one knight, let alone three? But instinct had driven me with one thought in mind—*save Papa.*

A dreadful howl arose from my father but he was cut off mid-cry. I soared into my room, directly into a shield held out by one of the knights. I felt an explosion of pain, and then nothing.

CALDER

Farmer Joshua had kindly allowed Calder to spend the night, despite his current status as an escaped prisoner accused of the horrendous crime of telling a young woman the fortune she most wished to hear. The hay pricked at his skin, but at least it was better than the bed he'd occupied at the rear of the blacksmith's dwelling, full of hard lumps that jabbed his innards every time he shifted in his sleep. In any case he would not sleep there again. If the constable insisted on wasting the town's resources tracking him down, his former lodgings would naturally be the first place they would check.

However, he could not bed down on a block of hay for long. Last night had been warm enough, but the seasons were changing and soon the crisp autumn air would force him to find shelter indoors. Today, he must visit the locksmith and his wife, and then it would be time to decide. If all went well, he might never need venture to the place he dreaded most.

He rose sufficiently early to glimpse streaks of red and orange across the horizon. His plan was to find the locksmith family at home before their work began for the day. He would call on them under the pretext of delivering the promised fortune to Tessa—he had a story in mind he hoped would please her—and go from there. The sooner he resolved how Gillian Skye came by the fox bracelet, the better. It weighed on him to think Faline might have lost it, or worse yet, given it away, but perhaps she'd awarded it to Tessa's mother after the woman performed her some great service. He also had to consider the possibility that Gillian Skye had stolen the fox from Faline, in which case she would be highly unlikely to admit anything. Still, he must try to persuade her to speak using as much charm as he could muster (*ha, ha,* said the voice of Faline in his head), and if this failed, he would find a more devious approach.

He avoided the main thoroughfares, where soldiers would likely be making their rounds. Those villagers whom he passed along the back roads were intent on their business and paid him no heed. He made good time despite his meandering route, and approached the locksmith's as the sun poked above the house.

It appeared the door to the house was open, though Calder had to squint, as even his one good eye was only "good" as compared to the other, entirely unusable one. A few steps closer and he could make out a large piece of splintered wood jutting from the door frame, clear evidence that someone had broken into the place. He had no time to speculate before three burly knights tromped out of the house, the last one holding some sort of bag behind his back.

Calder slid behind a tree and waited for the knights to disappear around the corner. They'd entered the house using violent means and now there appeared no sign of the locksmith or his family. His skin went clammy with dread at the thought of what they might have done to that sweet-faced girl who saved him from the pillory.

The instant the knights slipped from view, Calder sprinted to the house. What he saw upon entering confirmed his worst fears. The locksmith lay on the floor with his head tilted back and his eyes staring up, empty of life. A great deal of blood had spread across his chest and onto the carpet that he lay on. Calder caught his breath and looked round the rest of the room, thankful not to spot any more bodies. He knew he must check the bedchambers, yet his feet pinned him in place like stone weights. He wasn't sure he could bear to see the girl or her mother splayed out in death like the father; neither could he allow himself to turn and walk away. Step by step, he forced himself to the threshold of each room, both empty, with no signs of any violence having taken place inside them. He closed his eyes and breathed out. When he'd steadied himself, he entered the girl's room and sat on her bed, lowering his head and gathering the will to do what must be done.

He glanced up sharply at the sound of footsteps entering the house. *Have the knights returned?* Calder rose and turned to the open window. He trod lightly toward it, meaning to make his escape. But the sound of a woman's sobs gave him pause, and drew him back to the main room. A plump, grey-haired woman, weeping over the locksmith, looked up and started at the sight of Calder.

He hastened to reassure her. "The lord's knights did this," he said.

"Aye, I saw them leave," she said. "Where's Tessa?"

"Not here, thank the gods. Madame, accept my deepest condolences for your loss."

A veil of suspicion lowered over the woman's face. "My loss?"

"I'm new to these parts. Are you not Gillian Skye?"

"Nay, I live next door. Bettina Flanagan."

"Calder Osric," he said. "I came hoping to repay a service. Do you know where Tessa and her mother have gone?"

"Oh my," Mrs. Flanagan said. "Her mother went away when the lass were not much more than a babe."

"Went away? Where?"

She shrugged. "No one has laid eyes on her since. Not that we ever saw her before. Since the day Donal Skye first brought her to his home, she kept to herself. Never left the house that I could tell. I glimpsed her through the window from time to time, just enough to tell what a fair lass she were."

If only Calder could speak to Tessa, perhaps he could begin to make sense of what had happened. He said, "Do you have any idea why the lord would order his knights to kill Donal Skye?" Over the years he had often found answers in unexpected places, and therefore he did not hesitate to question even the most unlikely sources.

"I can't imagine," Mrs. Flanagan said. "He has always been a law-abiding man." She lowered her voice and glanced behind her. "It must have to do with the strange visit last night. I thought it were an ill omen then, I did. The royal carriage rode up and stopped on our very road, directly outside this house. Never have I seen it happen before."

"Lord Fellstone's carriage? Did anyone get out?"

She shook her head. "Not that I could see. It waited for a moment, then moved on."

Calder squeezed his eye in concentration. There could be no further delay. He turned to Mrs. Flanagan. "Can you help me lift him to the table? Let's not have Tessa find him like this."

Bettina Flanagan—salt of the earth—nodded and pushed up her sleeves.

TESSA

I woke to a throbbing head, feeling groggy and confused. It was bewildering and just a little bit terrifying to expect to be a person and instead find myself as a bird. Never having gone to sleep as a sparrow before, this was my first experience waking up as one. Worse—much worse—I realized I was in a net, which was bouncing off the back of the tree-trunk knight, who carried me as he walked alongside his two companions. *Why did they capture me? Where are they taking me?* I remembered what had happened, remembered my father's cry and how it cut off and… *I must not think about that.* I had to focus on a plan of escape, otherwise we might both be doomed. My first thought was to scrape my claw three times and change back to myself, but just as quickly I changed my mind. As a girl, I couldn't possibly fight off and elude three knights, but sparrow-me had the advantage of flight if I could escape from the net. I began to peck and chew at the string with frantic urgency.

"What do you think they want with the bird?" the grim-looking knight said.

"I dunno. Stuff it and mount it on the mantel?" the knight who carried me said. His words made me tremble, though the idea of me as some sort of trophy was absurd. Still, this reminder of my utter helplessness spurred me to work faster and yank harder at the threads of the net.

"I mean it. What's so special about it?" the first knight insisted.

His question echoed inside me. What *was* so special about me? Of course, no one at the castle could have any interest in a locksmith's daughter. But my amulet—the *windrider*—a magic charm which allowed its owner to shape-shift into a sparrow... I had no idea how unique such a charm might be. For all I knew, Lord Fellstone owned dozens... or none at all.

"He likes birds. I've heard he keeps one in his room." This from the blank-faced knight.

"The crow, you mean?" the largest knight said.

It sounded as if there *were* more windriders. *Couldn't his lordship spare one or two?* Of course not, he was a conjurer, and conjurers had proclaimed only they may perform magic. It was all very self-serving, insuring that no one outside their own inner circle could ever mount a challenge against them.

The knights slowed their pace, nearing a building which I knew to be a soldier's garrison. Once inside, I would have no chance of escape. I tore at the twine in a frenzy, while the knights halted in front of their commander.

"We have it, Sir Warley," said the knight holding the net. He swung me around to present to his superior.

Pressing as hard as I could against the section I'd been working on, I snapped the last connecting threads, creating a tiny opening. I squeezed through the hole, my right claw catching for an instant before I managed to shake it free. The grim knight swung his hand to grab me, but I slipped through his fingers and flashed up toward the sky. As I rose above my kidnappers, I heard Sir Warley slam one of the knights with the hilt of his sword, shouting, "Find another bloody sparrow if you value your life!"

I flew across the town square and straight toward home. I told myself over and over that surely Papa was safe. At Lord Fellstone's command, they'd come for the windrider, and to that purpose they'd captured sparrow-me. Once they had their quarry, they would have left Papa alone. No doubt he was worried, and angry at me for breaking my promise, but I would smooth it over when I returned, and then I would agree to leave Sorrenwood with him this very day, if he wished. Because even if I handed over the windrider to his lordship, I would certainly be arrested for having used it. Papa could be punished too, just for keeping it in our house. We had to run away, I understood that now. Ryland could come with us. He wouldn't hesitate, once he understood the urgency of our plight.

I landed behind a thicket and changed back into myself. But as I emerged from hiding and rushed toward my house, Mrs. Flanagan called out from next door. "Come, child. You don't want to go in there."

I paused and turned to her, my skin prickling with fear. "Why not?" She didn't speak—she didn't need to. The answer was written in her swollen eyes and care-worn face.

"Come away, Tessa. Sit with me for a bit," she pleaded.

"No!" I rushed inside and found the place dark with all the curtains drawn. Papa lay on the table with a blanket over him to his neck, his eyes closed, his face drained of color. I inched toward him, willing him to be alive, not believing he could be dead. I murmured his name, praying he would open his eyes and answer me. *Papa.* So still and icy with a tinge of blue to his skin. I drew down the blanket, terrified of what I would see. A ring of dark red surrounded the place where the sword had cut into his heart.

A ferocious wave of anger and grief swept through me. Three oil lamps in the room flared up of their own accord. How that happened, I didn't know, didn't care. I picked up the blue vase from the table and hurled it against the wall, where it smashed into pieces. I felt like a wild animal, ready to pounce, to hurt, to maim something. My eyes searched the room for anything else I could destroy.

Which was when I saw him, the one-eyed man from the stocks. *Calder.* He stepped toward me from the dark corner by the tapestry, muttering condolences.

My rage now had a focus, and I lunged at him, beating him with my fists. "It's because of you!" I cried out. It all became clear; it was nothing to do with the windrider. The knights had come to punish me for freeing this man. But Papa must have gotten in their way, trying to protect me. Or maybe… yes, this must be what happened… they believed *Papa* was the master of locks who had opened the pillory and released Calder. I'd been a blind fool to help the man. *It was his fault.*

"No," Calder said, grasping my hands. He was stronger than I expected, but still I fought him. "You think because you helped me? No. No one knew. It's nothing to do with me. I'm no more significant to Fellstone than an ant under his foot."

"Then why? Why did they kill him?"

"Perhaps they wanted something of his," he said.

My hand went to my windrider. I knew instantly that Calder was right, though I didn't want to believe it. From the moment I flew up to the castle window, and Lord Fellstone looked directly at sparrow-me… it still gave me chills to remember it. And the crow… the knights had said something about a crow… the crow that flew behind me, and turned back when I entered my house. I led that bird to my home, to my father. It was all because of me. I never should've used the cursed windrider. Papa was right. Magic was evil. *Only I'm to blame.*

"We don't have much time," Calder said. "They may return any minute."

I didn't care what happened to me now. Let them return and take me away. Let them set their boarmen on me and hunt me like the prisoner at the castle. I deserved their worst.

"He was a good man," Calder said.

Tears came unbidden to my eyes. "Did you know him?"

"I did not have that pleasure, but everyone said so. It means something when no one can think of a bad thing to say about you."

"He wanted to leave last night. I made him stay."

"God knows, few have wallowed in guilt more than I. Don't be like me. Come away and we'll save him." Calder opened his bag. Inside lay a huge jumble of strange and unrelated items, completely disorganized. He dug into the mess, searching for something. "But Calder, he's dead, you say. Well, there's a way to bring him back to life, but it must be done quickly." He raised a vial of green liquid, frowned, and put it back. "Blast! Where did I put it?"

Calder delved deeper into the bag. He pulled out a second vial, filled with something blue. "What is this thing that can restore life, you say? His lordship's dreadmarrow. Oh I know it won't be easy to get. He isn't going to simply hand it over to us. We'll have to sneak into Fellstone Castle and steal it." He pulled the cork from the bottle and sprinkled the blue liquid over Papa.

"What are you doing?" I said.

"This will preserve him for three days. Otherwise he could get quite stinky. We've no time to lose."

"Are you serious? Do you really think this dread—"

"Dreadmarrow," he said.

"Do you really believe it can bring a dead person back to life?"

"There are some who say it can."

"What does it look like?"

He glanced at me curiously. "A wand of black ironwood. Why do you ask?"

"I just wondered," I said. I didn't tell him I'd seen it work its magic in healing Lord Fellstone himself. I couldn't explain getting a private glimpse of the man. I didn't know how far I could trust Calder, and I'd never willingly shared the secret of my windrider with anyone, not even Ryland. But I needed little convincing that magic was real and that this dreadmarrow—surely the wand I'd seen—would work. Mama had left years ago, and now Papa was struck down. I had nothing further to lose. If I didn't act, the lord's men would most certainly return to arrest me and take back the windrider. Calder was giving me a chance to change the outcome—to bring my papa back to life. After that we could leave Sorrenwood as he'd wanted. Of course I would do it. I must swallow my grief for now and take action. There would be plenty of time to mourn in the end, if that was what it came to.

"Tell me your plan," I said.

ASH

The scribe grumbled upon Ash's return, then went back to ignoring him. Ash hunched over the desk that was too small for him, writing each upper and lower-case letter many times until he believed his were nearly as neat as the samples. Having bored of the task, he asked Mr. Ainsworth if he might copy out the page of a book, and in response, the scribe looked the same as if he'd been struck by lightning.

"Goodness no!" he said. "You're not nearly ready."

"May I show you what I've done?" Ash said.

But Mr. Ainsworth had no desire to see it. "You've barely begun. Expect many, many more hours of practice on the individual letters, and then you must learn how to connect one to the other."

Ash continued another hour until his hand began to cramp. "I should be returning now to help my father in the graveyard," he lied.

Mr. Ainsworth dismissed him with the wave of his hand. "You may come at the same time tomorrow," he said in the exact tone as if he were bestowing ten acres of land on a pauper.

Ash set out toward home, where he planned to retrieve his wooden sword in the hope of another afternoon practice session with Ryland. But as he neared the cemetery, his father saw him and waved him over.

Father peered down at the close-set graves of Gerald and Dorothea Skye. "We may have to place the casket on top of them," he said.

Ash's insides went cold. "What do you mean?" he asked in a hoarse whisper.

"You didn't hear?" Father said. "Donal Skye was killed today."

"He has a… he has a daughter. What news of her?"

"I don't know. Of course the poor child must be grieving." Father glanced behind them to be sure they were alone, and kept his voice low. "The lord's men claim Donal resisted arrest."

"I don't believe it. They'll use any excuse." He rubbed his forehead. "I told Ryland to warn him."

His father flushed with anger. "You…? Haven't you learned anything? Stay out of such matters."

"I didn't do anything." Ash turned away. "I need to go. I'll help you later."

"Stay away from that girl. And Ryland too," his father said.

Ash didn't like disobeying his father, but he refused to sit back and do nothing in the face of injustice. Even if the locksmith had broken the law, he should not have to pay for it with his life. Once upon a time, a person accused of a crime had been allowed to plead his case in front of a magistrate. Now, an accusation was equivalent to a death sentence.

Ash found Ryland at work inside the carpenter's shed, sawing through an oak plank. Ryland's eyes flashed with irritation when he glanced up to see Ash approaching.

"Can we talk?" Ash said.

Ryland looked over at his master, whose back was turned as he painted a table leg. Ryland nodded and followed Ash out of the building.

"Did you do what I said?" Ash held his hands at his side, clenching and unclenching his fists.

"My parents told me not to get mixed up in it," Ryland said, looking defiant. "How could I have known what would happen?"

"I *told* you. You should've gone there. What about Tessa? How is she?"

"All right, I suppose." He shoved his hands into his pockets.

"You suppose? You haven't seen her?"

"What are you, her mother? I can't go there. My parents have forbidden me from seeing her."

"Why?" Ash said, without admitting his father had done the same.

"Don't be an idiot. He was executed by the knights of our lord. I can't associate with the family of a traitor."

"Coward." The word slipped out of Ash without his thinking. In fact, Ryland's cowardice surprised him. He knew his friend was weaker than the image he sought to project, but he had believed him loyal to those he loved.

Ryland grabbed his collar and pushed him up against the building. "Take that back!"

"Ryland!" Tessa called out.

Both boys turned at the sound of her voice. Ash shoved Ryland off him.

Tessa hardly noticed Ash as she hurried up to Ryland and threw herself into his arms. It annoyed Ash to see Ryland so misjudged, but he wouldn't be the one to expose him. He slipped away around the side of the building, but then he paused, overcome with curiosity, wondering what Ryland would tell her. He leaned against the wall, listening in. A part of him wondered if Tessa would need consolation after this talk, and if he might possibly be the one to provide it.

"I'm sorry," Ryland said.

"Papa did nothing wrong," Tessa said. "They just went in with their swords, and—"

"Were you there? Did you see what happened?"

"I… no, I'd gone out. I found him when I came back."

Ash pictured Ryland with his arms wrapped around her.

"I need your help," Tessa said. "There's a way to save him."

Ash leaned in closer, wondering if he had heard correctly.

"Who?" Ryland said.

"Papa. I know it sounds crazy, but—"

"Isn't he dead?"

Tessa lowered her voice, causing Ash to strain to hear her. "There's magic that could bring him back," she said. "Have you heard of the dreadmarrow?"

"It belongs to Lord Fellstone."

"What if we could use it?"

"He isn't going to share it with you," Ryland said. "You should be at home. Mourning your father."

"There's no time. I need your help to sneak into the castle and steal the dreadmarrow. You're a fighter and I'm not."

"All I have is a wooden sword."

"I have one made of steel," Tessa said.

Excitement surged inside Ash. *A sword of steel.* Only Lord Fellstone's men could have them. Were Tessa and her father involved in some sort of rebellion? He would need to find out more. It might prove the chance he'd been waiting for.

Ryland shushed her. "Get rid of it. What if you're caught with it?"

"Help me," she said.

"If you do this thing I can't save you."

"Ryland, please… I beg you." Tessa's voice was thick. Ash pictured tears spilling onto her cheeks.

"My family needs me," Ryland said.

"*I* need you."

"I know death is hard to accept, but—"

"I won't accept it. I won't! Not ever! If you don't help me, I'll do it myself!"

Ash peered out to see Tessa leaving in a fury. Ryland stepped toward her. "Don't go," he said.

She paused. "Are you coming?"

Reading his answer in his silence and frozen stance, she spun around and hurried away. Ryland picked up a rock and hurled it at a tree beside the workshop.

TESSA

I wiped angry tears from my face as I left Ryland behind. It had never crossed my mind that he might refuse to offer help when I most needed it. If it was the other way around… if he had asked me to join a hopeless-sounding quest that would mean the difference between life or death for anyone in his family… I would have accepted without hesitation.

I would not let myself think about him now. If I did, my heart would break and Papa would be doomed. I must lay aside my feelings and push forward, one simple goal at a time. If I looked at the vastness of what we had to accomplish, I might weaken and give up before we even began. Instead, I focused on the first task: to find a swordsman. Since I had no idea how to use a weapon and neither, apparently, did Calder, it was essential that at least one person among us had the skills to fight and even to kill, if necessary.

A swordsman would expect to be paid, but I hadn't brought sufficient coin to entice anyone to risk his life. Papa's savings were at the house, stored in a lockbox hidden under the pantry floor. Calder had warned me not to return home, but I didn't see the harm if I were quick about it. I could change into sparrow-me if I heard anyone approaching while I was inside.

I was startled by footsteps running up behind me, but it was only Ryland's friend, Ash. He fell into step beside me, lowering his head, his eyes on the ground. "I can help you," he said, his voice wavering a bit.

I didn't know what to say, unsure how much he knew and what he was offering.

"I heard you talking to Ryland," he continued.

"You were listening?" Calder had also warned me of prying ears. I should've been more careful.

"I'm skilled with a sword."

"Right. I saw you with Ryland." Now that he'd abandoned me, I could allow myself to acknowledge that Ryland himself was no better than mediocre at sword play. Yet he'd beaten Ash decisively. If I allowed him to join our quest, Ash would be worse than useless.

"That was… I was distracted then," Ash said. "Trust me, I'm good."

"Even if you are, why would you want to come? Chances are we won't be returning from this." It seemed kinder to let the prospect of danger dissuade him, rather than to spend time arguing his merits as a swordsman.

"Got my reasons," he said. His face brightened. "We? Do you mean there are others?"

"There's no rebel army, if that's what you're hoping. Just one other. I do appreciate your offer, but… I wouldn't want to get you into trouble." I began to cross the road toward my home.

Ash grasped my arm. "Wait!" he said.

"I told you—"

"Look," he said, pointing at a grey stallion beside a tree just beyond the house. "Look at the saddle."

It bore the royal crest of Lord Fellstone.

"*Quick*," he said. All at once he yanked me off the road and dragged me into a clump of prickly hedges which scraped my arms.

"What are you doing?" I cried.

"I think I know whose horse that is. She's dangerous. We need to hide. Trust me." He scrambled further into the undergrowth. I hesitated, but then, not quite sure why, I followed him. "You're crazy," I hissed.

"Shh," he said.

We peered through the branches at my house, and a moment later, a tall woman stepped out. It was she who had wielded the dreadmarrow for Lord Fellstone, dressed as before in dark green leather and a cowl of the same color. Her mask made her seem not quite human; the way her sinister eyes peered through it sent a chill through my spine. She looked around from the top of the steps, and her head tilted back as if she were sniffing. She turned and tread toward us, drawing out her sword.

My hands went clammy. A shrill voice inside my head urged me to run. Ash's face tightened and his eyes went cold. He saw my panic and touched my arm.

The woman continued in our direction, while her gaze appeared to fix on something in the distance. I wondered if she sought to fool us by keeping her eyes averted, so we wouldn't know whether she saw us or not, and it would be all the more alarming when her glare suddenly snapped onto us.

Ash looked down and saw a rock protruding from the dirt. He dug around it with his fingers, pulling at it until it came loose. His hand wrapped around it. It might not be the most effective weapon, but better than no defense at all.

The woman paused on the road just above us. She stared at the horizon, raised her sword, and swiveled her head until her unsettling mask faced us directly. Ash and I exchanged a nervous glance. His grip tightened around the rock.

I heard footsteps running along the street. Mr. Oliver came into our filtered view, rushing toward my house. The masked woman turned away from us to look at him. He saw her and slowed his pace, but still continued forward. She sniffed, lowered her sword, strode to her grey stallion, and lifted herself onto the saddle.

"Hiyah!" she cried, stabbing the sides of the horse with her spurs. The animal leapt forward and carried her away at a gallop. I was left with the impression that her goal had been to frighten, rather than attack. To what purpose, I couldn't imagine.

Mr. Oliver disappeared into the house.

"Sorry for pulling you," Ash said.

"You were right," I said, forcing my way through the heavy growth to reach the road. I ran toward the house with Ash just behind me. Inside, we found Papa as I'd left him. Mr. Oliver had pulled up a chair beside him, and sat with his head lowered. He stood as I approached and stepped toward me. Papa's friend was clean-shaven, except for a beard that formed a neat circle on his chin. Fresh lines of grief crisscrossed his face. He opened his arms and gathered me in a tight embrace, which brought tears to my eyes. I didn't know why, but the scent of tobacco that emanated from the pipe and pouch he always kept inside his jacket pocket, brought with it a measure of comfort.

I drew back after a moment and wiped my face with my sleeve. "Mr. Oliver," I said. "I'm leaving to perform an urgent task that… Papa would wish me to do. May I trust you to look in on him? He should not be buried before I return."

"I won't leave his side till you come back," Mr. Oliver said.

"It might be dangerous to remain here. You saw the woman?"

"It doesn't matter. I'll take my chances."

"Papa never had a better friend than you. There's food and drink in the pantry."

He nodded and took out his pipe to prepare it.

I turned back to Ash, who wore a sorrowful look as he gazed at Papa. His reaction touched me, especially since, being the sexton's son, he must've seen many corpses before. That he hadn't grown cold and detached in the presence of death made me think well of him.

"Come," I said, leading Ash into my room. It was in a terrible mess, with the mattress upended and items from my wardrobe strewn about the floor.

"The woman must've done this," I said. "Who is she?"

"Fellstone's apprentice," Ash said.

"Why do you think she wears that mask?"

"Because her face is a window to the wickedness of her soul."

I looked at him curiously. *How does he know so much about her?*

"What do you think she was looking for?" Ash said.

I shrugged, though I believed I knew precisely what she wanted, and it was hanging from my neck, tucked under my shift, at this very moment. When we returned to the main room, I turned toward the hidden alcove where Papa had stored the sword. Its door swung downwards on one hinge, exposing an empty compartment.

"Did she take anything important?" Ash said.

CALDER

Calder thrust at the hay bale with the locksmith's sword. He'd never fenced before and never intended to learn, but he was interested in the sword's construction. It was a knightly sword, a one-handed straight sword, lightweight and well-balanced. It had a shark's skin grip, a simple crossguard, and a fine steel blade. The metal appeared to be of superb quality. A sword like this would not come cheap, particularly given that it would have to be purchased in secret. He wondered how the locksmith had been able to afford it.

He slid the sword back into its scabbard and set it aside. *Why hasn't Tessa returned?* She'd promised to come here directly after gathering her friend. She'd vouched for his trustworthiness and skill with a sword, but Calder felt wary nevertheless. The true mettle of a friend could never be known until he was asked to face the possibility of death on a quest of your choosing. In Calder's experience, this was when you learned you were, in fact, friendless.

He heard voices outside the barn, and a moment later, Tessa entered with a tall boy who looked familiar. The boy's eyes lit on the sword immediately, and he restrained himself with some difficulty from reaching forward and touching it.

“I expected you sooner,” Calder told Tessa.

“I went back to the house,” she said with a shade of defiance.

Calder sighed. “Sometimes I wonder why I waste breath giving advice.”

“Ryland wouldn't come,” she said. “I thought we might have to pay someone. My plan was to gather more money from home.”

Calder nodded at Ash. “We're paying him?” Looking the boy over, Calder didn’t think his services could be worth very much.

“No, he's free,” she said.

“Didn't know payment was an option,” Ash said.

“Interesting,” Calder said. “Why have you joined us, if not for silver?”

“I’ve got my own reasons for despising Fellstone and his minions. I’m not afraid, if that’s what concerns you,” Ash said.

“I’ll vouch for his bravery,” Tessa said.

Ash looked surprised by her defense of him. Suddenly, Calder remembered where he’d seen the boy before. “Aren't you the gravedigger's son?” he said.

“Aren't you the fortuneteller?” Ash said. “Is it harder to see into the future with only one eye?”

“He has a sharp tongue, I'll give him that.” Calder was beginning to warm up to the lad. He raised the sword in its scabbard. “Do you know how to use this?”

“Better than most,” Ash said.

Calder handed him the weapon and the boy strapped it over his shoulder.

“We have to be clever in any case,” Tessa said, making her lack of confidence in Ash’s abilities painfully clear. “Obviously we can't fight our way onto the castle grounds. Do you think we could scale the wall?”

“Scale the wall?” Calder said, shaking his head. “It's taller than the elm on Howorth Green, and quite sheer.”

"I've climbed walls before," Tessa said. "If we could find a long enough rope, I could throw it down to you."

"I don't think I could manage it, even with a rope," said Calder.

"Do you have a better plan?" Ash said.

Calder always had a plan, and everyone agreed it was better than Tessa's. It began with a meal, as all good plans must, for what quest ever succeeded on an empty belly? Farmer Joshua's wife served up fried eggs and potatoes, greasy strips of bacon, and thick slabs of rustic bread onto which they piled heaps of blackberry jam. Calder exhorted everyone to eat their fill, after which he returned to his favorite hay bale for a nap. When the sun dropped low on the horizon, they gathered again and prepared to set out for the castle.

Calder and his two companions lay on their sides inside Joshua's cart, crammed together between crates of vegetables, and covered by a tarp. Once they were underway, he cursed himself for not padding their conveyance better; he had underestimated the discomfort of bouncing against wood planks as the cart rode over cobblestones. Worse, they were squeezed too tightly for Calder to avoid Ash's elbow, which poked him every few minutes, despite the complaints he hissed at the boy. At least he'd managed to position his head next to a thin tear in the tarp, where the sliver of fresh air helped keep his stomach settled.

Before long, he glimpsed the massive gate set into the castle's outer wall. A powerful jolt followed, nearly throwing his shoulder out of joint. "I'd swear he's aiming for the potholes," he grumbled.

"He's *your* friend," Ash said, as if Calder were to be blamed for anything Joshua did. Ash's elbow jabbed Calder again.

"We share a mutual enemy," Calder snapped. Actually, he barely knew the farmer. But like many others in Sorrenwood, Joshua bore a heavy grudge against the Conjurer Fellstone for past injustices. When the opportunity arose for action, he didn't hesitate, though he well knew he put his livelihood at risk by helping them.

"Why are you here, Calder?" Tessa asked. "Revenge for the pillory?"

"That was all in a day's work. I've come seeking a friend."

"Is he at the castle?"

"She. I don't know. Perhaps."

"A scullery maid?" Ash said.

"Whoa!" Joshua shouted before Calder could reply. The horses halted abruptly, jarring the three companions hidden inside the cart.

Calder pressed his finger to his lips and squinted through his peephole. They'd ridden through the gate and were paused on the road which would lead them past the Cursed Wood to the castle. Six boarmen bearing two-handed great swords were on guard, three to each side of the gate. They were lined up like pillars, their eyes resembling cold dark pebbles, never blinking as far as Calder could tell. He stifled a shiver.

A guard wearing a spotless, well-pressed uniform and shiny leather boots approached the cart. His yellow hair was precisely parted and had been greased to keep it flat, but one errant strand had popped up in the back. He stopped next to Joshua and stood rigid while demanding in clipped tones that the farmer identify himself.

Joshua sounded confused when he spoke. "Is Orson about? He usually minds the gate."

"I'm Captain Yoxall. I mind the gate now."

This was not good at all. Joshua had assured Calder that Orson would be at the gate, and Orson was a nearly pleasant fellow who, for a mere half liter of Joshua's award-winning whiskey, would wave him on his way with nary a glance into his cart.

"Identify yourself," the captain repeated.

"Joshua Ferriman. Been delivering fresh vegetables to the castle for nigh on twelve years, and my pa before that."

"What's in the cart?" said the captain, not about to be led into conversation.

"Like I said… potatoes, carrots, onions, barley." Joshua moved out of Calder's view and returned with a jug in his hand. "Captain, maybe you'd like a taste of my own home-brewed whiskey. It's quite famous round these parts. You must get thirsty standin' about here all evenin'." He poured some into a cup.

Captain Yoxall ignored the drink. "I need to see what's under the tarp."

Joshua took a swig from the cup. "Mother of gods, I've outdone myself with this batch. Sure I can't tempt you?"

"Untie the tarp or I'll have my boarmen rip it off with their teeth," the captain said in the same measured tone.

Inside the cart, the three companions exchanged frightened glances. Calder opened his bag and began a frantic search. "Blast, where is it?" he hissed. It was as if his possessions had minds of their own, and deliberately shifted to new locations whenever the bag was closed, solely to vex him.

"No need for violence. I'll get it for you," Joshua said loudly. He stepped away with the jug, then returned and leaned over the tarp, taking his time to untie it.

Calder whipped out a vial filled with green liquid and flung drops of it over all of them. "It covers our scent," he whispered. Boarmen had poor vision and relied on their noses to seek out their quarry.

Joshua flipped the rope off the tarp. "Go ahead, take a gander at my prize-winning potatoes," he said.

As Captain Yoxall lifted the tarp at the rear of the wagon, Joshua began to back away. He and Calder had agreed he should run at the first sign of trouble. Later he could claim he'd allowed Calder and his friends into his cart after they'd threatened the well-being of his children, but he was too terrified of the boarmen to make his explanation at the gate.

Joshua continued his retreat as the captain steadily rolled the tarp forward. Just as Calder was about to be exposed, he leapt up and slammed his bag into the man's face. The captain fell to the ground, stunned.

"Run!" Calder shouted. He jumped down with his bag and shot toward the forest. He could hear Tessa and Ash running just behind him until their footsteps veered off to the side. Separating was a good strategy, though they'd made no arrangements for how to find each other later. He could not worry about that now. He risked one glance back toward the gate to see Joshua bolting toward town and disappearing behind the first building. The six boarmen stood gawking, unsure who to chase without orders from their human leader. Captain Yoxall pulled himself up, brushed off his precious uniform, and patted down his yellow hair.

"After them!" he shouted. The boarmen still looked confused, until the captain pointed toward the forest. Two set off in Calder's direction, while the others thundered toward the place where Tessa and Ash had sprinted through the trees.

Calder dashed to a tangled thicket and dove beneath it. Wooden tendrils scratched his face and clawed at his clothing. A branch tore through his trousers and held him in place. *Do the plants also defend Fellstone?* He looked back to see the two boarmen crashing towards him. He swore and thrust himself forward, the sharp wood gashing his skin as he broke free of it. He scraped his way along the dirt and pine needles until the bramble gave way to a carpet of moss.

The boarmen couldn't fit under the heavy growth, but it wouldn't take them long to smash their way through it. Calder, with his bag looped over his shoulder, raced toward fallen trees that were heaped just ahead. He plunged into a pile of leaves between two of the logs, and burrowed deeper until the leaves and dirt covered him entirely.

Though sounds were muffled within these bleak woods, he could hear the boarmen approaching. Their unwieldy girth prevented them from ever naming stealth as one of their attributes. They kept up a steady stream of blows and snorts, unnerving Calder. He was too small, and his vision too limited, to fight them. He did carry a dagger but rarely had he used it. Still, he reached for its hilt so he would be ready if it came to that.

A branch snapped near him. Silence followed, which was more terrifying than any of the noise that preceded it. He prayed the green potion covered the smell of his fear along with his human scent. Leaves rustled. His instincts told him one of them must be leaning over him, waiting like a patient beast of prey for his quarry to twitch. The stench of the creature's foul breath reached him and caused his nose to tingle. His blood froze at the thought of a sneeze.

But then came a snarl followed by incomprehensible squeals, and the sounds of one boarman shoving the other. Their footsteps crunched against the forest floor as they trotted away.

Calder sneezed quietly into his hand before clearing an opening in the leaves to let in fresh air.

ASH

Tessa zipped up a tree as if she'd climbed a lot of them as a child, and flattened herself on a branch that was nearly as high as the chapel tower. Ash followed her, feeling clumsy by comparison, though he had the excuse of being unaccustomed to having a sword strapped to him. He stretched out on a branch below hers, unsure whether there weren't still parts of him that would be visible to peering eyes from below. Perhaps it wouldn't occur to the boarmen to look up. With human bodies, they were capable of climbing, but their boarish instincts might revolt from such an action.

Ash remained as still as he could, as four boarmen followed a rough path not far from their tree. Three kept a fixed pace, glancing around and sniffing the air without pausing. The fourth hung back. His two sets of tusks looked longer, sharper, and deadlier than those of the others. The beast slowed close to the tree, and took several wheezy breaths. He glanced upwards without seeming to see Ash or Tessa, and a moment later, he continued after the other boarmen.

For several more minutes, neither Ash nor Tessa moved. Finally he looked up to see her leaning over the edge of her branch. Her attention was focused on a small beetle crawling near her face. She picked it up, stared at it, and brought it toward her mouth.

"What're you doing?" Ash whispered. Anyone would have to be starving to eat a beetle, especially one that was still alive, but no more than a few hours could've passed since they finished their meal and set out in the cart.

"Nothing," she said, dropping the bug. "You didn't think I was going to…?" She looked around. "Where's Calder?"

"Dunno. Thought he was right behind us."

"We need to find him."

Ash lowered himself from the branch, and she scrambled down after him. They began to make their way through the forest, but progress was slow through the dense undergrowth. Ash had hoped to find the north star and use it to guide them, but mist clouded their view of the heavens. A half-moon glistened through it, providing a small amount of light but not enough to give him any sense of the direction in which the castle lay. For all he knew, they could be headed straight back to where they started at the gate.

He was about to stop and consult Tessa when the ground shook and the boarman with razor-sharp tusks leapt in front of them. Tessa shrieked as the beast raised up his great sword with both hands. Fear paralyzed Ash as his mind flashed to another boarman, in another time and place. But Tessa calling his name brought him back to himself. With his hair tied back in the style Lance had worn, he felt his brother's strength surge through him.

"Get back!" he shouted to Tessa. He drew out the sword she'd given him and held it in position. Remembering the phrase he'd chosen for himself at Lance's urging, he cried out, "*From ash you came, to Ash you return.*"

Razor-sharp wheezed by way of a laugh and swung his mighty sword. Caught off-balance, Ash jumped backwards. The boarman came at him like a battering ram, attacking so fiercely Ash could do nothing but parry. Ash's movements were lithe and he could have danced around Razor-sharp given half a chance, but the beast gave him no opening. Razor-sharp slammed Ash's sword again and again, wearing him down, pushing him back. Ash slowed in his responses, growing less nimble. His practices had been all about technique, not endurance. He knew now that was a mistake. The boarman had no skills whatsoever, only sheer, unrelenting brute force.

Ash didn't know how much longer he could hold the beast off. *Where did Tessa go?* He half-hoped he'd given her enough time to save herself, and half-wondered why she didn't smack Razor-sharp with a heavy branch behind his head. In his distraction, he stumbled and fell onto his back. *My first and last battle, already over.* He watched the boarman raise his great sword to finish him off. Remorse filled him, not that he would die in combat, but that he had only fought *this* opponent—who meant nothing to him—and would never face the one who filled his nightmares.

Then a strange thing happened. A bird flew into Razor-sharp's face, scratching and pecking at his eyes, throwing off the boarman's aim. Ash rolled out of the way as the blow from Razor-sharp landed beside him. The bird flapped its wings in the boarman's face, continuing to peck and claw. Razor-sharp tossed his head, nearly slicing the little bird with his tusks. It darted away at the last second.

Taking advantage of the boarman's distraction, Ash bounded to his feet and drove his sword through the boarman's ribs. Razor-sharp toppled backwards, thrashed in place for a moment, and then died. Ash stood over him, gulping in air, his entire body trembling. It took a moment to settle himself. When he had, he drew back his sword and wiped it on the dead boarman's uniform.

He glanced around. "Tessa?"

She walked out from behind a tree. "Are you all right?" she said.

He wasn't sure. "First time I've killed anyone... anything?" He didn't really know how to define a boarman. Though the creature was half man, half beast, Ash derived no pleasure from taking his life. Lord Fellstone's magic had created them, and forced them into his service. Only he was accountable for their actions.

"You were amazing," Tessa said.

"Really? You were watching? Didn't know where you went."

"Sorry, I was frightened."

"Thought you might hit him with something." He hoped that didn't sound like criticism. He meant it more as a suggestion for the next time he engaged in battle.

"I should've," she said. "I don't know why I didn't think of that. I just froze up."

He looked around nervously. "Let's get out of here. I was lucky this time. A bird flew in his face."

"That was some brave bird," she said, smiling.

CALDER

Calder rose from his place of hiding and retrieved his bag. He brushed the leaves off himself, ignoring the small twigs still stuck in his hair. He opened his bag and searched through its contents for several moments, cursing repeatedly, until at last he pulled out the object he needed: a handheld compass. His plan was to head toward the castle, hoping his friends would do the same. They had little hope of finding each other inside the forest. He raised the compass close to his face and held it under the moonlight to read its dial. If he had not gotten too turned about, his destination ought to be due south from this point. But if he was wrong, he could end up deeper inside the Cursed Wood, which circled the castle. He would have to take that chance, he decided, slinging his bag over his shoulder and setting out.

"Tessa? Ash?" he called out in quiet tones, in the off chance they had not gone far after all. The wind sighed and the branches went *scritch, scritch* against each other, but no one answered him. He walked on.

During his long travels across the sea, he had managed to contain his memories of Faline underneath his daily thoughts and concerns. But the closer he came to the place she might be, the more those memories pushed forward, so that he could barely think of anything else. Even now, her image appeared to him in the sweep of a willow tree's branches, looking as she did when he last saw her, an enchanting young woman, sixteen years of age.

By then he'd fallen hopelessly in love. Worse, as a mere lad of seventeen himself, he had been foolish enough to believe his feelings might be returned, despite the enormous differences between them. Her rank, her wealth, her beauty and refinement… these should have told him what insanity it was to believe he had a chance with her. Instead, he convinced himself they had a unique bond that went deeper than any earthly considerations. His practical side understood that when nothing was ventured, nothing was gained, and so he resolved to risk humiliation and heartbreak by confessing his feelings to her on her sixteenth birthday.

A grand ball was held in her honor that night. Faline wanted to invite him, but her parents would have burned the hall down before allowing Cook's son to enter it as their guest. Calder watched through the glass at the terrace door while she danced in the arms of other men, as light and graceful as a cloud, with her billowy white gown whirling round her. As entrancing as she was, he preferred her in the simple garb she wore during their walks, when mud would stick to her slippers, and leaves catch in her hair.

Every gentleman, young and old, waited for his turn to partner with her. But Faline showed particular favor to Daniel, a young man who had claimed the most number of dances by far. Daniel belonged to a well-to-do family in the neighborhood. Faline's parents treated them like poor relations: they were tolerated as long as they acknowledged the vast superiority of the Eldreds in every way.

Seeing Faline's face brighten whenever Daniel approached, Calder suppressed twinges of jealousy. She'd known the boy for several years; naturally she was friendly with him. But Calder had noticed the frequency of Daniel's visits increasing over the last few months. When he'd mentioned it to Faline in an offhand way, she had brushed his concerns aside.

"We talk about books," she said. "His family is dull and hardly owns any."

Every birthday since she turned ten, Faline had snuck out of her house at midnight to meet Calder under the alder tree. He had left the terrace early to go there and wait for her, but it was not till several hours later that she finally arrived. Her face was flush with joy as she approached.

"Oh Calder," she said. "This has been the most perfect night of my life."

"Happy birthday," he whispered. He had planned to pour out his feelings, but her words made him hesitate. He was not such a fool to ignore that the most perfect night of her life had not, up till now, included him.

She clasped his hands. "Tonight, we're going to elope."

"We…?" Calder said. For one exquisite moment, he was the happiest man alive.

"Daniel and me, of course. We've tried to cover our feelings, but I thought you must see it. You know me so well."

On the contrary, he now understood he knew her heart no better than she knew his. He turned away, bracing himself against the tree, as he absorbed the blow. He kept his face in darkness so she wouldn't see the lines of despair that must have formed over it.

"He's gone to fetch the carriage," she said, oblivious of his suffering.

"Why?" The word arose from him like a cry for help.

"My parents would never approve of him," she said. "This is the only way."

Calder heard the carriage approach. At the same time, Faline's brother Mace ran toward them from the house. "Stop!" he cried out.

Calder wanted to welcome Mace's interference. But something inside took hold of him. Some code of behavior that had planted itself without his even knowing. All this time spent with Faline had clearly given him ridiculous notions that didn't fit with his station at all. Her parents would consider a black adder more capable of noble action than he... and yet he felt compelled to do the honorable thing.

"Go," he said. "I'll hold off your brother."

Her eyes glistened. "Dearest Calder. I'll never have a better friend." She kissed his cheek and squeezed his hands before letting go. Then she turned to the carriage, which had slowed to a halt on the road several yards away.

Calder reached into his bag, and for once, he didn't need to search. He only had one of the item in question, and it lay on the top. Quickly he lit the pouch with his flint and threw it on the ground in front of Mace. Thick smoke poured out from it, blanketing the boy. Its odor threw him into a fit of coughing and no doubt stung his eyes. Calder turned back and saw that Faline had gotten into the carriage. He grabbed his bag and prepared to run.

But Mace was faster. Half-blinded, he emerged from the dense cloud surrounding him and leapt at Calder. He grabbed his arm, pulled him around, and thrust his sword into Calder's eye. It might not have been where Mace intended the blade to go, but he could hardly be blamed for his poor aim at the moment.

Calder had no memory of anything that happened after that. A few weeks later, when he lay in his room recovering, Faline came to see him. With his one remaining eye, he looked up at her in surprise.

"You've come back," he said, annoying himself by stating the obvious.

"I never went away. When I saw what my brother did to you... I couldn't leave you like that. I made the driver stop. He and Daniel carried you up to the house."

Calder meant it when he told her he was sorry. A shroud had fallen over her eyes since he last saw her.

"My parents told us they would cut off my inheritance if I married him. I haven't heard from Daniel since then. He didn't love me at all, it seems." A tear slipped down her cheek, and she swiped it away.

He wanted to tell her it was all for the best, even given the loss of his eye, but he knew she wouldn't thank him for judging Daniel unworthy.

"Since then… my parents made me a match," she said. "I shall marry the man in a fortnight."

And with that, the tiny bubble of hope was pricked once more. "Who?" he croaked.

"A man of great wealth and power. The Conjurer Lord Fellstone," Faline had said.

#

With his mind wandering, Calder wasn't sure how much time had passed. He had given up on the compass and moved onto a rough trail. Now he noticed a strange-looking tree atop an incline on one side. It had a sinister aura about it, with many bare and spindly limbs that gave it the look of an enormous spider. He was about to turn away and continue without drawing any nearer, when he noticed a figure moving at the base of the tree. *Can it be one of my companions?* From where he stood, he wasn't certain, and therefore his only choice was to approach with caution, hoping to get a closer peek at the person without their glimpsing back.

Strange oval shapes hung from the tree's lower branches like dreary decorations. The figure—he could now confirm it was a woman—cut one down and cradled it. Her mane of curly black hair seemed to move with a life of its own. Fascinated, Calder drew nearer still.

The woman wore layers of clothing: pantaloons under a skirt, two blouses covered by a vest, several scarves and a shawl. Calder's gaze shifted to the bundles hanging from the tree. They looked like animals—squirrels, rabbits, raccoons—wrapped up in some sort of greyish yarn. Movement from the woman attracted his eye. With her back to him, she hunched over the thing she'd cut down, making a strange sucking noise. She now appeared to be bald.

He'd seen enough to tell this was not someone likely to help him find his friends or complete his journey. As he crept backwards, a branch cracked under his foot. He froze in place, silently cursing. The woman twisted around and glowered at him. Her face was ancient and hoary. Her hands had spider webs between the fingers, and long, deadly-sharp nails.

But the thing that drew his eye and made the blood curdle inside him, was one of several bracelets on her left wrist: a leather wristband with a fox's face in pewter, matching his own pewter cat. He stared at the hag with a growing sense of horror, as thousands of spiders swarmed up her skirt from the thing that she had dropped—a half-eaten rabbit—and settled over her scalp to resemble undulating hair.

TESSA

I As Ash and I made our way through the shadowy landscape, every crackle of a twig, hoot of an owl, or scrabble of a nocturnal animal made me start. Under normal circumstances, I didn't scare easily, but the Cursed Wood had fed my nightmares as a child. It was known to be so dense and dank that sunlight had little effect, and daytime could hardly be distinguished from night. When we began our trek, there had been a half-moon guiding us, but somehow its light had gone dark, and I could not have said whether it was blocked by trees or clouds or incantations. It was a forest thick with thorny undergrowth and huge mossy canopies, with air that stank of decay. Worse—oh, so much worse—was the aura of menace that hung over us like a shroud. We inched forward along a path of sorts, watching for roots that would trip us, and branches that might reach out to slash our skin. We spoke in whispers, anxious not to wake the forest demons.

"I don't think this is the right way to the castle," I said.

"Do you think we should look for Calder first?"

"He would expect us to continue on. I'm sure he's doing the same."

"Okay, well our best bet seems to be this path," Ash said. "It must come out somewhere. I don't think the forest is very wide."

"Not wide, no. If we followed a straight line to the castle, I imagine it's no more than half a mile. But it surrounds the castle. What if the paths are meant to lead us round and round the circle?"

"That's impossible. Sooner or later we'd come back to the road that cuts through it."

"The paths might double-back before reaching the road," I said. "Haven't you heard the legends? No one who enters here is ever seen again. But if the paths led straight through the wood, or back to the road, don't you think people would find their way out?"

"Those could just be tales to discourage intruders."

"I hope so. But in any case, I think we should go this way." I pointed at an angle to the left of our path.

"Why?"

"I saw the castle. When I was, um, up in the tree." In truth, after Ash had killed the boarman and before turning back into myself, sparrow-me had flown up high enough to view the fortress. I knew when I landed which way we needed to go, though admittedly I wasn't certain if we were still following the same course.

"That was a while ago," Ash said. "I really think we should stay on the path."

I stopped to look at him. Maybe he thought, because he was a boy, he should get to make all the decisions. But that wasn't my opinion. "I do feel strongly about this," I said. "And it is my quest, after all. It was nice of you to come… why did you come, by the way?" I paused, but when he didn't reply, I barreled on. "Whatever the reason, as last-chosen, you can't expect to be the leader."

"I suppose you would have rather had Ryland." Ash's voice was thick with resentment.

"He is the better swordsman." I regretted the words as soon as they left my mouth, especially knowing they were false.

"The better...? If he were here instead of me... well he wouldn't be here, he'd be back there dead on the ground, and you'd be helpless with no one to protect you."

"Protect me? I seem to recall you would've lost that battle if not for the lucky arrival of a little bird."

"If Ryland were here, I'd prove in an instant who the better swordsman is. But he isn't here, is he?"

"Only because his father forbade him to come," I said, suddenly finding virtue in what I'd viewed as cowardice just a few hours earlier. "We'd all be better off if we listened to our fathers." I smothered the realization that it was the height of hypocrisy for me—whose Papa was dead because I'd failed to obey him—to be lecturing anyone on this subject.

"My father forbade me too," Ash said quietly.

His words took me by surprise. *Why did I even start this argument?* I didn't feel like myself in this place. It drained me of all happy feeling, leaving only the negative emotions of anger, fear, and suspicion. Unlike Ryland, Ash had defied his father to join my quest. He deserved my respect and gratitude, even if he couldn't slay a mouse with that sword of Papa's.

Ash blurted, "It's because of Ratcher."

"What?"

"You asked why I came. It's because of her. Fellstone's apprentice. It was something that happened three years ago, when Lance and I were—"

"Lance was your twin? I heard he died. I'm sorry." Without brothers or sisters myself, it was hard to know what that would feel like. But if Ash and Lance were anything like the widow Hawley's twin daughters, Margaret and Anna... well, those two were inseparable. I couldn't imagine one of them without the other.

"One day we were working, digging a grave," Ash said. "At least

I was digging. Lance usually got distracted. I called him to take over for a bit so I could rest. The sun broke through a cloud, and then he saw it in the soil I'd loosened up."

"Saw what?"

"A huge ring… an emerald with gold coils wrapped around it."

I looked at my finger, trying to imagine such a thing. "Was it a woman's ring or a man's?"

Ash snorted. "What difference does it make? We weren't planning to wear it."

"How do you think it got in the graveyard? Was someone buried with it?"

"I don't know. It wasn't on anyone's finger."

"I just wonder how someone could be so careless to lose a ring that must be worth more than Papa would earn in three lifetimes," I said.

"No idea. In any case, I thought we should tell our parents," Ash said, "but Lance had the idea to bring it to the swordsmith and trade it for two steel swords."

"It must've been worth much more than that."

"Dunno," he said. "Swords were priceless to us. But we were idiots. The swordsmith's livelihood depends on Lord Fellstone and his army. Who else can commission weapons from him? The ring must've tempted him… but not enough to overcome his fear of arrest, if we were ever caught with his swords. So instead he snitched."

A cold chill crept up my neck.

"Ratcher came to our house the next day. She had the biggest, meanest-looking boarman with her… she called him Scarface, for obvious reasons. She told us everything would be forgiven if we turned over the ring and showed her where we found it. We weren't sure whether to believe her, but one thing we knew… she and her boarman would slaughter our whole family in an instant if we hesitated. So we confessed and brought them to the grave where the ring had turned up. It seemed as if we were in the clear… she took a step like she was going to leave… then she nodded at the boarman." Ash looked away and continued in a thick voice, "He speared Lance through the chest."

"Why? Why did they have to do that?" My eyes filled with tears.

"She said one of us had to pay for not turning the ring in to the garrison. Lance just happened to be nearer the boarman."

"So your goal… the reason you're here… is revenge?"

He nodded.

"She's wicked. I could tell when I first saw her at the castle. I'd like to kill her myself," I said.

He shot me a glance. "You saw her at the castle?"

My mouth dropped open as I realized my mistake. A moment passed while I searched wildly for an explanation that did not involve sparrow-me pausing in flight to perch on a castle window and spy on Lord Fellstone and Ratcher. At last I muttered, "I meant, the house. When you and I saw her at my house."

He looked as if he didn't believe me, but he didn't comment. We walked on in silence.

Our pace quickened as the way opened around us and the ground grew softer and more pliant. I took a step and cried out as my foot sunk deep into a mud patch, forcing my other leg down onto its knee. I looked up at Ash for help and what I saw behind him froze my blood. A man but not a man. A shimmering form, not quite solid. Its clothes in tatters. Dark holes where its eyes and nose and mouth should be. *A wraith.*

Ash saw my look and spun around to see what caused my fear.

"I'm stuck!" I said. It felt as if powerful hands gripped my foot under the earth, refusing to release it.

Ash turned back to me, knelt and grabbed my leg. I leaned on his back to keep my balance while we both pulled.

The wraith tread straight toward us, as if it could see us with those empty sockets. I gasped in recognition: this was the poor, starved prisoner who was chased and killed by the boarmen outside the castle.

"We don't have time, get out your sword!" I told Ash. I yanked my hardest but my foot barely moved.

The wraith was steps away from us. I drew back from its path as far as I could. Ash—brave Ash—moved in front of me and took out his sword.

"Halt or I'll kill you!" he cried, though his words made no sense, the wraith was already dead.

The creature continued steadily. It knew Ash was powerless against it, or perhaps it didn't care. Ash slashed at the wraith, but wounds sealed instantly, the moment the sword was withdrawn.

The wraith passed through Ash's arm and then through my leg, bringing with it a paralyzing chill, colder than anything I'd ever felt in my life. I shivered convulsively as the creature appeared on my other side, and kept moving forward at the same measured pace.

"What's it doing?" I said.

Ash stared after it. "Lance and I saw one once in the cemetery. It reached out of its grave… gripped the sides… pulled itself out. It didn't pay any attention to us. Like this one. It went in the direction of the castle. They say Lord Fellstone calls them up."

I looked back down. "Help me," I said. "Let's try pulling slowly." We made steady progress so that I broke free moments later. "Hurry now," I said, wiping my boot on the grass as a short burst of triumph flashed through me. "He isn't following the path. The wraith knows the way."

I grasped Ash's hand so that we wouldn't lose each other as we ran through the darkness. But I was surprised at the warm glow that coursed through me when, after a second's delay, his long fingers folded over mine.

CALDER

Every instinct inside him told him to run. It took all his strength of will simply to stand there and not turn away from the revolting scene playing out before him. But he had to do more than that. He needed to step forward, speak to the hag, and somehow pry from her the answer to his question: *How did you come to have that bracelet?*

Calder lowered his bag to the ground and tucked his distinctive wristband under his sleeve. His hand brushed the hilt of his dagger as he padded toward her. He gained reassurance from its presence, though he hoped he wouldn't have to use it.

The ancient woman eyed him, holding herself motionless except for the mass of spiders on her head.

"That's a pretty bracelet you have. The one with the fox," he said.

Her gaze shifted between Calder and the bracelet. "The one-eyed man likes Arachne's cunning fox?" Her mouth made clicking sounds as she spoke.

"Yes, I wonder where I might find one like it."

"There is no other. It once belonged to the pretty princess, but she has no more need of it." Arachne pretended not to watch him. She was a devious one and he would need to be wary. He struggled to hide how sharply her words pierced him. *She has no more need of it.*

"Who is the pretty princess?" he said. "Do you mean Lady Fellstone?"

"The pretty princess who is the master's wife," Arachne said.

"Where has she gone?"

"Why do you not ask her master?" She sat down upon her stool, entirely heedless of the spiders moving in ripples and waves over her head.

Calder did his best to suppress his revulsion. He held out his arm, revealing his own wristband. "Tell me, and you may have this one too."

Her eyes gleamed with avarice. "I will show you, one-eyed man. The pretty princess is right here."

Calder caught his breath. "Where?"

"Look, we made a special place for her. You see?" Arachne directed Calder's eye past her to a heap of bones beyond the tree. He gasped in dismay.

Web shot out from Arachne's fingers. She spun like lightning, pinning Calder's arms to his chest before he had time to react. "Help!" he cried out. "Help me!"

Arachne spun web over his mouth, silencing him. "There will be no help for the one-eyed man." As the sticky strands whipped round and round his body, she said, "The pretty princess ran away from the master but we caught her. We took her cunning fox and green sparkly ring and saved her for eating later."

She hung Calder from a sturdy branch of the tree with a thick loop of her web, so that he was lifted off his feet and left to dangle like the other poor animals she'd caught. When she finished, only his nose, eyes, and wrist were left uncovered. No doubt she wanted to keep him alive until she was ready to devour him. She extracted the bracelet from his wrist with her long claw-like fingernails, and secured it on her own arm beside the fox. He didn't know why she allowed his eye to remain open, but he guessed she might enjoy an audience to her debaucheries.

Arachne resumed her seat and picked up the half-eaten rabbit. The spiders swarmed down from her head and attacked the meat in a feeding frenzy. An instant later they returned to Arachne's scalp and she tossed the skeleton onto the heap of bones.

She raised her wrist and gazed with satisfaction at her matching bracelets. "The curious cat and the cunning fox," she said. Her gaze shifted to Calder. "We are grateful for your gift and shall tell you something in return." She cringed and backed away from some shadow in her own mind. "We never ate the pretty princess. Master sent his swinish swine-men to take her back. Dreadful, loathsome swine. We hid in the tree and they ate our food. They took our pretty princess and her sparkly ring."

She caressed the band. "But we kept the cunning fox for ourselves."

There could be no better consolation than the knowledge that Faline had escaped the repugnant Arachne and her arachnid army. The thought of her poor defiled bones scattered here amongst the rest of Arachne's victims had been too much to bear. But he cursed his carelessness in allowing himself to be caught. He did not believe he could look to his friends for rescue, as they seemed to have lost him entirely, nor could he even hope for a band of swinish swine men to save him. Fellstone would not be sending them out for him.

ASH

Ash heard it first, a thin cry for help. He couldn't say for certain if it was Calder's voice, but who else could be stranded in the Cursed Wood tonight? A second cry came and this time Tessa reacted.

"Calder!" she said.

"That way I think," Ash said, pointing.

"We'll have to lose the wraith," she said, peering at his face, uncertain if he might object.

But Ash would never question the need to save one of his own. "So be it," he said. Appreciation flashed in Tessa's eyes before they turned and ran through the heavy brush, branches slapping against them, scratching their skin. They needed to reach Calder soon. His cries had stopped and there was nothing further to guide them to him. Ash prayed to the gods his life had been spared.

They spied movement beneath a huge, spindly tree ahead of them. Ash grasped Tessa's arm to slow her, and placed his finger on his lips when she looked around. She nodded, and the two of them slunk toward the tree. As they drew closer, they made out the shape of a strange, witch-like woman, who busied herself beneath the branches.

"There's something strange about her hair," Tessa whispered.

Ash's gaze was fixed on something else. "I think that's Calder... hanging from the tree." He stared at the largest bundle.

Tessa followed his eyes and gasped.

"Let's get closer," Ash said. They picked their way toward where Calder hung.

Tessa grasped his sleeve and pointed to the side at Calder's bag, lying where he'd left it on the ground. She darted forward and opened it.

Ash had seen enough. He straightened and drew out his sword, preparing to attack.

"Wait," Tessa whispered. "There might be something here."

Ash didn't believe there could be anything in Calder's bag more effective than his sword. He'd already defeated a boarman in combat. *How can an old woman compare to that?* If there was a difference between bravery and foolhardiness, Ash had not yet caught on to it. He bounded past Tessa, while she snorted in frustration, digging into Calder's bag.

The hag turned at the sound of Ash's approach. He vaulted across to her, lifting his sword. "Release our friend from the—"

He lost his voice abruptly, as he had the dreadful realization that what he'd thought of as her hair was instead a vast spider's nest.

She gave him a twisted smile, recognizing his fear. She laughed with a clicking sound as her spiders swarmed off her head, onto Ash's sword, up his arm, and all over his body. He cried out, dropped his sword, and threw himself on the ground, twisting and rolling. *They're everywhere.* His face, inside his clothing... he couldn't see, couldn't breathe, as he writhed in agony.

He heard Tessa shout from what seemed like a distance: "Call off your spiders." Still they teemed over him, crawling and biting. He swatted wildly and pounded himself against the ground. If only there were a cliff nearby, he wouldn't hesitate to jump and make the torture end.

Someone made a choking sound and then Tessa spoke again: "Call them off or you die!"

The spiders moved off him in a pulsating mob. He opened his eyes to see the black mass scuttle across the forest floor and climb onto a pile of bones, where they settled and went still. His body still prickled and itched, and he continued to bat at phantom stragglers.

Finally Ash was able to look up. Tessa stood behind the hag, gripping a thin rope around her neck. She wrenched the rope harder, making the woman choke and sputter.

"Don't even think of bringing them back here," Tessa said. "They don't frighten me."

Ash pulled himself up, retrieved his sword, and hurried to Calder. He cut him off from the tree but didn't manage to catch him as well as he would've liked—he expected to hear from Calder about that later. Once he had his friend on the ground, he cut through the webbing with little difficulty, though it would take some time to fully remove the sticky residue from his sword and Calder's clothing and hair.

As soon as he could move again, Calder drew out his dagger, stalked to the hag, and placed the sharp point under her chin. "Perhaps this will teach you not to trap people," he said.

A gasp from Tessa drew Ash's eyes to her. She was staring at the matching bands Arachne wore, one with a cat, the other a fox.

Calder spoke as if he wished to reassure her. "It's all right, Tessa. Your mother escaped."

"But how do you—"

"I'll try to answer all your questions later." Calder turned back to the hag. "Tell me where the princess is now."

Tessa loosened the rope just enough to allow her to speak in a raspy tone. "It has been ever so long since she was here. But we heard she ran away once more after her master took her back."

"Did he find her again and return her to the castle?" Calder asked. When she didn't answer, he pressed the dagger into her putrid skin. Green blood seeped out.

"We don't know," Arachne said. "We keep to ourselves. Leave us alone."

"Keep to yourselves? You were going to eat me."

"We do not mean any harm. We must eat. The one-eyed man and his friends must eat too."

"Tell us how to reach the castle from here," Ash said.

Arachne's eyes lit with a devious glint. "Follow the path," she said.

Calder slammed down the knife on the tree root beside her, stabbing one of her spiders that lingered there. She cried out as if he'd cut her own flesh. "Don't hurt us!" she whimpered.

"Don't lie!" Calder said.

"The web leads to where the master lives," she said, nodding toward what looked like a thin rope tied around the tree trunk. The rope—which had to be tightly woven spider silk—continued toward another tree. *Terrific,* thought Ash. *More spider stuff.*

There was no further information to be gotten from her. With hemp from Calder's bag, they tied Arachne into a bundle and hung her from the tree. As they walked away, her spiders swarmed over her.

"See how you like it," Calder said, looping his bag over his shoulder. He grasped the rope made of spider silk with one of his hands. "At least it isn't sticky. I'll keep hold of it. We might lose sight of it in the darkness." He led them forward, following the line from tree to tree.

Ash still brushed at imaginary spiders. Red welts from their bites sprouted up on his hands and face.

"You must encounter spiders when you're digging graves," Calder said.

“Spiders, yes,” Ash said. “Coordinated attack battalions, no.” He shivered and turned to Tessa. “Why aren't you afraid of them?”

She answered with impatience. “They're just bugs. Birds eat them.”

He had thought she might be more sympathetic. He was grateful she’d saved him, but felt ashamed she’d seen him at his worst, rolling on the ground, helpless, whimpering like a baby. All because of a million tiny creatures that any bird could eat.

He moved aside as she pressed past him and stepped beside Calder.

TESSA

Calder had reclaimed both bracelets from the horrid spider lady, and gave me the one belonging to my mother. I put it on my wrist directly, while questions whirled inside my head. I now felt certain it was no accident that Calder's bracelet matched hers. *If he knew her, why hadn't he told me sooner?*

I drew up beside him to speak to him. "How did she get my mother's bracelet?"

"She stole it from her, just as she stole mine."

"If so… how did my mother escape?"

"Fellstone's boarmen came to her rescue," Calder said.

"Why would they do that?"

"They acted on Fellstone's orders."

"What was she to him?"

He paused to give me all his attention, his single eye full of sympathy. He said gently, "She was his wife."

His words made no sense. I thought I must not have heard him correctly and I asked him to repeat it.

Calder spoke in the same tone he might use to a small child. "Your mother was my friend Faline, who became Lord Fellstone's wife."

I thought Arachne had somehow addled his brain. Perhaps her

spiders had injected him with their poison. "That's ridiculous," I said. "My mother's name was Gillian and she was married to my father."

"If only your parents had told you. Why must I always be the bearer of bad news?"

"It isn't true!"

Calder sighed. He drew out a faded note from his pocket and handed it to me. I read the note aloud, feeling a tremor building inside me. "Dearest Calder, I've escaped from Fellstone. A kind locksmith has taken me in. Come to me, be my savior. Faline."

"The letter was sent years ago to the house where I once lived," Calder said. "They had no idea how to find me. A chance meeting several months ago put the letter into my hands."

"Maybe my father helped your friend. It doesn't make her my mother."

"Think about it. Your mother hid herself from everyone. Why? Because she didn't want Fellstone to find her."

"My mother's name was Gillian," I protested weakly.

"Of course she couldn't use her real name. Take heart, Tessa. She escaped Arachne. She may yet be alive."

We walked on in silence while I tried to wrap my head around what Calder had told me. *It can't be true.* But if it were… it explained why Mama almost never left the house. Why, on our last afternoon together, she *did* go outside without seeming to feel any ill effects whatsoever. Why, when meddlesome neighbors stopped in, trying to get a glimpse of her, she would remain in her room and make up excuses not to come out. It all made sense if she meant to hide herself from anyone who might recognize her.

Then there was the windrider and the question of how Mama came to own such a powerful piece of magic. *Because she was the wife of the Conjurer Lord Fellstone.* Of course it must have been his, only a conjurer could've made it. She took it and perhaps even used it to make her escape.

And now, because of my carelessness… because I had flown right up to Lord Fellstone's window and shown myself to him… he knew where the windrider was, and he wanted it back so badly he had killed my papa for it. I was not only to blame for refusing to run away with Papa, but for everything else that led up to his death. And yet, just when my thoughts were at their lowest, as I blamed myself for every terrible thing that took place since the day I discovered the power of the windrider, a small tendril of hope crept into my consciousness. If Lord Fellstone's men had found Mama at our house and taken her back… *she could be alive. She might be here at the castle, perhaps imprisoned, but still… alive.* I knew it was greedy to wish for the recovery of both my parents, and yet that hope took hold of me hard and refused to let go.

Before long, we reached the end of Arachne's line. The trees opened up and the castle, in all its grim majesty, soared before us. Somehow we'd passed through the Cursed Wood without dying and now we must find a way to enter without detection. I needed to concentrate on that goal and not allow myself to be distracted by thoughts of Papa inching closer to the point of no return, laid out on the table back home.

Calder beckoned us back behind the cover of trees, in case there might be eyes peering out of the castle's black windows.

"Let's gather our strength for a moment," he said. "We need to determine our next step."

We retreated to a small clearing, where we found logs and stones to sit upon. Calder took out a whiskey flask, while Ash found some beef jerky in his pocket to nibble on. I opened my pouch and took out a packet of sunflower seeds. I had started eating them recently and quickly learned to shell them with my teeth, sucking out the seed inside. I turned to Calder, determined to learn more of my mother, though I wasn't yet ready to pronounce myself convinced.

"How did you come to know my… Faline?" I said.

"My mother was cook in her parents' household," Calder said.

"I suppose it was a grand place to live."

"For them it was. My mother and I slept in the garret. But Faline… she was nothing like the others in her family. We were close from early childhood."

I looked toward the castle, which loomed above the trees. "Why did she marry that tyrant?"

"Her parents assured her not all conjurers were evil. They told her she would grow to love him in time."

"I can't imagine her believing that." Mama would not have been so naive.

"I blame myself," Calder said, squeezing his wristband. "Like a fool and a coward, I let her go." He lowered his head.

I wondered suddenly how much Papa knew. She must have explained who she was, or else how could he have accepted her strange behavior? But if he knew… why had he left me in the dark? *He should have told me.*

An overwhelming exhaustion came over me. I sat beside Ash and leaned with him against the base of an oak tree. Before I knew it, we had nodded off.

#

I wasn't sure how much later it was when I jerked awake and found my head resting on Ash's shoulder. We pulled away from each other awkwardly. I rose and began gathering leaves and small branches while Ash and Calder talked.

"How do you plan to get us in?" Ash said.

"Uh, let's see. Since the drawbridge is up and the outer windows are barred… we only need to swim across the moat, scale the tower wall to the ramparts, kill the sentries who are sure to be there, and finish before someone sees us and raises the alarm," Calder said.

"I don't think we can do that."

"Really? It sounds so easy."

"What if we create a distraction?" Ash said. "Something that makes them open the drawbridge."

"Like what?" Calder said.

"Dunno. We could start a fire, and when they come to put it out, we sneak behind them into the castle."

"Do you think they'd leave the entrance unguarded as they all race out? If they see a fire, they'll expect an attack. They'll be looking for the enemies who started it. Admittedly, it would be hard to imagine a less likely group of stragglers to storm a castle than us, so perhaps we'll simply pass under their notice."

Let them figure it out. I whistled softly to myself, forming a pile out of the sticks and leaves I'd gathered.

"What's your idea then?" Ash said.

"If you recall, we started out in the vegetable cart. If no one had searched it, we would have been rolled right into the castle courtyard," Calder said.

"That was it? No other plan?"

"What's yours? Charge the castle? We saw how well that worked against Arachne."

"Says the man we found wrapped in her spider web."

"Exactly my point. That's what happens when you let your emotions get the better—" Calder stopped speaking abruptly. Absorbed in my whistling, I didn't bother to look over and see the cause. I sat on the pile of leaves and branches I'd made.

"Look at you," Calder said with an air of bemusement.

I glanced over to find that he and Ash were staring at me. "What?" I said.

"Making your little nest. You're just like a bird."

"That's ridiculous," I said, rising immediately and kicking the branches out from under me. Just because I didn't want to sit directly on the dirt didn't make me a bird. And plenty of people liked to whistle. Mama used to do it all the time. Unless I was using the windrider, I was a person, one hundred percent.

Calder continued to watch me with growing curiosity. Finally he said, "Is there anything you'd like to tell us?"

"No, of course not," I said.

"Something that might help us get inside the castle?" His gaze lowered to my amulet.

I touched my sparrow defensively. "I'm not sure what you mean."

Calder let the moment sit. "Very well then." He turned away.

Did he know what it was? It seemed that way. And he was right… I could easily swoop into the castle as a bird. But I'd never told anyone. Even Papa had to discover it on his own. There was something about the transformation of man into beast—or girl into bird—that felt intensely personal, like taking off my clothes in front of them. Maybe the use of magic was always like that. I didn't know; I had no other magic.

Ash still looked at me. "Is it true?" he said quietly. "You know something that might help us?"

He had already faced death twice for us. The second time he'd had to endure spiders. My weakness was snakes… I couldn't begin to imagine the horror of hundreds of them slithering all over me. And Calder… my mother's dear friend. Both had risked everything to come with me on this quest to save Papa. Perhaps they had other motives as well, but still we were sworn companions and it would be unfair—nay, unforgivable—to hold back any skill or knowledge that might further our goals.

"I suppose I should've said something sooner," I began, "but I've never told anyone before."

"About what?" Ash asked.

I held up my windrider. "This. It's magic. It lets me change into a sparrow."

Ash stared for a moment and then laughed. "Did you get into Calder's whiskey?"

"You have to admit it explains a few things," Calder said.

"You've imagined it." Ash told me. "You were just sleeping, you must have dreamt it."

"You'll see for yourself," I said.

"I believe her," Calder said. "I've heard of such magic before. It's called a windrider, isn't it?"

"Yes," I said. And then to Ash, "The bird who helped you against the boarman. That was me."

He stared at me, clearly trying to remember the bird and its precise actions.

"I can find an open window and fly into the castle. If there are bars, I'll fit through them."

"If it's true, I don't like it," Ash said. "You'll be all alone in there. What if you're caught? We won't be able to help you."

His concern annoyed and pleased me at the same time. "I'll just look around," I said. "I'll be careful to stay out of sight."

"I agree," Calder said. "Try to find a place where we can enter. But do nothing. Come back and report. You'll be our scout."

I nodded and lifted the windrider to my lips, but then I hesitated. "Can you turn around?" I said. I had always changed in private. Once I tried staring into the mirror, but my vision clouded before the moment of transformation. As a result, I had no idea how the process would appear to others. It always began with a strong tingling sensation, and then my mind would grow murky, making me unaware of my surroundings, until suddenly I would find myself as a sparrow. What if I became naked for an instant before the change was complete? Anything was possible.

But there was another reason I wished them to turn away. I did not want them to see how to activate the magic. A small part of me feared one of them might want to try it himself.

Calder turned away immediately. Ash hesitated, probably because he still didn't quite believe me and needed to see it for himself. But when Calder grabbed his sleeve and pulled him, he too looked away. Then I blew on my windrider three times, and became the russet sparrow. When I cheeped, the two men turned to look at me, their faces bright with awe. Calder opened his hand, and I flew up and landed on it. He smiled at me, while Ash reached over and smoothed my feathers with a tentative caress. Then I lifted off and flew toward the castle, its black, imposing form outlined against the sky, growing lighter with approaching dawn.

Even the gravity of our situation could not keep me from feeling the thrill I always experienced when the wind rushed through my feathers. I tried to stay focused on the task… straight to the castle, fly into the first open window, and explore from there. But then I noticed an odd, shimmery sort of movement forming at the base of the castle walls… dusky shadows that were hard to distinguish against the darkness behind them. I would need to find out what this was before continuing. If it were some sort of magical defense, it could prove to be a barrier to Ash and Calder. I flew lower and circled once, straining to make out the shapes.

My sight went black. When it returned an instant later, I lay in the dark cavern my mind had visited before, on the night Fellstone's carriage appeared outside our house. My head restrained, my body strapped down… the sickly odor of decay. I struggled to move, but my bindings were too tight around me. I heard a sound like before, which became the scrabble of clawed feet over rock. Fear shot through me as I pictured rats finding me, climbing over me, scratching and biting as I lay helpless to run or fight. A candle flickered suddenly, and then came a deep, low, terrifying rumble… impossible to tell if the noise came from man or beast. I strained with all my might to burst out of my bindings. *Hopeless.* Heavy footsteps trod toward me. A scream formed in my throat.

Phoom! I was sparrow-me again, tumbling from the sky after a black crow rammed me. I beat my wings furiously, but the left one felt as if it were broken. Try as I might, I could not stop my fall. I stretched my good wing, straining to glide, trying to slow my descent… I was coming down fast, too fast, and when I hit the ground it was hard enough to stun me for a moment.

I glanced around to see the shadows drawing nearer. I tried my wing again but I could not get any lift. Without flight, I had no defense, and so I scraped the ground three times, transforming back. I stood up to run but now the shadows surrounded me, and I could see they were not shadows at all, but human beings, or what remained of them. Men, women, children… without eyes or noses or lips.

Calder's shout echoed from a distance. "WRAITHS!"

They closed in tight around me, leaving no gap for me to slip between. I thought, perhaps I could walk right through them, as the other wraith did to me in the forest. But if it turned my insides to ice as it did then… *how can I make it past so many?*

I recoiled as the same wraith we'd seen in the Cursed Wood stretched his hand toward me. Behind me, others reached out. The man came forward and touched me. I dropped to my knees as his hand pushed into my chest, like a frozen knife cutting into me. Gasping for breath, I fell backwards, trembling uncontrollably. The wraith knelt over me, glowing from the warmth he'd stolen from me. A spasm ripped through me as his hand wrapped around my beating heart, and I felt no more.

CALDER

After watching Tessa get knocked from the sky by a suspiciously aggressive crow, Calder had opened his bag and begun rummaging through it. By the time he glanced up again, he saw the ghostly forms approaching her and cried out. But he feared his warning came too late.

He dove back into his bag. "Blast!" he said.

Behind him, Ash unsheathed his sword and set off at a run toward the wraiths. Calder looked up too late. "Ash, no! Come back!" The boy didn't lack bravery, but he needed some sense kicked into him. While Calder watched, Ash plowed into the field of wraiths and slashed at them with his sword, but wherever the blade made contact, the gash sealed as if it never occurred.

The drawbridge was lowered and knights poured out onto the field. *We created a sufficient distraction after all*, thought Calder. "Bloody hell," he muttered, continuing to search inside the bag. Seconds later, he drew out a container with holes punched into the top. He used it to shake a fine white powder onto the bag, and then all over himself.

Calder and his bag began to fade until they were invisible. He felt around for the bag's handle, picked it up, and ran toward the circle of wraiths, leaving impressions of his footsteps in the mud and on the grass.

The first knight reached Ash and prepared to engage him in battle.

"*From ash you came, to Ash you return,*" he shouted, clashing swords against his opponent. Calder slipped past them unseen, intent on reaching Tessa.

Calder had felt the touch of the wraith before. It was something he would never forget and prayed never to feel again. He looked for a path to reach Tessa, but he could not see her through the swarm. He lowered his bag, resolving to walk through them if it came to that, when abruptly the wraiths began to part.

Fellstone's apprentice rode up on her grey stallion. Calder had never seen her before, but he'd heard talk of the mask she wore. She glanced 'round the field of battle while the wraiths spread apart and made way for her, as if she'd sent a signal only they could sense. They faded and grew dim until a moment later, they were gone.

Only then did Calder see Tessa, lying prone and lifeless on the grass. The sight pierced him through the heart. *Did we survive the wicked forest only to die at the gate?* The fault lay with him. What had he been thinking to bring two youths on this futile quest?

A boarman missing half an ear trotted up behind the apprentice. At the woman's command, the boarman lifted Tessa over his shoulder and carried her toward the castle.

Is she alive? Now was not the time to lose hope. He must carry on as planned, with or without the help of the others. He swiveled around to catch Ash in battle with more knights. Strong and lithe, swirling and slashing with the grace and power of an acrobat. *What a swordsman we found without even realizing.* But as Ash spun to block a thrust from yet another attacker, he came face to face with a wraith that had not faded with the others. The wraith was smaller than Ash, a mere boy. Ash went pale and doubled over, struggling for breath, though no soldier had struck him.

"Lance!" he called out with a voice so grief-stricken it would break the heart of any feeling person. Calder understood then that this was Ash's twin, though not a twin any longer as he would forever remain the age of his death. Ash reached out to him, but Lance faded now, as the other wraiths had before him. A soldier knocked the sword from Ash's hand, and another slammed his head with his shield. Ash fell, unconscious, perhaps even dead.

Calder could do nothing for his companions at the moment. Only pray for their lives, and the hope of reaching them within the castle. He rushed toward the drawbridge, weaving his way past the knights and boarmen. As he drew near, a devious-looking boarman sniffed the air and turned his way. The boarman bent down to look closer, noticing the impressions of Calder's feet in the dirt. He drew in a long, wheezy breath, his snout an inch from Calder's head.

Another boarman came behind the first and shoved him to the side to make way for the returning knights. Calder dodged just in time to avoid being pierced by the boarman's keen-edged tusk. Then, quick as he could, Calder sprinted across the bridge and into the castle itself.

His goal must be to learn the fates of his companions, but first he had to negotiate the castle grounds and orient himself. The vast outer courtyard teemed with activity, both human and animal. He noted a stable, hen house, and pigsty, but the bulk of the area along the perimeter was occupied by soldiers' barracks. Men on foot, knights leading horses, pairs of boarmen, and a surprising number of chickens crisscrossed the region as the invisible Calder picked his way toward the entrance to the castle proper. It took a great deal of last minute jumping out of the way to avoid collision, and he credited his frequent evasion of law enforcement with giving him the skills to succeed in this.

The enormous double doors leading to the Great Hall, and beyond that, the inner courtyard, were open. This appeared to be the norm for when the castle was not under siege. The Great Hall was exactly that; an expansive receiving area for visiting hordes, Calder supposed. Even the furniture seemed larger than life, with wooden tables that stretched the length of the hall, and huge padded chairs next to a giant hearth. Four sentries guarded a large, ornate wooden door on one side, which Calder suspected might be the entrance to Fellstone's private chambers.

He crossed the hall quickly and left by way of open doors leading to the inner courtyard. He paused at the top of the steps and scanned the broad area. On the opposite side, a tower was set between the castle walls. An arched opening flanked by two guards armed with spears and daggers provided entry at the base of the tower. As Calder watched, two soldiers approached carrying Ash, and spoke to one of the guards, who then left his post to lead them into the building.

Calder flew down the steps after them. He ran across the stone courtyard, around a fountain, and past some sort of staging area with a viewing platform. He preferred not to think of the type of entertainment Fellstone might be in the habit of watching. Slowing down as he drew near the guards, he took silent steps between them into the tower. Inside, he found a plain circular room from which one set of stairs went down, and another went up. From the sound of things, they'd taken Ash below. Calder descended the stone steps cautiously; it wouldn't do to fall down them and make a ruckus. Or break his neck.

At the bottom, he came to a row of iron doors cut into the stone. The guard stood waiting by one that was open, and a moment later the soldiers emerged from the cell carrying Ash's boots, coat, and sword, which they tossed into a corner. The guard locked the door, then slid the key onto a hook. Calder pressed himself and his bag against the wall as the three men trooped past him and clomped up the stairs.

His first thought was to applaud himself on his good luck. Ash must be alive or they would not have put him in the dungeon. Secondly, they left the key right there. He pulled himself up to peer through the peephole of Ash's cell. The boy lay on the floor unconscious, with his wrists shackled and chained to the wall, and his ankles manacled to each other. The prospect of escape did not look quite so easy anymore. The key on the hook must be for the doors only; it was much too large to work on the small padlocks that held the chains together. But there were no other keys in sight. Moreover, Calder did not have enough invisibility powder to cover Ash. Since the stuff cost an arm and two legs, he'd only purchased the amount needed for himself and his bag, with a little extra for touch-ups. So even if he could somehow get Ash out of his manacles, he would not be able to whisk him past the guards at the tower entry.

He briefly considered taking Ash's sword, but just as quickly rejected the notion. He did not want to waste what little powder he had left, in making the sword invisible, and in any case, he was better off defending himself with his dagger.

The boy and his sword would have to wait. He was passed out anyway; it couldn't hurt to let him sleep it off. At least Calder knew precisely where he was and could work on a plan to break him out. In the meantime, he needed to find Tessa. He checked the four remaining cells to make certain she hadn't already been brought here. Surprisingly, all were empty. He took this as an indication that prisoners were dispatched with little delay. He would need to work fast. There would be no forgiving himself if they dealt with Ash before he managed to return.

The dungeon was not the only thing down here. At the bottom of the stairs, the stone corridor branched off in another direction, and

Calder meant to explore it. He set out along its clammy interior, glancing into dark rooms as he passed. A rat scampered across one chamber, which was filled with broken weapons in need of repair. The next housed instruments of torture. His insides turned to jelly at the thought of himself or either of his companions being taken here. He'd been tortured once before and would rather die than allow it to happen again. But he would deal with that problem if and when it arose.

The stench of rot and putrefaction increased as he approached the final chamber along the passage. It was the morgue, the place which he'd hoped to find, though he dreaded to enter it. His heart skipped a beat as he glimpsed a body on a table across the room, with a white sheet spread over it. He had to pause and lean against the wall, steadying himself. *Please, I beg you... let it not be Tessa.*

He had to be certain. Calder stepped forward as two men appeared from another part of the room and approached the body, muttering between themselves. The older man had white hair and a grizzled appearance, while the other was quite young and suffered from the deformity of a club foot. The latter man carried a bucket of water toward the table, sloshing as he went.

As Calder drew nearer, he became convinced the form was simply too large for a girl. Clearly a man lay under the sheet, a fact that was confirmed as soon as the white-haired worker lowered the cloth to the corpse's chest. The deceased was a person of middle-age, with strong shoulders, grey hair, and a pointed beard. It took a moment for Calder to recall where he'd seen him before. The man was Sir Warley, formerly captain of the garrison. Whenever he came to a new town, Calder made it his business to find out who was in charge of enforcing the law, though it had not helped him to avoid the pillory this time.

The two undertakers stood with the bucket of water between

them at the end of the table, and each dipped a cloth into it. They washed the corpse one section at a time, gradually lowering the sheet until the cut in his stomach that must have killed him was exposed.

"His lordship said we was to give him all the respect of his station," the old man said.

The other man snickered. "Even though the lord's own apprentice gutted Sir Warley?"

"Where'd you hear that?"

"Jamie the footman told me. Seen it with his own eyes."

"Why would she do that?" the old man said.

"Jamie said, it were all about a bird. Sir Warley brought Lord Fellstone a sparrow in a cage. His lordship and Ratcher looked at each other and said, 'Wrong one.' Then Ratcher turned to Sir Warley and stuck her dagger in 'im."

"Over a bloody sparrow? I don't believe it."

"I've seen stranger round here," the one with the club foot said. He lowered his voice. "I were here last night when they brung in Sir Warley's body. Ratcher came after they left. She didn't notice me behind the stack of ledgers. When I looked over, she were squeezing blood into a vial from Sir Warley's vein."

"Did she see you then?" the old man asked sharply.

The younger one shook his head. "She left right after."

"Best not to wonder about their goings on. Less you know, the longer you live."

Calder could not argue with the man's wisdom. From what he'd heard, half the conjurers' potions required blood from someone or something. It wasn't his concern; he'd seen what he needed to see. Tessa was not in the morgue. He still couldn't be certain she was alive, but there was hope now, and he would not rest till he found her.

ASH

When he first opened his eyes, he couldn't understand where he was or how he got there. It felt as if someone were pounding the back of his skull with a hammer, over and over and over. He came to realize he was lying on his back on the cold stone floor of a dank cell, chained to the wall. It took a while longer before his memory came rushing back, bringing with it a surge of cold fury. *Lance.* It had not been enough for Ratcher to have him killed; she must condemn him to eternal torment as well.

Ash pulled himself up, sending another piercing stab of pain through his head. He raised his shackled hands and felt his scalp; a significant welt had already risen. But at least he was alive and uncut. *What of his companions? What of Tessa, surrounded by the horde of wraiths?* She'd fallen from the sky, and it seemed she could no longer fly. Only Calder could have saved her with something from his bag of tricks. Surely he had an ointment or talisman in there that could repel wraiths. *But what if he hadn't reached her in time?*

They were alive; they *must be* alive. Only their lifeless bodies laid out before him on a slab would convince him otherwise.

The clang of metal rattling in the keyhole made Ash look up. A guard with heavy-lidded eyes and hollow cheeks opened the door and made way for Ratcher to enter the cell. He closed the door behind her.

She stood staring down at him. Ash felt a loathing so strong, he wanted to leap up, throw his arms over her, and tighten his shackles around her neck until she breathed no more. He held himself back, mainly because he doubted the chains were long enough to allow him to reach her. The time would come for his revenge, but first he must find out if she would reveal anything about the fate of his friends.

He wondered if she remembered him or his brother. He didn't think they were any more remarkable to her than many others whose deaths she must have ordered without remorse. But the emerald ring must be unique, and its recovery a significant event. When she came to their house, he had thought at first that the ring belonged to her. But later when he learned she was only an apprentice... *what apprentice could afford a ring at all, let alone one with an enormous emerald?* It had to be Fellstone's. Having robbed the residents of Sorrenwood of all their worth, he could afford to line the fingers of both hands with precious gems.

He kept his eyes averted from Ratcher, determined not to let her rattle him. To his surprise, she began to laugh. He couldn't help but look up at her then, at the strange spectacle of the blank mask that hid everything but her eyes and mouth. She laughed harder and harder until the laughter became coughing that sounded like the caw, caw, caw of a crow. She stopped as abruptly as she'd begun and caught her breath.

"I haven't seen anything so amusing in many a month," she said. She spoke in low, honeyed tones that oozed into his ears. It was not a voice to be trusted: heavy sweetness layered over bile.

"You and your friend, that silly girl, expecting to breech the castle defenses, with nothing more than your sword and her...? Oh that's right, she had no weapon, not so much as a sharp toothpick," she went on. "So really it was just you in charge of slaying our entire army. It might've worked too, if each soldier had waited patiently in line to face you one by one. Was that your plan?"

Ash looked away. He would not give her the satisfaction of showing any reaction to her mocking.

"A plan must have some chance of success," Ratcher said. "The odds must not be entirely against you," she went on. "If your goal was to die, you could've chosen far easier ways. Now that we have you, that's no longer an option. Only the most excruciating deaths are meted out here."

Ash stared at a point on the wall. He refused to let her frighten him.

"Was there anyone else? An army of three-year-olds hiding in the woods? A legion of rats trained to do your bidding?" She laughed again. "I suppose you're wondering about the girl. The wraiths can be overzealous. Sometimes even we can't stop them. They're drawn to human warmth like moths to the light. If given a chance, they'll drain it out of you until your body freezes solid. Again, not an *easy* way to go."

Beads of sweat gathered on Ash's forehead. He could easily resist the taunts against himself, but not Tessa. Though he tried his best to block out Ratcher's words, the image of Tessa lying frozen and alone near the castle moat flashed before his eyes. His right arm flinched.

It was enough to satisfy Ratcher. She opened the door. "Welcome to Fellstone Castle. When I return, I expect you to talk. If you'd rather not, I'll invite Scarface the boarman to join us. I think you may remember him."

The door shut and the keys jangled in the lock. Ash punched the air, yanking at his shackles, picturing Lance and his defilement again. His rage was the impulse that would keep him alive.

TESSA

I snapped awake, my hands beating at the air. *Wraiths all around… intense cold… don't touch me!* I rocked back and forth, fighting an invisible enemy, until I realized they were gone and I was alone. I rubbed hard to heat my chilled limbs but the worst was inside, where it felt as if I'd swallowed a block of ice. It would take time for the warmth to seep all the way through me.

What place is this? I lay on a lavish canopied bed within the most exquisite bedchamber I'd ever seen. It was larger than our entire house, and filled with costly and elegant furniture. A tray of luscious fruit and nuts rested on the center table, which, like the dresser, was fashioned from fine oak, with flowering vines carved along the edges. The settee and chairs were upholstered in sky-blue brocade velvet, matching the color of the satin drapes. Parchment, quills, and an ink bottle were set out on the writing table. Sunlight poured in from the two windows, and a fire simmered in the magnificent hearth.

I grasped the thick white quilt that covered me, and pressed it against my face to warm my cheeks. I had no clue how I'd survived the ordeal of the wraiths, let alone ending up in this incredible room. *Are my friends in a similar place?* I wondered if the dark rumors surrounding Lord Fellstone's life and actions were all just a terrible misunderstanding.

I didn't have time to speculate. The clock was ticking down on the chance to save Papa's life, and I needed to get up. But when I moved to raise myself, I was rewarded by a jolt of pain in my left arm. I stared down at it and noticed a small puncture where my vein was, and a drop of crimson on the sheet as if a bit of my blood had spilled out. I wasn't sure, but I supposed it must be related to the injury I received outside the castle. The crow... that blasted crow again... had flown into me and damaged my wing. Would it heal when my arm healed? *What if I never fly again?* My hand shot to my neck, feeling for my windrider. *Gone.*

I leapt up, hardly noticing in my distress that I was clean and wearing a pretty white nightgown. I tore through the room in a frantic search for my beloved sparrow. My key pouch had been left on the table, but there was no sign of the amulet or any of the clothes I'd been wearing. I searched the drawers. There were delicate undergarments in the dresser, made of silk, satin, and lace, folded to perfection. I pushed them aside to look underneath, making a mess of everything. When I came to the last drawer, I found a book.

I should not have been surprised and yet I was. It was Mama's favorite, "The Trials of Kallos," which I had come to love as much as she. I opened its cover; she'd signed it just where she'd signed the copy we had at home. Here it was not "Gillian Skye," but "Faline Eldred Fellstone." Though the names were different, the handwriting was the same graceful script, ending in an identical flourish trailing from the final "e" in her surname. Part of me had not really believed Calder... had not *wanted* to believe him... but this proof was more difficult to deny. Her favorite book, her own writing... it had to be true.

My gaze swept the room again. How much cruelty had she

suffered at her husband's hands, to drive her away from all of this? How courageous she must have been to even attempt an escape from his fortress. I felt ashamed for doubting her, for thinking her capable of betraying Papa and running off with another man. Somehow… I felt quite sure of it now… Fellstone had found her and taken her away from us. I began to let in the faintest glimmer of hope that she might still be alive, might, in fact, be somewhere in this castle now.

I looked in the wardrobe. A dozen gowns hung on the rack in different colors and textures. I drew out one to examine more closely, its shade a lovely cream, its style smooth and unaffected. I pictured my mother wearing it at a grand ball, every man's eyes upon her. What a harsh fate that she'd been claimed by a wicked conjurer instead of a handsome, kind-hearted prince. I brushed the gown against my cheek and breathed in its scent, which reminded me of Mama's jasmine perfume, though perhaps I only imagined it by wishing it to be so. I closed my eyes and pictured her kneeling next to me, kissing my cheek, smoothing my hair back from my brow. My heart filled with love for her, in a way I hadn't allowed myself to feel for many years.

CALDER

One would think the ghastly odors Calder breathed inside the morgue would have quelled his appetite, but that wasn't the case. In search of something to fill his stomach, he made his way back across the courtyard, and into the Great Hall. From there he found his way to the main corridor, which wrapped its way around the castle. The place was constructed as a rectangle, with the inner courtyard creating a hollow in the center of it. Everything of importance appeared to be arranged on the main level. He took a staircase to the second level, and concluded from its plain appearance, low ceilings, and bare floors, that it served as a garret for housing the servants.

He returned downstairs, following his nose to the bakehouse, which was nestled between the kitchen and the brewery. He crept past two scullery maids and the baker to reach a tray that had just been removed from the oven. Waiting until they were distracted preparing the next batch, he snatched three rolls and stuck them into his bag so they would not be seen. Perhaps hearing him, one of the scullery maids glanced back and noticed the empty spots where rolls should've been. She shot a look at the other maid, wondering if she could have stolen them.

Calder hurried away with his prize before questions could be asked. He would've loved to fill a tankard at the brewery, but it would spill if he put it into his bag, and if he carried it in his hand, someone would be certain to notice it floating through the air. He passed on that with regret, and headed back upstairs to the servants' quarters. Rooms ought to be empty now, during mid-day when most were working, though there might be some who had night duty and slept in. The first door he tried must have been one of them. A man lay in his bed and opened his eyes groggily at the empty space that was Calder. He pushed the door shut and tried the next room. This one was unoccupied, with two beds neatly made. He slipped inside, closed the door, and took out his rolls. They tasted better than any he'd ever had before, and he wished he'd taken double the amount. But he did get lucky in finding a flagon which was half-filled with ale inside the room, and he gulped it all down with satisfaction.

Calder returned to the main level to continue his search for Tessa, but immediately spied Ratcher at the far end of the corridor, proceeding at a rapid pace. He sped after her. The woman had supervised Tessa's removal from the field; if anyone knew where she was, it must be her.

He stepped as softly as he could, but at one point a floorboard creaked and Ratcher paused and looked back. Seeing nothing, she continued until coming to an ornate door, over which a variety of strange symbols had been carved. She knocked and announced herself, and while she waited for a response, Calder snuck up directly behind her, trying not to breathe. She glanced back as if she sensed something, but shook it off when a man's voice coming from inside the room told her to enter. As she opened the door and stepped into the room, Calder squeezed behind her, almost brushing her with his bag.

A beast with the head of a crocodile and the body of a dog leapt up from the floor with a loud, menacing hiss. Its bones were sharply outlined, its skin scaled like a reptile, its long tail lined with deadly spikes. *Good god, what monstrosity is this?* Calder's instincts told him to flee, but when he looked back at the door, he saw Ratcher closing it. Instead, he scooted around a large vat, which was mounted over a flame, with steam rising from it. He glimpsed Lord Fellstone standing at the counter, grinding a purple flower with a mortar and pestle.

"Settle down, Fiend," Ratcher said, thinking the animal was reacting to her arrival.

"It's only Ratcher," Lord Fellstone told Fiend.

But the beast continued to hiss. From his hiding place, Calder could hear the tap of its claws on the bare floor as it drew closer to the vat. He had to do something before the croco-dog was upon him. But that meant getting into his bag without making a sound.

"Have you got her blood?" Lord Fellstone asked.

"Here, my lord," Ratcher said.

Calder heard her making her way gingerly past Fiend. Anxiety that he might be discovered and perhaps devoured any second, kept him from speculating on exactly whose blood Ratcher was delivering.

"I trust this will be sufficient, your lordship," she added.

"It will do."

The inside of Calder's bag was visible but hidden from the others' view behind the vat. Calder searched inside it as Fiend drew closer, hissing and salivating. He wondered if his forehead, damp with perspiration, was starting to show.

"What's wrong with you, Fiend?" Lord Fellstone said.

Just as the tip of Fiend's snout appeared, Calder whisked out the vial of green, scent-hiding ointment. It looked like it was floating in air as he uncorked it and shook it over himself. Wherever the droplets landed, Calder became visible. Bits of his arms, head, nose, and legs appeared.

"Are you certain there's nothing there?" Lord Fellstone said.

Ratcher said, "I'll check, my lord."

Calder threw the vial back into his bag and seized the invisibility powder. He shook it over all the visible parts, then tossed the jar back into the bag, closing it just as Ratcher peered around in his direction. Calder held his breath, unsure if he'd managed to cover himself completely. Fiend rounded the other side, uttering a guttural growl. It took all of Calder's willpower not to bolt in the face of Fiend's enormous maw, packed with crooked, razor-sharp fangs. Just as Calder thought he could bear no more, Fiend sniffed the air, grew quiet, and turned back. He settled into his corner and curled onto his bed.

"Did you have a bad dream?" Lord Fellstone asked Fiend. Then to Ratcher, with a harsher tone, "The girl could've been killed."

Calder peered round the side of the vat to watch them. This appeared to be Fellstone's conjuring room. The large chamber was filled with the tools of wizardry: jars of murky potions, vats of teeth, fingernails, hair, and eyes, goblets, hourglasses, ritual knives, and jewelry in the shape of symbols. Fellstone wore a smock over his tunic and trousers, which were of plain design but clearly sewn of the finest materials. He poured a noxious-smelling potion from a beaker into a vial which held a small amount of crimson liquid—no doubt the blood Ratcher had brought.

"My lord, she was never in any real danger," Ratcher said. "No lasting damage was done."

"She fell some distance."

"Only her arm was hurt."

Tessa's alive. It filled Calder with such joy, he felt liked shouting it out. Only her arm had suffered; she would get over that. They had all made it into the castle alive. Though Ash was imprisoned, and Tessa's whereabouts unknown, his heart rejoiced almost as fully as if their quest were complete.

"I suppose the dreadmarrow could heal her," Ratcher said. "But of course, that's only for your lordship's use."

"I'm not in the habit of sharing it."

"No one would ever expect you to, my lord. I'm sure it's quite out of the question."

"It isn't for you to say, Ratcher." Fellstone paused in stirring the potion. "On second thought, I rather think I might allow it. It's a small wound, isn't it?"

"Yes, but does that matter?"

"I say it does. I'm going to allow it. Just this once."

"If you're certain—"

"Don't make me repeat myself!" Fellstone stepped away from the vial and, using an elaborate key, opened a large cabinet made of heavy wood and decorated with gilded ornaments. "I see no harm in letting the child use it."

Ratcher bowed her head.

It was a stroke of luck to learn the location of the dreadmarrow. But Calder didn't like that it was to be used on Tessa. *Who knew what effects it might have on her?* Magic was known to take on a force of its own, and to influence those who used it for ill as well as for good. Bringing Tessa's papa back to life could also have negative consequences, but the alternative of certain death made it worth risking.

Calder was most intrigued by Fellstone's apparent interest in Tessa. He did not seem to bear resentment toward Faline's daughter; quite the contrary, in fact. It could be a sign that Faline was still alive and in good favor. He had seen no indication of her presence inside the castle, nor heard anyone speak of her, but much of the fortress remained unexplored. There was time yet… if no one caught him.

Lord Fellstone removed a thin leather packet from the compartment. A heavy, ancient-looking book with strange writing on the cover could also be glimpsed within. He handed the packet to Ratcher and relocked the compartment. Returning to his vial, he poured its contents into a cup.

"This ought to bring out the bloodbeast in me," he said. "The dreadmarrow has been leaving me drained of late." He chugged down the potion, grimacing as his face went pale and perspiration erupted on his forehead.

"Sire, I look forward to your transformation," Ratcher said.

TESSA

I had to pull myself together; this wasn't the time to indulge in grief. I needed to find Ash and Calder, and after that, secure the dreadmarrow. Every tear I shed—every non-essential action I took—ate into the precious time remaining to save Papa. As for Mama... there would be time to seek her later, if we managed to escape from here alive.

First I had to change into something besides this ridiculous nightgown. My own clothes had been taken, and so I must make do with whatever I could find in the wardrobe. I glanced through the gowns again until I came upon the plainest one, a simple brown muslin which laced up the front. I put it on and considered myself in the mirror. It fit surprisingly well; even the length was just right. Mama would've been pleased to see me grown up and wearing something of hers. I slipped on a pair of fine leather shoes. Unfortunately, my feet were larger than hers, but I could manage with the minor discomfort of pinched toes.

I attached my pouch to my waistband and hurried to the door. Not surprisingly, it had been bolted from the outside, but in no time at all, I unearthed a skeleton key from my collection that perfectly fit the lock. I peered out into the hallway to make certain it was empty before I stepped out.

Few who lived in Sorrenwood had ever viewed the inside of the castle, and yet everyone had an idea of what it must look like. Like most others, I'd pictured unlit hallways filled with unspeakable creatures crouching in the shadows, shabby doors that creaked when they were opened, and dismal rooms with broken furniture, spider webs in the corners, and rats scurrying across the floor. The reality could not have been more different than my imaginings. Sunlight poured in through rows of arched windows. Glittering chandeliers hung from the ceilings high above me. Bright frescoes portraying village life covered sections of the cream-colored walls. Rich red and gold carpets, so different from the ugly, threadbare floor coverings in my own house, overlaid the polished wooden floors. I marveled at every sight, and wondered if Mama, upon first seeing the castle, had believed she was the luckiest young bride in the world.

The first room I passed had these words painted on its door in red: "DO NOT ENTER UPON PAIN OF DEATH." I wondered what could possibly be in there, that would make his lordship want to kill you if you saw it. But I had enough strikes against me already; there was no point in breaking rules I didn't need to break. I would certainly not try to enter unless I learned the dreadmarrow was kept in there.

Just beyond this strange room, I came upon a large picture gallery with its double doors open to the hallway. Curious, I wandered into it and began to look about. The place was filled with the portraits of Fellstones through the centuries. Some had red hair, others yellow, brown or black. There were long faces, stunted faces, and fat faces… bulbous noses, upturned noses, hook noses, and pointy noses. Hairstyles changed; facial hair on the men came and went. But a powerful strain of arrogance ran through all of them. You could see it in their cold grey eyes, the arch of their brows, the lift of their noses and chins, even the placement of their hands.

At the end of the gallery I came to the portrait which put to end, finally and completely, any doubts I might still have held regarding my mother's identity. I whispered her name to myself as I gazed at her likeness. She wore a white gown with a lace shawl and her hair fell over her shoulders in ringlets. She gazed out at the world with a plaintive, haunting look: a sheep among Fellstone wolves. My heart broke for her.

Then I noticed the ring she wore. It was just as Ash had described it, an enormous emerald held in place by golden tendrils. Exquisite and repellent at the same time; a symbol of her servitude to a man of extreme wealth and power. I imagined what must have happened the day she managed to escape. She didn't run through the forest, as she had the first time when Arachne caught her, and Fellstone's boarmen retrieved her. Instead she stole the windrider, became a sparrow, and soared over the castle walls. She landed in a quiet place—the graveyard—and changed back into herself. She saw her ring and realized she'd neglected to leave it behind in her haste. Perhaps it crossed her mind to sell it, but doing so would lead him to her. She must get rid of it, the symbol of everything she hated. She yanked it off her finger and buried it in the dirt. A graveyard seemed a fitting place for an object that reminded her of trampled desires and a life that was more like death. Long after she left it, the wind blew, the soil shifted, and the ring rose closer to the surface. Twin boys would dig it up and see it as a means to achieve their dream of owning real swords… but one of them would die for it. How Mama would have grieved to know her thoughtless disposal of the ring led to the death of a child. But she could not have imagined such a crime. The killing lay at Ratcher's feet.

The sound of footsteps broke in on my reverie. I hurried to the doorway, filled with the hope that it must be one of my companions. When I looked out into the corridor, I saw to my surprise, that the door was open to the mysterious room which threatened death upon entry. I thought I glimpsed the shadow of movement inside. Now I was convinced it must be Ash or Calder. *Who else would take such a risk?* Perhaps the dreadmarrow was indeed kept within that room, and somehow, they had found it.

I approached the open door, paused at the threshold, and peered cautiously in. It was a gloomy place, more like the castle of my imagining, with the heavy scent of must and ruin. The curtains were drawn, the grate cold, and a thick layer of dust covered all the surfaces. It was a child's room, with both a crib and a bed, tiny clothes laid out on a dresser, and raggedy dolls heaped on top of a toy chest. The place felt bleak and abandoned, as if no one had entered it in many years. I saw no sign of my friends, but still I stepped inside for a closer look.

An arm whipped out from behind the door and wrapped around my neck. A dagger pressed against my back.

"If I killed you now, no one could say you weren't warned," Ratcher said.

"Let me go!" I cried out.

"Why should I?" Her words slid like oil from her mouth.

"I meant no harm," I said.

"Didn't you?" She lowered her arm and shoved me toward the crib. "Go ahead, feast your eyes on the forbidden room."

"What is this place?" I said. "Why are you here?"

"Why am *I* here?" She looked amused. "There are no restrictions on my movements in the castle, which is more than can be said for you." She nodded at the crib. "Regarding your first question, I don't think the answer could be any more obvious."

The sheet and blanket were perfectly folded over the tiny bed, which had turned grey from years of neglect. "Yes, I can see it's a child's room. But why was it left like this?"

"It was closed up before the child ever got to use it."

"Did the baby die?"

Ratcher gave a hard laugh. "Hardly. In fact she's standing right here before me."

I whirled around to check behind me, but no one was there. Ratcher's gaze fixed on me. "I don't understand," I said.

"This is your room," she said. "Is that clear enough for you?"

I still didn't comprehend.

"His lordship ordered that no one, not even the maids, should enter this room, after your mother left with you," she said.

"Left? I've never been here."

"You have, but you couldn't see it, nor could you walk through it on your own two feet."

"Must you speak in riddles?" I said, my impatience growing.

"When you left, you were still inside your mother's womb. It broke your father's heart when she stole away with you."

"My father…?" I trailed off. *Papa?* She didn't mean Papa. *Fellstone?* No. It couldn't be, I would never believe it. I shook my head furiously. "My father is Donal Skye, the locksmith," I told her.

She shrugged. "If you say so. It's nothing to me." She moved toward the door. "Come along now. I have orders to heal you."

Tears gathered in my eyes and I wiped them away fiercely. Ratcher was lying. Of course she was. The woman was evil and she would say anything to hurt me. I must not listen to her lies. *Papa is my father.*

"Come with me," Ratcher said. "His lordship wishes to heal you out of the goodness of his heart, and not because you're any relation of his. Definitely not."

I followed her in a daze back to the room where I'd woken up. She ordered me to sit by the window, took the dreadmarrow from its case, and used it to direct a beam of sunlight over my injured arm, just as I'd seen her do with Lord Fellstone's boils.

I struggled to return my thoughts to the problems at hand. *Find Ash and Calder. Steal the dreadmarrow. Save Papa.* "What happened to the boy who was with me?" I said. I knew Ratcher must already be aware of him, as I'd heard his battle cry on the field while the wraiths surrounded me.

"His accommodations are not quite as lavish as these," she said.

He's alive. I suppressed a surge of excitement. "I want to see him," I said.

"That will depend on the grace of his lordship."

"If my friend isn't treated well, I won't cooperate with any plans Lord Fellstone has for me." If he chose to pretend I was his daughter, my cooperation would not come easily.

"You must tell him in your own words," Ratcher said. "I'm sure he'll welcome your demands and conditions."

I wanted to ask about Calder, but what if he had managed to sneak into the castle without being seen? My question would give him away. I would need to seek him out for myself, as soon as I could get away from Ratcher. In the meantime, I had another object to pursue. "Something was taken from me," I said. "A necklace I'm fond of."

"The windrider?" Her eyes gleamed with amusement.

I should not have been surprised she knew exactly what I meant. "Yes, you saw it?"

Ratcher gave a cawing laugh. "It belongs to his lordship."

"Oh? Is he always so careless of his possessions?"

"Your mother stole it, as I'm sure you know."

"I suppose he could just make another," I said.

"You underestimate the difficulty involved. Creating powerful magic comes at great cost."

Then indeed, it was of more value than I'd imagined. I wondered about the crow; it had to be another windrider. Was it Ratcher who used it?

"I've heard conjurers can change into an animal at will," I said.

"Every conjurer has a bloodbeast, which is unique to him or her," said Ratcher. "It isn't like a windrider. Those are all birds, and anyone, even a simple girl like you, can use one."

"What is your bloodbeast?"

"An animal that would relish making a meal of your little sparrow." Ratcher lowered the dreadmarrow. The bruising on my arm was entirely erased and the pain had disappeared. I watched as she restored the dreadmarrow to its case. My fingers itched to snatch it away from her; I would've done it if I still had my windrider. Without it, I would need to run from the room and then... well, I didn't even know how to find my way out of the castle. Ratcher had only to shout down the corridor, and guards would no doubt appear and block my way. The theft of the dreadmarrow would have to wait.

"Am I a prisoner here, Miss Ratcher?" I said. "I'd like to know."

"Just Ratcher. I would not presume to answer for your father, I mean, Lord Fellstone."

"He isn't my father." Papa was my father and always would be.

"Then by all means, tell him how much happier you were as the unremarkable child of an insignificant locksmith, and how greatly you prefer the friendship of the gravedigger's son over anything his lordship might have to offer you."

She walked to the door. "His lordship expects you for dinner. A handmaid will help you prepare. I recommend you wait here till then. You never know who—or what—you might encounter in the hallways." She let herself out.

I went to the bed, lay down, and stared at the canopy. Everything I'd believed to be true about my life and family had changed since I'd set out from home. Ash and Calder might need my help, but first

I had to think. Nothing had turned out as I'd expected. *Nothing.*

What if my father really was Lord Fellstone? It would never change my feelings for Papa. He had raised me and taken care of me and taught me my trade. He loved me, protected me, nourished me. He would always be my true father, no matter what my relationship to Lord Fellstone might be.

I wondered how the lord would feel about me. He'd put me in the beautiful room that must once have belonged to my mother. The neglect of the nursery seemed to indicate a man whose heart was broken by the loss of his child. Did he truly wish to claim me as his daughter? Would he try to earn my love? Such feelings went against everything I'd learned about the conjurer and his wicked ways.

On the other hand, if he wanted my presence in his life badly enough, he might go so far as to make me his prisoner. I'd found the door of my bedroom locked, and there were bars on the windows. It seemed I might be forced to escape as my mother did before me. If I did, he would surely send his men after me. If I succeeded in saving Papa, we would have to flee Sorrenwood as quickly as possible.

Perhaps, though, I might use his interest in me as leverage to get what I wanted. I could agree to return to the castle and even live here for some time, if he would only give me the dreadmarrow and allow me to use it on Papa. And of course, he must tell me what happened to Mama, and set her free, if she were a prisoner here. My friends must also be allowed to leave the castle. If I meant that much to him, he ought to be willing to grant these requests, which should not affect him one way or the other.

Beyond all these considerations, there was something deeper that grated at my soul. *Who am I?* If I were Fellstone and not Skye, did that change anything about me? I'd never aspired to anything beyond work as a locksmith, and marriage to Ryland. It could be that I had no greater ambitions because I believed I came of humble origins.

But if the blood of Fellstones ran through me... did that mean I could be a conjurer? It was said that one had to be born to it.

Before I discovered the power of the windrider, the very thought of magical incantations terrified me. But now I knew that magic could be used for something that was pure and innocent and joyous. Some conjurers were rumored to be virtuous. If I had that power... well, of course I would use it to make the world a better place for myself and everyone I cared for.

There was so much to consider. My mother also had a pedigree that I could not have imagined before. She came of a wealthy, aristocratic family. They didn't sound like people I would wish to know, but perhaps they'd changed and might welcome a granddaughter. I would like to learn more about them, perhaps from Calder, who must know a great deal from his time growing up in their household. My mother might have a sister or cousins who I could visit at their estate someday.

But my mind was wandering far and wide again and I had to force myself back to the problems at hand. *Find Ash and Calder. Get the dreadmarrow (perhaps stealing was no longer necessary). Save Papa.* These came before any other consideration. After I dined with his lordship, I would make my requests, and if he refused them, it meant following through on the original plan, no matter what the risks might be.

The handmaid, Mary, arrived shortly thereafter and insisted I change into more formal attire for dinner. At first I resisted, until she threatened to call "my father." It horrified me to learn that everyone in the castle already knew me as his daughter. How soon would word spread through Sorrenwood?

Mary then drew out the most beautiful gown I'd ever seen, a silk lavender in a style that would flatter my figure. I used to think I didn't care for such finery, but I suppose it's easy to say that when there's no chance you'll ever own such a thing. I decided there was no harm in treating myself this one time. No matter if the lord granted my requests, I could never see myself settling into life as a spoiled lady of the castle.

I'd managed to dress myself since I was four, and thus I found it difficult to stand like a helpless doll while Mary adorned me. She scolded me whenever I tried to help, until I gave up. When she was done, she held up a mirror of polished metal, and the girl who stared back at me seemed like a stranger. Perhaps clothes do make the man, or the woman. After that, Mary insisted on arranging my hair, and I was forced to sit in front of the mirror for another hour as she brushed my locks and arranged them in coils.

"What a pretty lass you are," she said.

I bristled at the compliment and lowered my voice. "Can you help me? Have you seen any prisoners who were brought into the castle?"

Mary continued as if I'd said nothing. She took out a pearl necklace and earrings from a box. "His lordship sent these for you to wear tonight." She clasped the pearls around my neck. I couldn't help but stare at them and admire their luster, though I was determined not to be impressed by the jewels.

"I have money I can give you," I said. "Please. It's important that I find them."

It was like speaking to a statue. "Don't you look beautiful?" she said. "Let's try the earrings with it." She clipped them onto my lobes. "You're very lucky, you know. You're going to sup with all the lords and ladies."

The thought made my body stiffen and my stomach clench.

ASH

A year ago, Ash had sewn a nail into the waistband of his trousers. He knew that in his quest for revenge against Ratcher, he was likely to end up imprisoned someday. The nail was thin enough and small enough that it might not be noticed in an inspection of his belongings. He was right. His jailers had taken his belt and shoes, and must have searched him while he was unconscious, but they had not found the nail.

It took some time to pick away at the threads of his waistband. He should not have sewn it in so tightly, but he'd wanted to be sure it remained in place. Finally he opened enough of a hole to push the nail out. He went directly to work on the cuffs around his ankles.

A nail had seemed a wholly practical item to sew into his clothing. It could be used to pick a lock or to gouge out an eye. He would do that to Ratcher if he ran out of options; at least then he'd have the satisfaction of seeing her blinded before he died. And if for any reason they chose to let him molder in a cell for years instead of killing him, he could scratch the number of days that had passed on the wall, and slowly—ever so slowly—dig a passageway out. He knew how farfetched it was to imagine such an escape, yet any idea that gave him even the tiniest flicker of hope must be worthwhile.

After what must have been at least an hour of poking and scraping, his cuffs were still locked, and his respect for Tessa's trade had grown by leaps and bounds. He swore under his breath. *How could it be this difficult?* He should've asked for instructions while they wandered about the forest. If she could learn locksmithing skills from her father, surely she could have passed them along. But he never asked, barely spoke to her at all, in fact. He was not afraid to face Ratcher in hand-to-hand combat, but had been petrified to raise his eyes to a young woman who made his heart beat faster.

She was unlike any girl he'd met before, as brave and clever as a man. Braver and cleverer than Ryland, come to think of it. He wished he could have met her under different circumstances… in a world where Lance was still alive. In a place of peace and harmony overseen by a just and kind-hearted ruler instead of a despot. A place where he could make an honest living as a scribe. Or better yet, he could learn to write poetry, although he could not imagine anyone ever paying for a volume of his poems. In this perfect world, Tessa could work as a locksmith if she wished, and perhaps even consent to be his wife.

Then again, if Fellstone hadn't killed her father, there would have been nothing to come between Tessa and Ryland, and Ash would never have had a chance with her.

The key rattled in the door and Ash thrust the nail into his pocket. The jailer entered carrying a metal dish and slid it across the floor to him before ducking back out. Ash stared down at the unappetizing meal of soggy gruel resting on the stone floor beside him. *Is that a moth floating in it?* The sight made his stomach want to heave. But he knew he had to keep up his strength so he would be ready when the moment arrived to escape. He picked up the dish and removed the bug. Unless he too could turn into a bird, he was not ready to eat anything so revolting. He took a small spoonful of the gruel. It tasted as bad as it looked, but still he forced himself to take another swallow. And another.

TESSA

I lifted my spoon over a bowl of consommé, at a dining table so lavish King Midas would gratefully sup from it. The room was lit by golden candelabras. Red wine had been poured into cut crystal glasses. Real silverware, gilded cutlery, hand-painted porcelain, embroidered silk napkins... the list went on and on. No wonder the taxes in our village had gone up. One place setting at Lord Fellstone's table was worth a great deal more than our house.

The footman had seated me to the right of the empty chair at the head of the table. Six others had already taken their places across and next to me, people I'd never seen before, dressed in rich satins, silks, and velvets. They looked as if they were of noble birth, but I held my head high. Papa taught me not to fear the wealthy, nor ever to cower to them.

The boy to my right looked roughly the same age as Ash. His blond hair was neatly combed back and he had a dark shadow where he apparently hoped to grow a mustache. There were lions embroidered on the cuffs of his white silk tunic. His soft, thick, pale hands compared poorly to those of Ash, which were tanned and fine-boned. I even preferred the marks of honest labor that Ash's chipped fingernails and creased skin revealed.

The boy wore a mischievous expression as he leaned toward me and spoke into my ear. "We don't begin until his lordship arrives."

I lowered my spoon.

"I'm Malcolm Harlan," he continued. "Allow me to present Countess Bracken, seated across from us."

The countess, to the left of the empty chair and directly opposite me, was a tiny woman bent under the weight of her thickly jeweled necklace. Her earlobes hung down unnaturally, stretched by heavy golden dewdrops. Her wrists were similarly overloaded with bracelets, and I wondered how she would eat her soup without submerging them. Her eyes—too large for her head—skewered me with a malicious glare.

"The hideous young fellow next to her is my younger brother, Edmund," Malcolm said.

The young man, perhaps a year less than his brother, scowled across at us. He seemed to have spent a good deal of time arranging his appearance. Oil had been applied to tame the natural curl of his hair and his lips were red enough to make me wonder if he had dabbed them with rouge. He wore white, puffed silken sleeves and a purple embroidered vest. I felt quite certain that if I looked under the table, I would find him to be wearing matching purple satin breeches and white hose.

"That's my mother, Lady Harlan, beside him," Malcolm added. "And father, Sir Harlan, next to her."

Lady Harlan was striking in her beauty and appeared quite young. She had sensuous eyes, generous lips, a straight nose, and yellow hair coiled at the base of her neck. Unlike Countess Bracken, she showed good taste in the application of makeup and jewelry, with nothing more than a simple gold chain round her neck and small diamond earrings.

Her husband, Sir Harlan, was her opposite in every way. At least twice her age, he likely had never been a handsome man, even in his youth. Perhaps to compensate for his thinning hairline, he had thick sideburns of the type that were called "mutton chops" and a bulbous red nose that required constant application with his handkerchief. His dun-colored tunic strained at the seams over a plentiful belly.

"Good evening, young lady," said Lady Harlan. She drawled, affecting the manner of an older woman, enunciating each syllable, as if trying to impress people with her education.

A young lady on Malcolm's other side leaned around him to look at me. "Don't forget me!" she said in a high-pitched squeal. Her silk gown was of a bright pink color, with playful cats embroidered along the neckline. Her hair was dull brown, her face narrow and pinched, and her eyebrows plucked down to a faint outline. She wore gold kitten earrings and a gold kitten necklace. I wondered if blowing on her necklace might turn her into a kitten.

"I'm Lady Nora," she said. "Malcolm and I are engaged to be married. The countess is my grandmother. Delighted to make your acquaintance, Lady Teresa."

"That isn't my—" I began to say, but a footman interrupted by announcing Lord Fellstone's arrival. Two liveried servants held open the door as his lordship glided through it. He was richly but not ostentatiously dressed, in a black silk tunic with pearls on the cuffs. His fine wool breeches were also of plain black, and his leather shoes as well. He had a kind of feline grace, with silent and smoothly controlled movements like that of a wild cat stalking its prey. He did not so much sit in his seat at the head of the table, but melt into it.

Aside from what I'd viewed as sparrow-me, I had only seen him at a distance before, at public events which were carefully arranged to present the illusion of Lord Fellstone as a popular leader of the people. Close up, he looked handsome for his age, which I would guess to be mid-fifties. In reality, he might be five hundred years old and kept alive by the magic of the dreadmarrow. Certainly the skin of his face looked tight, as if the wrinkles had been unnaturally stretched out. His eyes were lively as he turned toward me and raised his glass.

"To my daughter, Lady Teresa. Welcome home," he said, giving me a delighted look.

The guests raised their glasses and echoed his toast: "To Lady Teresa."

Why did they insist on calling me that? "It's just Tessa," I said, trying to keep the anger out of my tone.

Lady Nora hissed at me behind Malcolm's back. "Pick up your glass."

I'd never had wine before, nor any other form of spirits. Papa had been strongly against it and never kept any in the house. At the moment, I was a little afraid of the effect it might have on me. I'd watched the twins Margaret and Anna drink heavily one night, take off their clothes, and dance naked in the town square. Afterwards they were so ashamed, they kept inside their own house for months.

Everyone sat frozen, their glasses lifted with nowhere to go. All eyes rested on me except those of Sir Harlan, who gazed longingly at his soup. Malcolm was clearly entertained, and Lord Fellstone continued to smile.

I had nothing to gain by being stubborn, but if I relented it would show my willingness to adapt and the action might inspire a similar spirit of cooperation on the part of his lordship. I raised my glass and Lord Fellstone tapped it with his own.

"Let us be bound by the ties of blood, forever and always," he said.

Everyone drained their glasses except for me.

"It's rude not to drink," said Lady Nora. I wanted to tell her it was rude to criticize other people, particularly those who had recently arrived and never been schooled on the behavior expected at the table of a mighty conjurer, but I held my tongue. I would do what was expected, come what may. I threw back the contents of my goblet all at once and lowered it with a gasp. From the heat that suffused my cheeks, I could tell my face must have flushed beet red.

Malcolm snickered as the servants poured more wine for all. Spoons clinked against china as everyone began to eat.

"Use the outermost fork for the next course," said Lady Nora. "Let me know if you have any questions about the meal and I'll be happy to assist."

I began to feel sympathy for Malcolm, her betrothed. How long could one bear her brainless patter? He would regret their union by the morning after they spoke their vows.

"She's not a half-wit," Malcolm said, referring to me. It was hardly a compliment and yet I felt almost grateful for his championship.

"She hasn't been brought up like we have, has she? I'm only trying to help," Lady Nora continued.

Sir Harlan paid no attention to anyone. He slurped his soup, disposing of it in no time, and glancing at the footmen as if he hoped to hasten the arrival of the next course with a look.

"I suppose this must all be quite overwhelming," Lady Harlan said.

Lord Fellstone's eyes narrowed.

"What do you mean?" I shifted to the side as a servant took my soup bowl.

"Goodness," said Lady Harlan. "I do not suppose you have ever been to a place this grand before."

"I don't measure the worth of a place by its size," I said. "Nor by how much money was spent in decorating it."

Edmund sneered. What an amiable fellow he was. "How would you measure it, then?" he said.

"By how warm and welcoming it feels," I said, not to be deterred. Out of the corner of my eye, I witnessed Lord Fellstone studying me.

"What a charming sentiment," said Malcolm. I couldn't tell if he was being sarcastic or not.

"I'd like to see you try living in a hovel," Edmund said to his brother.

Lady Nora gasped as she stared at my place setting. "Your napkin should be opened up and placed in your lap," she said.

I lost patience with the lot of them. Anger surged inside me and red flashed before my eyes. I heard a cracking noise, followed by a sharp cry from Lady Nora.

Her wine glass was broken in her hand. A jagged sliver stuck out from one of her fingers and blood was smeared around her palm. She gulped out loud sobs.

I stared at her in confusion, realizing I'd pictured the glass shattering in her hand an instant before it happened. I tried to shake off the feeling of unease that came over me. *It's just a coincidence.* Somehow I'd noticed she was pressing too hard, and the inevitable consequence had flashed through my mind. *That's all.* I was sorry she'd cut herself, but it had nothing to do with me.

"You may be excused, Lady Nora," Lord Fellstone said. He actually looked amused by her distress. At his signal, a footman hurried over and helped her out of the room. Immediately after, two more servants arrived, bringing with them a giant roast pig, which they set in the center of the table. Countess Bracken squealed with delight.

I stared at the poor animal in revulsion.

The countess noted my expression. "Have you never eaten pork? Your childhood certainly has been deprived."

"I've had pork," I said. "I never had to look at the poor pig's face though."

"Imagine how you'd feel if you were a boarman," said Malcolm.

For the first time, I felt sympathy for those beasts.

"I'd like to start with a slice of its cheek," Sir Harlan said.

"Would you?" Lord Fellstone said. He wore a smile, and yet something in his tone carried an undercurrent of danger.

Sir Harlan apparently thought so too. "I uh… um… I… I didn't mean…" The man trailed off, lowering his head.

Lord Fellstone rose. "My daughter said she was disturbed by the pig's head. What do you think we should do about it?"

Sir Harlan spluttered, having no idea what answer his lordship was looking for.

Lord Fellstone sauntered toward him. "I asked you a question, sir."

"It's nothing to me, whatever you like… whatever she likes," Sir Harlan mumbled.

"How would you feel if it was your head upon that platter?" Lord Fellstone said.

Beads of sweat formed on Sir Harlan's forehead. Around the table, all eyes were veiled, all expressions tense. Lord Fellstone must have acted this way before; they feared what he might do. They all knew it: *the tyrant is unbalanced.*

"Hold him," the lord said to the two who had carried in the platter. They grasped Sir Harlan's arms behind his back, pushing his head forward onto the table. Lord Fellstone turned to a guard standing by the door. "Give me your sword." The guard rushed forward and handed over his weapon. Lord Fellstone raised it above Sir Harlan's neck.

"*I beg you, my lord…*" Sir Harlan whimpered. His wife, Lady Harlan, left her chair and moved out of the way. Her gaze fixed ahead of her. Sir Harlan's sons kept their heads bowed.

"Answer the question," Lord Fellstone said. "What shall we do about the pig's head?"

"*I... I... I don't know,*" Sir Harlan said.

"Shall we take it away, my lord?" Malcolm said, keeping his eyes averted. I admired his courage for daring to speak up.

"Ha! Who says the old are wiser than the young?" Lord Fellstone said.

"Yes, let's take it away, that's it," repeated Sir Harlan.

Lord Fellstone lowered the sword and nodded at the footmen to release Sir Harlan. The man straightened and dabbed at his forehead with his napkin.

"Well?" said Lord Fellstone.

Sir Harlan cowered. *What now?*

"Buffoon! You said you would take it away."

Sir Harlan looked around hoping someone might come to his aid, but no one did. He rose, leaned over the table, tore the pig head from its torso, and carried it out of the room, while its grease soiled his jacket and dripped onto his shoes.

Lord Fellstone resumed his seat as if nothing had happened, and waited to be served a slice of pork. When no one spoke, the lord said, "Let's not forget this is a celebration."

Countess Bracken began to talk about the weather, and the others joined in with forced jollity. I suppress a shiver and remained silent.

CALDER

He wasn't accustomed to going more than three hours without a meal, and now it was approaching five since he had a few meager rolls. When the smell of roast pork wafted into the corridor where he'd been taking a short snooze against the wall, he thought he would die if he didn't get a taste of it. He followed the scent to the hall outside the formal dining room and watched while the footmen carried it in. He hurried to the entrance but the doors fell shut right in front of his invisible nose, nearly catching it between them in fact. He'd hoped to snag scraps that fell from the table, or even to snatch a bite or two off someone's plate, but now there would be no pork for him, unless he could find leftovers in the kitchen later. Calder didn't think he could bear to wait that long.

Leaving his bag in a corner, he padded his way into the kitchen to find Cook and her scullery maids preparing the next course, a luscious fig pudding. Other staff were seated at a long dining table in the servants' hall, digging into plates of boiled chicken parts. He tiptoed over to the serving tray, which rested near the elbow of a stern butler with eyebrows shaped like wings. Just as Calder reached up to swipe a piece of chicken, a maid with a voice like nails on slate asked the butler to pass the meat. The plate was whisked up and sent down to the other end of the table, leaving Calder struggling to suppress a curse. He was now forced to follow the chicken to its new resting place, all the while dodging newly arriving servants who came to take their seats at the table. Once within arm's reach, he had to wait until one of the footmen made a joke, distracting everyone's attention. His hand shot to the tray, and he grabbed two legs before running from the room.

"Well, knock me over with a feather…"

Calder glanced back as he rounded the corner. A young kitchen maid stood behind him with her mouth open.

"What're you rattling on about?" asked the stern butler from the table.

"I just saw two chicken legs flying through the air," she said.

The footman laughed. "Oh really, Molly? Where?"

"They're gone now. They ran out of the room," she said.

"'Course they did. They were legs after all," the footman said. Others broke into laughter.

"I think we need to check the lock on the liquor cabinet," the butler said.

"This isn't fair. I haven't had a thing," Molly said, but her protestations were buried under the loud mocking that followed.

Calder ducked into a small, empty room tucked behind the kitchen, which held only a table and chair. He sat down and raised one of the legs to his lips, but an instant before he could chomp down on it, he heard steps approaching from the hall.

Blast! He dropped the legs onto the table so they would not appear to be suspended in mid-air as he held them, and scooted over to the wall. Ratcher—of all people—stepped into the room carrying her meal on a tray. She paused and stared down at the chicken. Had she seen them floating? She glanced around the room, appeared satisfied, and sat down with her food.

For the sake of all that's holy, why is she eating here? The servants might not have welcomed her presence but they could hardly bar her from the kitchen. Probably she considered herself above them. Having grown up among servants himself, he knew the fear of association. One minute you're dropping in to swipe a chicken leg, and the next, someone has ordered you to clean out the chimney flue. Yet, neither had Fellstone invited Ratcher to join him and his guests in a feast that included a tantalizing roast pig. She was neither master nor servant, but somewhere in between. It had to be a lonely life. He almost felt sorry for her.

He didn't dare sneak past her to the door in case she'd glimpsed the floating legs and was now on alert, listening for the movements of an unseeable person. After all, invisibility could not be terribly surprising within the abode of a conjurer. There were probably a dozen spells that could accomplish it. Thus he remained pinned to the wall, as still as he could manage, while his throat grew dry and his stomach hollow. It was torture enough watching her scrape every last crumb off her plate, but then, when she reached for the legs, he feared he could stand no more and would have to kill her for them. Somehow he held himself in check while she cleaned the meat from them so thoroughly, it was as if the bones had been dropped into a vat of burning acid. He would've wept if he could've done it in silence. At least she could've taken off her mask while she ate, to satisfy his curiosity if not his hunger. But her mouth wasn't covered, for this very purpose he supposed, and she could eat perfectly well as she was. He wondered if she even slept with the blasted thing on.

At last she finished and rose up. She bent to adjust her tunic and left the room. He waited a moment and was about to set off himself when he noticed a shiny object resting on her seat. It surprised and puzzled him to find, on closer inspection, that the object left behind was none other than Tessa's windrider.

TESSA

I had been hoping to speak privately to Lord Fellstone, but the display during dinner made me reluctant to approach him. In the end it made no difference, as he came to *me*. His manner was cheerful, but I now knew how quickly that could change. He took me across the courtyard to the center tower, and I followed him up the stairs—of which there were many—until at last we went through a door that led outside, onto a domed balcony high above the rest of the castle. Here he directed my gaze out over his vast domain, eerily lit by the glow of the moon. The view was stunning; even the Cursed Wood looked appealing from this vantage point.

"I hope you can forgive the careless actions of my knights," Lord Fellstone said.

"Careless?" I said, forgetting in my anger that my responses should be more guarded. "Is that how you describe the murder of my father?"

I could tell he didn't like to hear me use that word for Papa. But he held himself back from correcting me. "Irresponsible, then," he said. "They were meant to take the locksmith in for questioning regarding his role in your kidnapping. But he resisted them."

"An unarmed locksmith against three of your knights?" I would have also liked to challenge his use of the word "kidnapping," but I realized I must let some things go if I had any hope of gaining his lordship's cooperation.

"You are right," said Lord Fellstone. "They were overzealous and will feel my wrath."

His concession gave me hope, and I blurted what was closest to my heart: "Please let me save him."

Lord Fellstone stiffened. "Save him?"

"Allow me to use your dreadmarrow," I said.

He frowned. "Out of the question."

"Sir, I beg you with all my heart."

"You don't know what you're asking. You would not want it if you did."

"But you let Ratcher use it on me."

"What, you think reviving the dead is the same as healing a bruised elbow? Only a powerful conjurer could bear the effects of a resurrection for long."

I turned away, struggling to swallow my anger. At that moment a crow flew down and landed on the cupola above us. Without noticing the bird, his lordship placed his arm over my shoulders. It took all my self-control not to recoil from him.

"Dear child," he said. "You shall feel my generosity. I have decided to release your young friend without consequence."

"Thank you. But—"

"Do you know anything about the lord who is master of all conjurers?" he said.

"Lord Slayert," I whispered. As much as the people of Sorrenwood hated and feared Fellstone, they would've pledge their loyalty to him for an eternity if it meant keeping us safe from Slayert. His subjects were bound to him in slavery, and his torture chambers were infamous.

"He means to expand his realm. If I wait, if he perceives me as weak, he will soon set his sights on Sorrenwood. I need to act quickly, before he suspects me. I've been gathering my forces to oppose him," Lord Fellstone said. "His reign has lasted too long and I intend to replace him." He looked at me. "But I need your help."

Nothing could've surprised me more. "What could I possibly offer?"

"The Fellstone blood runs through you. Tell me, did you picture Lady Nora's glass breaking in her hand before it did?"

"I never thought it would happen." *How does he know what was in my mind?*

"Strong emotion feeds your power. Directed thought gives it focus. I will teach you."

I couldn't believe I made the glass break merely by thinking about it. I'd certainly never done anything of the sort before. Except… I'd been too angry and grief-stricken to consider it at the time… but it was strange how the lamps in our house had flared up, the moment I discovered my dead Papa.

There had to be an explanation for that. I'd left the door open; a breeze must have blown in and whipped up the flames. In any case, whether I had powers or not, I didn't want Lord Fellstone teaching me his foul magic. I wouldn't wish to hurt anyone with my thoughts, even if it were possible.

"What about Ratcher?" I said. "Isn't she your apprentice?" She must have far more magical skills than I would ever possess, and most likely she'd relish going to war with another despot.

"She has talent as a conjurer, but she is low-born and can never be our equal."

"Is that why she wasn't at dinner with us? Does she dine with the servants?"

"She's neither servant nor master. She sups alone."

I glanced up at the cupola, wondering if the crow were still there. If I was right, and the crow was no mere crow, it was not a conversation to be having now.

"I would like to help you, my lord," I said. "But another matter aches at my heart. Please… tell me what happened to my mother."

Lord Fellstone lowered his arm, and his voice hardened. "She went from here sixteen years ago."

"But four years after that, she disappeared from our home."

"I advise you never to think of her again. She abandoned us both. I haven't seen her face since the day she stole away with my unborn daughter like a thief in the night."

Is it true? If she were not here at the castle, I had no idea where to look for her. And if Lord Fellstone were to be believed, she had no wish to be found. The thought of never seeing her again drained me of hope, which, combined with the lingering chill of the wraith's touch, brought on a fit of trembling. I rubbed my arms to settle myself.

"Forgive me," Lord Fellstone said, his manner instantly pleasant again. "You must be exhausted after what happened at the castle walls." He nodded toward the stairs. I looked back once before descending them, to see the crow flying away.

His lordship delivered me back into the hands of the same footman, Thomas—a swarthy person with a trim mustache—who had escorted me to dinner. Thomas returned me to my room while I asked him questions about how he came to work at the castle. He was as tight-lipped as Mary, though I understood at the end that he was born into service and therefore would always be in service. I told him it was possible for some people to rise out of their stations in life, but he showed little interest in my opinion.

Once inside my room, I removed my jewelry and was preparing to change into the plainer gown I wore earlier, when a soft knock sounded on the door.

Calder's voice came through from the hallway. "It's me," he said. "Calder."

I opened the door but no one was there.

"I'm here," Calder said. "You just can't see me." He brushed against my arm, making me jump. "You can shut the door now," he added.

I heard footsteps and then I saw an apple rise from the fruit bowl.

"I'm starving," Calder said. Crunching noises followed, as bite marks began appearing in the apple.

"Incredible," I said. "Where did you learn magic like this?"

"My tricks aren't magic, they're science." It sounded more like "shy-ants" because his mouth was full of food. "Listen, I've gone 'round the whole castle. I know where to find Ash and the dreadmarrow." He finished the apple, pulled a folded piece of parchment out of his bag, and handed it to me. "I made maps. It was amusing to watch my quill and parchment appear to float in the air. Here's yours." He picked up a large bunch of grapes and began popping them into his mouth. Once inside, they also disappeared.

"What about my mother?" I explained what Lord Fellstone had told me. "I don't know if I believe him. He might be holding her prisoner."

"I don't know. With luck we'll soon have the dreadmarrow as a bargaining tool—once you use it, of course."

I needed to tell Calder what I'd learned, but I found it hard to even know where to begin.

"Sit," he said, seeing my distress. He took an orange before drawing me down on the divan beside him.

"Did you know about my…" I said. "I learned my father is really… oh, it's just too awful."

"Oh dear," he said. "I was afraid that would turn out to be the case. Stay strong, Tessa. Your father is the man who has always filled that role in your heart."

I nodded tearfully. He was right, of course he was. Papa would always be my father. How much stronger must be the love that encircles the child who was born of another man.

Calder, peeling the orange, said, "Now, we need to free Ash and—"

"Lord Fellstone said he would let Ash go," I interrupted.

"This from the man who ordered your papa's death?"

"He claimed that was a mistake," I said.

"Fellstone's men don't make mistakes like that. They value their lives too much."

I began to perceive a faint shimmer of Calder. "I can see you. A bit."

"It's wearing off." He took my hand. "I know now why I liked you instantly. You're very much like your mother. Trust her judgment. I'm certain she ran away from Fellstone to protect you. She would not have made that decision lightly."

I agreed with him. No more delays; little time remained to save Papa. I rose and snatched my key pouch from the table. "Can you make us both disappear?"

Calder shoved the two halves of the orange into his mouth in rapid succession. He shook his head. "Too little remains. No matter how much I pack, invariably I run short on something." He reached into his bag, pulled out my windrider, and smiled up at me. "However, I did manage to find this."

I snatched it from his hand and had it round my neck faster than Calder could blink. My face felt flushed as powerful feelings of relief and happiness flooded through me. I could not remember when I'd ever wanted anything so badly. "Thank you," I said, my voice intense.

Calder was now sufficiently visible for me to see his face cloud with doubt. I realized I should've been more guarded; he thought me too needy. *How can he understand what the windrider means to me?* His judgment was unfair. Despite how much I loved it, I knew I could live without it if I must. *Of course I can.*

Still, it was with great happiness that I changed back into sparrow-me, after Calder explained the plan. When we left my bedchamber, he was no longer transparent. I flew above him as he slipped across the corridor to an outer door that led to the courtyard. Outside, he waited out of sight while I fluttered toward the tower, entering over the heads of the two sentries. One of the guards glanced up, saw that I was just a harmless bird, and looked away. Thanks to Calder, I knew precisely where to find Ash. I swooped down the stone steps, landed on the peephole of his cell, and looked in. He was seated with his eyes closed, leaning against the wall not far from the door. I dropped down to the floor and changed back into myself, noticing with relief that Papa's sword was stashed with Ash's coat and boots in a corner; he would be glad to get his things back. I found the key on the hook, just as Calder had described, and tried to insert it into the lock. The key met with resistance and first I thought it might not be the right one, but with a bit of pushing and jiggling, I managed to force it all the way in. With the turn of my wrist, the cell door swung open.

ASH

Ash did not take confinement well, having spent much of his life outdoors. He liked it that way. His work in the cemetery was hard, but when the sun was out, and the flowers blooming… it was tolerable. In truth, almost any other job would be preferable. It just showed how much he hated being restrained inside this cold, sunless pit, that even grave digging was starting to look good to him.

He wasn't sure—because it was always dark inside his cell—but he thought no more than a day had passed since he was imprisoned. Yet already he grew impatient. He feared his friends were dead, or shackled in the cells next to him. Or, even if they were somehow safe outside the castle walls, there was little they could do to help. Neither of them had a weapon larger than a dagger, nor knew how to use one. He was on his own. He had one tool—the nail—and he would only get to use it once.

The guard who delivered his meal had worn a key ring. If Ash attacked him with the nail, he needed to take action that would silence the man instantly. An eye-gouging would only make the guard shriek and draw others to his side. Ash felt the nail in his hand, wondering how firmly he could hold it while he plunged it into his victim. He tried gripping it and pressing it against the floor, but it slipped through his fingers.

When he picked up the nail to try again, the metal restraints round his wrists caught his eye. There was a small gap where the cuffs clamped together. He looked back at the nail, getting an idea. He picked it up and forced it into the gap. Its width was perfect to hold the flat end tightly, so that the pointed end jutted out. When it was ready, he pressed the nail against the stone floor, and it remained firmly in position.

All he needed to do was ram his wrist into the guard's neck.

He worked a while longer, making certain the nail was just right. After that, he dozed for a bit, until the sound of the lock rattling woke him. He quickly checked the nail again, then moved as close to the door as he could manage. For some reason, the guard was taking longer than usual with the lock. Perhaps it was another guard, with less experience, who would be easier to overwhelm. But he could not rely on that. He sat poised and ready.

The door came open and Ash lunged, grasping a leg, dragging the figure toward him, and leaping on top, all in one swift movement. He raised his wrist to finish the man off, but at the last second, the gasp of a woman stayed his hand. He stared down into the face of his victim, and made out Tessa's features in the dark.

"Ash!" she said. "It's me!"

He couldn't believe how close he'd come to killing her. How he would have lived with himself after that colossal blunder, he didn't know. But she was all right, and now a new feeling coursed through him, an intense awareness of the shape of her body… the sweetness of her breath… the soft touch of her hands on his arms. It seemed that her lips parted as she gazed up at him, and he wanted to kiss her, wanted it even more than revenge against Ratcher. Tessa looked as if she wanted it too, or maybe that was wishful thinking on his part.

He came to his senses before he made an idiot of himself. He had tackled her, and now he had her pressed against the filthy floor of a dungeon. When he kissed her—if he kissed her—it should be in a place that made her feel at ease, a place they both would want to remember. He moved off her.

"Did I hurt you?" he said, taking her hand to help her up. He released her before he could be tempted to draw her close again.

She shook her head and moved to close the door. When she turned back, he stared at her in awe, realizing she was wearing a gown that made her look like a fairy tale princess. "Where did you get that?" he said. He knew as soon as the words left his lips, that it should not have been the first thing he asked, when so many more important questions remained to be answered.

Tessa laughed softly. "You didn't waste any time planning your escape. I think it would've worked, too. Thank the gods you realized it was me."

"Sorry. I had to act fast for the plan to work."

"Of course. And it's very dark in here." She sat down, spilled out keys and picks from the small bag that she wore, and lowered her head over his wrist manacles. "Not easy to see what I'm doing. Stay still."

"Where's Calder? Is he all right?"

"Outside. He's fine. I had to become a bird to get past the guards."

Ash looked at her curiously. "How is it you still have your clothes?" Then realizing how his question must've sounded, he stammered, "Not that I was hoping they'd be gone or anything."

"That's how the magic works," she said. "Whatever I'm wearing, or carrying, stays with me." She worked with a small, thin sheet of steel that she inserted into the shackle of the lock. She twisted it until the latch released.

"What's that?" he said.

"It's called a shim. Works well with spring locks."

He felt vindicated for failing to make any progress with the nail and told her about his efforts.

She handed him a key from her pile. "Take this. It opened my bedchamber door. Most likely the locks on the inner doors are all the same. It should get you into *her* room." She smiled at the nail. "You won't be able to open it with that."

"Don't you need it?" he said.

"I have a similar one. I think it will work well enough."

He slid the key along with the nail back into his waistband. He watched while Tessa opened his locks one by one, and listened as she told him what she'd learned since they separated outside the castle. It was difficult for her to speak of it, but gradually she revealed that Lord Fellstone was her father. The news came as a shock to Ash. *How could someone so lovely and innocent be the daughter of a conjurer?* He had thought evil was an inborn trait: the sins of the father visited on the sins of the child. But clearly he was wrong. She had the character of the man who brought her up.

His wrists and one ankle were now free. As Tessa worked on the last manacle, he brought up the subject which had been weighing heaviest on him. "I saw my brother outside the castle walls."

"You mean Lance? How could he…?"

"He's a wraith." He spat the words out in disgust.

Tessa gasped.

"I can't leave him like that. Have to find a way to save him." It was no longer a simple matter of killing Ratcher. Not that it would ever have been simple.

Tessa touched his wrist, bruised and raw from the metal that chaffed against it. She leaned her forehead against his. "We will save him," she said. "Somehow we will."

CALDER

Too much time had passed since Tessa had flown into the dungeon. Calder prayed her locksmithing skills would prove sufficient to the task at hand.

In the meantime, it fell on him to prepare a distraction. Behind the cluster of trees next to the fountain, he searched for sticks and leaves and any discarded bits of parchment. There was precious little flammable material to be found, a testament to those who maintained the castle grounds. What he did find, he arranged into a pile beside the fountain, out of view of the tower guards. He lit the fire with his flint before dashing away and hiding behind the steps that led down from the kitchen.

Calder waited, watching for the sign and thinking how easy everything had been earlier, when he was invisible. A moment later he glanced back at the pitiful fire, which was already running out of fuel. Putting himself at further risk of being spotted, he darted to the single tree directly across from the Great Hall, gathered the broken twigs that lay beneath it, and tore back to his fire. The flame had nearly extinguished but he managed to revive it with some heavy blowing. It flared up as he added the twigs one at a time.

Calder had only just returned to his hiding place when Tessa flew out from the tower and perched on the roof. This was the signal.

He took a piece of bamboo filled with powder from his bag and tossed it at his fire. Unfortunately, the bamboo missed the flame entirely and rolled away. *Blast.* He crept out of hiding to retrieve it, when suddenly a sinewy man approached from the other side of the fountain, and Calder barely had time to scoot back into safety. Watching anxiously, Calder judged the man to be a knight based on his mode of dress, and his disregard of good sense in growing a long mustache that hung in two thick strands below his neck. The knight gave every impression of being potted, strolling unevenly toward the fire. He paused beside it, swaying and rubbing his hands over the flames. *Don't look at the bamboo*, Calder shouted inside his head, but it was as if the opposite thought hit the knight, whose gaze immediately shifted. He stared down curiously at the unfamiliar piece of wood, and then scooped it up for closer inspection, nearly knocking himself off balance in the process.

The plan is going to fail. Calder had no more gunpowder. He racked his brain to think of another trick that might cause a sufficient distraction. Meanwhile, Tessa waited on the roof, watching.

The knight grew bored, and perhaps wanting to see how the strange wood would burn, tossed it onto the flame.

The bamboo exploded. The knight spiraled backwards, while Calder dashed into the castle. He vaulted up the steps to the second floor and watched out a window as the tower guards left their posts, and ran to the knight's aid. The gunpowder continued to blast while Ash emerged from the tower, bolted out across the courtyard in the opposite direction from the disturbance, and entered the castle. Tessa was to have given him a map, and instructions on where he should go. With luck, he'd find his way without being seen.

Several servants emerged from their rooms and gathered at the window beside Calder. "It's nothing," he said. "Something in the fire popped." He slipped away while they continued to stare outside.

Calder had spent much of the afternoon checking the servants' quarters until he had found one he could safely assume was not in use, since the drawers were empty and the mattress had no linens. Now, he made sure no one was watching as he let himself into the room. Ash was already there, seated on the bare mattress, looking over his copy of the map.

"How are you?" Calder said.

Ash felt the back of his head. "Better," he said. "Thanks."

Calder nodded and sat beside him. "You're safest up here. There are so many servants, they don't seem surprised when they don't recognize someone. Or perhaps they've simply learned over time that it's better not to ask questions."

Ash stared at the map for a moment longer.

Calder said, "She told you where to meet us?"

He nodded. "But… don't wait for me."

"Tessa won't leave without you."

"She *must.* She has to save her father."

"I'll do what I can to convince her," said Calder, not looking forward to the task.

"Convince her for Lady Fellstone's sake."

The boy was cleverer than Calder had imagined. To appeal to his affection for Faline… that was the way to get him to do anything. And he had no doubt Faline would put the survival of her daughter… and the locksmith… above her own. When he'd first set out, the search for Faline had come before every other consideration. But now, insuring Tessa's safe return to her papa was the priority.

He nodded to Ash. "If you don't make it in time… I'll be back for you," he said, and he meant it.

Ash began to rise, but Calder put a restraining hand on his shoulder. "Wait a bit. Until things have settled down."

ASH

Once all was quiet within the castle, Ash made his way to Ratcher's bedchamber, fittingly located on a landing in between the two floors, neither upstairs nor downstairs. The door was locked, but he had no problem opening it with the key Tessa had given him. He was glad Ratcher wasn't there; it would give him the advantage of surprise. Her chamber was large enough but surprisingly plain compared to the opulence of the rest of the castle. Except for its size, he would have thought it belonged to one of the servants. The simple bed was tucked into a corner, leaving space in the center of the room for performing incantations, he supposed. A small stone fireplace warmed the place well enough, with a smoldering flame that must have been lit in preparation for her return.

He'd planned to hide in her wardrobe, but she didn't have one. Several dark green jackets and trousers—she did not seem to own another color—hung from hooks along the wall, and a meager dresser inclined beside the bed, but aside from these there were few possessions on display. He stood behind the door—his only option—hoping she didn't swing it wide upon her return. While he waited, he filled his mind with happy memories of Lance. These thoughts fed his determination and helped keep him alert and ready for the moment to come.

It wasn't long before he heard Ratcher's key inside the lock. She opened her door and stepped into the room. He didn't hesitate, kicking the door closed behind her with one foot, and raising his sword to her neck just as she whirled around toward him. He pressed the tip firmly against her jugular. "Don't move," he said.

Ratcher went still. "This is impressive. I almost regret mocking you earlier."

He would not allow her banter to distract him. "My twin, Lance, was made into a wraith," he said. "Tell me how to free him."

"I should've thought you would enjoy the family reunion."

Ash pressed the sword closer, nearly cutting Ratcher's flesh. "Tell me or I'll kill you now."

"It's rather obvious, isn't it? Kill Lord Fellstone and all the magic he wrought will die with him. He called forth the wraiths, and only his death can release them."

"How do I kill him?"

"Stronger, braver, and wiser men than you have tried and failed," she said. "Even if you can get past his sentries, he has set spells to protect himself and everything he values."

"There must be a way," he said.

"He trusts no one. Even I don't know his methods. Kill me if you must, but my death won't further your goal."

Ash lowered his sword. "Defend yourself."

"Oh this is tedious," Ratcher said.

"Would you rather I just killed you?" He would do it if he must, though it would not give him as much satisfaction.

Ratcher sighed and stepped backwards, drawing out her sword. "I warn you, I'm good at this."

They took their positions and Ash raised his weapon. "*From ash you came, to Ash you return,*" he said, his voice thick and low.

"Oh my, a catch phrase," said Ratcher. "I wish I had one. How about, 'Die, you despicable slug!'"

They began to duel, feeling each other out, testing, looking for weaknesses. Ratcher quickly showed herself to be skilled with the sword, perhaps even better than Ash. "I always wondered what it would be like to have a twin," she said.

He tried not to listen to her.

"Like two halves of one person," Ratcher said.

Her talk made him impatient. He didn't want to hear her, didn't want to look at her either. The cowl and mask covered most of her face, except for her cruel mouth and the dark slashes of her eyes. *What's she hiding?* He pushed harder, forcing Ratcher into a defensive posture but at the same time, opening himself up to mistakes.

"Twins compensate for each other's deficiencies, do they not?" Ratcher said. She inched backwards toward the door as the battle continued. When her back was nearly against it, she cawed like a crow three times.

Ash nearly had her pinned, until she slammed his sword and slipped past him to the other side. His back was now to the door.

"Strong as a pair, but weak as a singleton," said Ratcher. "Without your twin, you're only half a man." She slipped her sword under the tie that bound Ash's ponytail and sliced it off.

He reached up and touched the hair on his shoulders, realizing what had happened. It was true, what she said… he'd always felt weak without Lance at his side. Her action brought him back to himself, Ash Kemp, the quiet reader, the soulful star-gazer. Lance was the fighter, and no matter how hard he tried, he could never be as skilled and determined as his brother. As his self-confidence slipped away, he began a frantic defense. Ratcher attacked with renewed energy. He didn't hear the door opening, didn't know the boarman had entered until he grabbed his arms from each side and pinned them around his back. Ash looked up to see Scarface looming behind him, the boarman he loathed most in the world.

Ratcher said, "I see it all now. Lance was the strong one. You were only pretending to be him."

It was what he himself had known for years, but to hear it from his enemy's lips cut nearly as painfully as the sword she thrust into him.

TESSA

I flew back through the open window into my bedchamber as soon as I saw Ash had made it safely into the castle from the dungeon. The noise was bound to attract attention, and I would be the first person Ratcher would think of, especially since Lord Fellstone had given me free reign of the place up till now. I landed on the floor, changed back into myself, leapt into my bed, and pulled the covers to my chin.

A moment later, I heard my door being pushed inward. I pretended to be asleep, but half-opened my eyes to see who might enter.

No one did. Something scraped across the floor, and then the door was closed again. I waited a moment before jumping up to see what was there. I nearly cried out when I realized what had been dragged into my room.

It was the head of the roast pig from dinner. At first it baffled me, and then I had an idea who might bring me such a gift. I cracked my door open and peered out. Across the hall in the shadows, Malcolm and his brother Edmund huddled, snickering among themselves. *Of course.* I stuck my tongue out at them. They moved on, clearly disappointed that their prank had not evoked more of a reaction.

They must have hoped I would run screaming from my room.

I shut my door and leaned against it, waiting to give them time to clear out. I checked Calder's map for the nearest stairway to the upper floor. He'd advised me to cross the south wing along that corridor. I took a cloth from the table, wrapped the pig head inside it, and carried it with me out of my chamber. The hallway was empty, and I hurried toward the southwest tower. The staircase was tucked behind an alcove, probably to discourage its use by general visitors to the castle. I hurried toward it, but before I could start up the steps, a hand grasped my arm from behind.

"Did you like my gift?" Malcolm whispered into my ear. He spun me around and held me close to the wall.

"Let go of me," I said, keeping my voice low so as not to attract the attention of anyone else.

He sniffed the air and looked down at the round shape I was carrying inside the cloth. "Why, here it is! You did like it. But where are you taking it?" He glanced up the stairs. "Do you have a starving friend among the servants who might like a bit of tongue? I confess I'm wounded you're not keeping it for yourself."

"I'm getting rid of it. Now leave me alone."

"Tell me what your errand is. I can be trusted."

"There is no errand."

"Then leave that and allow me to entertain you in my chamber," he said.

"I would not wish to make Lady Nora unhappy," I said.

"She need never find out."

"Remove your hand or I'll scream for help."

He looked amused. "Will you? Go ahead then," he said, calling my bluff.

I tried to pull away from him, but he pressed me against the wall. "As I thought," he said. "You do have some hidden purpose. Well, if you're going to sneak about the castle, do be careful to avoid the monsters."

He stepped back, releasing me from his hold.

I hesitated. "Monsters?"

"Have a nice evening." He moved away.

"Wait," I said. "Tell me about them."

He paused and turned back. "If I do… and you survive… will you remember this favor?"

I nodded. With luck, my friends and I would be leaving soon, and I would not see Malcolm again.

He drew closer and lowered his voice. "They live in the passageways under the castle. I've never seen them; I can't tell you what they look like. But I knew a boy who went down there and never came back."

"How does… how does one find these passageways?"

"They were designed as a secret means of escape in case the castle fell to invading forces. There's an entrance from most rooms. Mine is behind a tapestry, with the door raised above floor level so it can't be seen."

I should've been glad of this information. *What better way for my friends and me to escape?* Certainly one of the passages must lead outside the castle walls; otherwise, it would only be a matter of time before the invaders would find those who were hiding, and slaughter them.

But a cold dread spread inside me as I recalled my vision. *I lay bound on a table in a cave beneath the ground.* Lord Fellstone had told me I had powers. Could I see my own future? Was this the fate that awaited me in a grim tunnel carved into the rock below?

Malcolm smiled at me. "I can see I've frightened you. Good. Because otherwise… it would be a shame if you were to die so soon after your rebirth as a Fellstone."

I turned away, shutting his words out and forcing the horrid vision from my mind. I hurried up the stone steps. It was much darker in the garret, and the hall felt claustrophobic with its low ceiling and close walls. The floor creaked as I scurried past the shabby wooden doors of the servants' bedchambers. Moments later I reached the staircase that would lead back down to the conjuring room. Calder was there, waiting so still in the corner, I almost didn't notice him. He looked at my bundle curiously and bent over it, closing his eyes as he breathed in the scent of pork.

"Sorry, I didn't bring it for you," I said. "Where's Ash?"

"He'll meet us later," he whispered. He gestured for me to keep quiet and moved ahead of me, leading me down the twisty stairs. I wondered about Ash and if he had gone to confront Ratcher. I would've liked to find him and help him, though I sensed he would insist on carrying out his revenge entirely on his own.

We reached the conjuring room without incident. The door was locked, and I had a moment of panic when my skeleton failed to open it. The key was not as perfect a fit as the one I'd given Ash, but with some manipulation, I managed to turn the lock. I looked back at Calder, who touched the handle of his dagger.

"I hope we won't have to hurt the poor dog," I said.

"Croco-dog," he corrected. "Maybe he won't be here." He stepped in front of me, insisting on entering first, and I followed carrying my bundle.

"Good croco-dog, good Fiend—"

Fiend sprang at us, coming out of nowhere, his jaw snapping.

I leapt behind the table, knocking everything off it. Calder dropped his bag and jumped the other way. Fiend slid into the door, slamming it shut.

Calder picked up a wooden chair and held it out. "Down, boy!" he shouted. Fiend came after him and bit the chair, chomping it into bits.

"Use this!" I cried, tossing him my bundle.

Calder held it out to Fiend. The croco-dog spread open his giant jaw and Calder rolled the roast pig head into it. He jerked his arm away a fraction of a second before Fiend snapped his mouth shut. "You're welcome," Calder said.

Fiend chomped once, crunching on bone, before swallowing the head whole. *Done.* He stared down Calder, who drew out his dagger. Fiend pounced and Calder flew backwards, banging his head on a cauldron, and instantly passing out. Fiend approached him, snorting and salivating, looming over Calder's unconscious form.

What now? My gaze swept the room and fixed on a ritual knife left out on the counter. I sprang for it, gripped the weapon, then hurtled toward Fiend from behind. I stabbed the creature's back, but the knife broke on his tough scales. He whipped his tail sideways, knocking me into the corner, where I cowered as he advanced on me, his gait menacing, his open mouth exposing a deep, dark pit of razor-sharp teeth. I pressed back against the wall, perspiration spouting from my forehead as Fiend's massive snout drew close. I said my last prayers, certain he would dispose of my head exactly as he had done with the pig. Only then did I notice the small cannonballs—five or six of them—stored in an open box near where I stood. If I could grab one of them and drop it on Fiend's head… I inched toward the box and lifted one out, but it slipped out of my hand and rolled along the floor.

Fiend's eyes shifted to the ball. Suddenly, he whirled around and ran after it. He stopped it with his snout, then rolled it back toward me the same way. He directed it to my feet, paused, and looked up at me expectantly.

He's a dog after all. I rolled the ball along an empty path which had probably been cleared for just this purpose. Fiend followed it with his eyes before scrambling after it.

Calder groaned and pulled himself up. He started at the sight of Fiend returning with the ball.

"It's okay," I said. "Are you all right?"

Fiend dropped the ball next to Calder and wagged his tail.

"Why, you're nothing but a great big, mouthy puppy," he said, rolling the ball away. He turned back to me. "The only permanent damage is to my self-esteem." Calder hurried to the door and bolted it to hold back any sentries who might have heard the noise. "Quick as you can," he said. He lit a lamp with his flint and continued rolling the ball for Fiend whenever he returned with it.

"Why isn't Ash here yet?" I said.

"I don't know. Revenge is a tricky business." Calder took my hand and led me to a cabinet. "This is it. Can you open it?"

After checking the lock, I took out my ring of master keys. Outside the room, footsteps thumped along the corridor.

"Hurry!" said Calder. "Time's running out."

I tried keys as fast as I could. If we did not get the dreadmarrow now, we would not get another chance and Papa would remain dead forever. I focused my concentration on the tasks before us: *open the cabinet, take the dreadmarrow, escape the castle.*

I went through all my keys with none of them coming even close to fitting. I would have to try my tools now, but that would take time, and my hands were already shaking. Perhaps I needed to go through my keys again. Frozen by indecision, I stared at the golden oval plate surrounding the keyhole, which had an intricate geometric pattern carved into it. *Where have I seen that before?*

"Can I help?" Calder said.

"I'm thinking," I said. "It was all so easy till now."

"Well there was Fiend," Calder said, frowning.

I kept staring at the lock.

"Are you sure you've tried every key?" Calder said.

It hit me then. The familiar pattern. I had seen it before, on the handle of the golden key Papa gave me. How could I have forgotten? I drew it out from the chain under my shift and placed it in the lock.

A perfect fit.

"You're right," Calder said, sounding distracted. "It *has* been too easy. It's almost as if someone planned for us to…"

I glanced back at him and saw his face transform with a jolt of realization. As I began to turn the key, he vaulted toward me and knocked my hand from it. His own hand touched the compartment as the door came open.

There was a flash and Calder disappeared.

"Calder!" I shouted. I looked around, then down at the floor. There was a cockroach in the spot where he'd been standing.

"No!" I cried. "No, no, no…" Not this. *Not Calder.*

Loud banging began on the door. Fiend, like the good guard croco-dog he was, positioned himself next to it and let out a low, threatening growl.

I reached down to pick up Calder, but he streaked away and disappeared into a crack between the floorboards. "Come back!" I cried.

The pounding on the door continued, and I didn't know how much longer it would hold out. I dropped to my knees to peer into the crack. "How can I save you if you won't come to me?" I said. I could no longer see him and I didn't think he would be coming back. He wasn't himself anymore; he had the brain of a cockroach now. "Don't leave me alone," I said into the hole in the floor.

"Tessa? Ratcher here," she shouted from the other side of the door. "I imagine you're surprised to hear me. I did study under his lordship's fencing master, one of the most accomplished swordsmen in the world. But how can my skills compare to those of the self-taught son of a gravedigger? By all rights your ashy friend should've been the victor, but somehow, while paying very little attention, I managed to kill him."

I flung myself at the door. "You're lying!"

"He went on and on about his brother being a wraith. I'd say I did him a favor. They can both be wraiths now. Problem solved."

She could not have known about Lance unless Ash had spoken to her. If he spoke to her, he would've challenged her. And since she was still alive… it must be true. *Ash is dead.*

I slumped down against the door, grief overwhelming me. I saw Ash in my mind, as he'd looked inside his cell, his face inches above mine after he tackled me. I'd wanted him to kiss me. That it would never happen now… that I would never see him again… filled me with the suffocating sensation of drowning.

Tears streamed down my cheeks. It was my fault. Why had I agreed that he should come? Why had any of us set out for this cursed place? I slammed my fist against the door. *Ash.* I'd barely given him credit when he was alive, and now, for the first time, I saw him clearly. His strength and bravery, his loyalty to his brother and to us…

Loyalty. That thought drew me out of myself. I *had* to continue without them, I owed it to them to complete the quest. I could not, under any means, allow their loss to be in vain. I looked up, pushed myself back onto my feet, and then… *blackness.*

I was inside the dreaded cave again. Everything as it was the first two times. The sensation of being utterly and terribly alone. The stench of death. The restraints from which I had no hope of escape. As before, I saw a candle flicker, followed by the awful sound that came from deep down inside the monster who must've imprisoned me here. The heavy footsteps approached. I wanted to scream, but nothing came out, not even the smallest sound. A moment later, a hooded form loomed over me, its face shrouded in blackness. An enormous, gloved hand was raised up. A knife glistened in its grip.

A mighty thump at the door took me out of the nightmare. The wood splintered and nearly gave way. I caught my breath, leapt forward, and grabbed the dreadmarrow from the compartment. As I did so, I noticed the book beside it: its title, in beautiful script, was "THE CONJURER'S BOOK OF INCANTATIONS." Part of me wanted to steal it, but no, I would only take that which would be used for good. I dashed to the window and struggled for a moment with the latch before swinging it open. At the last moment I remembered Calder's bag and turned back. I scooped it up, thrust the dreadmarrow inside it, and blew on my windrider three times.

I lifted off and flew out just as the study door crashed open. A moment later, as I set my direction toward the forest, I saw Ratcher at the window staring up at me. She clutched the tome of magical incantations to her chest.

TESSA

Upon my return, I found the house reeking of tobacco. Mr. Oliver sat awake with his smoldering pipe, shivering in Papa's armchair, huddled inside several layers of wool, and a fur hat and mittens. He'd been afraid Papa would decompose faster if he lit a fire. In fact, Papa looked rather better than Mr. Oliver did.

There was no time to waste. Ratcher had no doubt informed her master of the theft, and forces had likely been dispatched to retrieve it. I needed to move Papa from our house without delay.

Together with Mr. Oliver, we managed to set Papa in the wheelbarrow. It was undignified but restoring his life trumped all other considerations. Fortunately, the hour was late and we saw no others on the street except for one stumbling sot, who thought Papa was another like himself, passed out from too much drink. I carried Calder's bag over my shoulder while we wheeled Papa to Mr. Oliver's lodgings, a one-room apartment behind the small cobbler's shop where he worked. There we transferred Papa to Mr. Oliver's bed. After starting a fire from logs and kindling that were stacked outside, Mr. Oliver—the best friend a man could ever hope to have—left us alone, saying he would stay with his sister's family for as long as we required the use of his home.

I piled blankets on Papa to keep him warm until the fire could fully heat the place. It would not help to bring him back to life, only to have him freeze to death. I lit a lamp and placed it beside him.

Soon after, the first rays of light from the rising sun entered the house. *It's time.* I took the dreadmarrow out of its case, and lifted Papa's shirt to expose where the sword had cut through him. I raised the dreadmarrow and held it as I'd seen Ratcher do. At first there was nothing. But after several moments, the wand caught a beam of light from the window and spread it in a wide circle over Papa's wound.

As I watched in wonder, the wound began to heal. I continued to hold the dreadmarrow over him until the scar was entirely gone.

I lowered the wand. "Papa?"

He looked no closer to life than he did before. His skin felt slightly warmer to the touch, but that might only be due to the higher temperature in the room. His color had not come back; more heat must be needed. I hurried to the fireplace and added a log to the flame.

I sat beside him and whispered into his ear. "Wake up, Papa. I need you to wake up." I waited a moment, while he lay there as still as ever. "I should've listened to you. We could've been safely in Blackgrove." I took his hand and rubbed it. "I beg you to wake up. If not for you, then for me. If not for me, then for Mama… and Calder… and Ash."

My gaze shifted to the dreadmarrow. I picked it up and tried again, this time spreading the healing light over him entirely, from head to toe.

Still there came no response from Papa.

It looked as if it had failed. Perhaps it only worked in the hands of a conjurer. I was naïve to think I had the power to use it. Of course it wouldn't respond to me, a simple girl, the daughter of a locksmith no matter what anyone said.

Of a sudden, a thought came to me and I realized what I must do. I unclasped my windrider, kissed it, and held it over Papa. "I give you my sparrow," I said. "May its flight bring you joy and swift passage into the next world." I would bury him with the thing I loved most in the world. He had wanted me to give it up, and I would do so as a final gesture of my love. It wouldn't bring him back, but it was the right thing to do. He'd warned me of its dangers, and perhaps he was right. But more importantly, giving Papa the windrider made me feel as if a part of me would be with him forever.

As I leaned over him to fasten the windrider round his neck, his lip twitched, and before I even had time to react, his entire body went into a spasm. I dropped the amulet.

Papa's limbs started shaking and I hastened to tighten the blankets around him. I placed my hand under his nose, checking for breath. "Breathe, Papa." I pressed his chest gently to help him. He opened his mouth and sucked in air.

His eyes snapped open and he stared at me in confusion. Tears of joy streamed down my cheeks. "You're going to be all right," I said. "You're going to be all right." I smoothed back the hair from his temple. His body trembled.

He opened his mouth to speak and what came out was a croak: "*Cold.*"

"I'll build up the fire. You're going to be all right," I said.

On my way to fetch another log, I bent and snatched up my windrider. There had been no need for sacrifice after all.

#

It took hours for Papa to warm up but at last he did. I had gotten him to move to a chair by the fire, where he sat with a blanket on his lap, sipping from a cup of hot tea. I stepped up behind him and patted his shoulders. "I have to go out," I said.

"I don't think you should," Papa said.

"I must. I won't be long."

His face contorted in anger. "I'm your father. Obey me."

My mouth dropped open. I'd never seen such an expression on his face. He'd been a stern father, but never, ever harsh. *Has death changed him?*

But just as quickly, his face relaxed and he seemed himself again. He didn't appear to remember what happened only seconds ago. "What were we saying?" he said.

I kissed the side of his head. "Try to get a little sleep."

He closed his eyes as I let myself out of the house.

I dreaded the task that lay before me, but I knew I must do it. Taking miniature steps to put off the moment for as long as possible, I walked until I came to the graveyard and the little house next to it where Ash's family lived. At least it had been a family once upon a time. Now it would be nothing but a mother and a father mourning the loss of their two sons for the rest of their lives.

I tapped on the door. Ash's mother opened it and greeted me warmly. She led me into the kitchen where I sat at a table with three chairs which would become a table for two. Ash's papa joined us and his mother poured us tea. As we sat together, I told them about Ash's bravery, and the love for his brother that had driven him to seek revenge. I told them of his fearless stand against the boarman, and how he had charged into a battalion of soldiers at the castle walls. His mother wept quietly through all of it, and his father too, though he covered his face with his handkerchief. At the end, I reached across and held his mother's hand.

I left out only one thing. I could not bear to tell them Lance had been made into a wraith, and that Ratcher had threatened the same for Ash. There were some things a parent should never be told about their child.

ASH

He woke to find himself flung over Scarface's shoulder, bouncing against the boarman's back as he was carried along a wide corridor. His side ached where Ratcher had stabbed him, but he did not think he was in any danger of dying, unless he lost too much blood. She'd bested him and then, to complete his humiliation, she'd given him a flesh wound instead of killing him. His cheeks burned with shame that he'd passed out over something so minor.

He let himself flop against the boarman, careful not to reveal that he'd woken. It was essential for him to act now, while no one else was around. Scarface was careless. He carried his great sword on one side, and a bollock dagger on the other. Ash considered going for the sword, being the more powerful weapon, but he realized it would be too heavy, and by the time he yanked it entirely from its sheath, the boarman would have flipped him over and subdued him. It must be the dagger.

Ash took a deep breath and steeled himself for the pain that movement would cause him. Then, acting with great speed—his one advantage over the beast that carried him—he snatched the dagger from Scarface's belt, raised it with both his hands, and plunged it into the boarman's back.

Scarface let out a deep groan and dropped to his knees. Ash didn't hesitate. He leapt up, pulled back the dagger, bent over the boarman from behind, and slid the deadly edge across his throat. Blood gushed out as the creature fell forward. An instant later he was dead.

Ash heard voices coming from the far end of the corridor; there was no time to spare. He dashed the other way, turning a corner, racing to the end of the hall. He peered out to find a sentry posted along the next passage. Fearing he was trapped, he retraced his steps, past several closed doors, unsure which ones to try. Then he came to the one marked DO NOT ENTER UPON PAIN OF DEATH in red paint.

It must be the nursery; the door was as Tessa had described. Although, for all he knew, the castle could be teeming with rooms that threatened you with death upon entry. But his options were few at the moment. With fumbling hands, he retrieved the key she'd given him, which took precious seconds because he'd stupidly forced it back in his waistband when he should have just stuck it into his pocket.

A shout rang out from around the corner. Someone must have found Scarface's body.

He shoved the key into the keyhole and turned it, but nothing happened. He dropped down on his knees to look more closely, and jiggled the key in the lock. The bolt still refused to turn. *What now?*

There were more shouts, closer now, and the sounds of soldiers gathering to begin a search. He breathed deeply to calm himself and drew out the key. He inserted it again, without forcing it this time, carefully feeling for the path of least resistance. He turned it and the lock clicked open. He slipped into the room, glancing back at the same time. There were shadows at the end of the corridor, and the clomp of boots approaching. He shut the door silently behind him, praying he had not been seen. He glanced around; it was indeed the nursery, just as Tessa had described it. Noises grew louder outside the room. Ash turned back and slipped the key in the lock, hoping it would not be heard over the sounds made by the soldiers. This time it turned without difficulty, and he carefully withdrew it from the slot. It would not do for someone to look through the keyhole and see that the door had been locked from inside.

He positioned himself behind the door, still as could be, Scarface's dagger at the ready. If they came in—and almost certainly they would—he would not go without taking some of them with him. He listened as the soldiers approached, banging on doors, checking each room. Moments later they paused outside his door. The knob began to turn.

"What're you doing?" one soldier said. "Can't you read?"

"I know what it says," said another.

"We can't go in. Last one who did lost his head."

"What if he's there?" the second man said.

The knob rattled as someone tried to open it.

"It's locked," the second one said with relief. "He can't be in there."

Never underestimate your enemy. But clearly they wished for an excuse to move on past the forbidden room, and a locked door was as good as any. They continued their search down the corridor, and soon enough, the castle grew silent.

Ash exhaled and looked down at his wound. He felt weak from blood loss, but at least it seemed to be an injury of the flesh only. There was a general ache, but no sharp pains as he poked around at it. Getting an idea, he found a relatively unspoiled sheet tucked into the crib, underneath the filthy bed cover. He cut a strip from it with the dagger, then looked about the room for vinegar or anything else to keep his wound from turning foul. There was nothing. He briefly considered lighting a lamp and holding the fireplace poker over it until it was hot enough to cauterize his wound, but the amount of time that would take and the risk of making things worse rather than better, stayed his hand. He also wasn't certain he could bear a jolt of agonizing pain right now. Instead, he simply bound the strip of cloth around his waist to keep the wound covered.

Exhaustion began to overwhelm him. He knew he ought to move on. The soldiers could easily report that they'd checked all rooms but this one, and others might be sent back to do the job. However, it was equally dangerous for him to go out and wander the castle corridors while the search continued. In the end his need for rest made the decision for him. He folded himself onto the child's bed and closed his eyes, thinking over all that had happened. He'd failed against Ratcher. He should've killed her straightaway, without allowing her to arm herself. She had not shown Lance that level of respect. His death had been an execution, and hers should've been the same.

His brother would not have been such a fool. Lance had been the practical, determined one. He had teased Ash for always having his head in a book, which was where he got those old-fashioned, ridiculous ideas about chivalry and honor. Lance was smarter. If he were to fight, he would have made sure the fight was balanced in his favor, even if it meant cheating. His brother believed the means didn't matter if you achieved your ends. He always won, because he never gave up until he could declare himself the winner.

Still, Ash's disappointment was balanced by satisfaction in another respect. Scarface had killed Lance, and now Ash had killed Scarface. Because he was following orders, the boarman's death wasn't nearly as satisfying as Ratcher's would be, yet Lance's murder had clearly given Scarface pleasure, and for that simple reason he had deserved the fate he received at Ash's hands.

His thoughts drifted to Tessa. She'd been dressed like a princess, but what he remembered most was the determined cast of her face as she worked to free him of his shackles, and the way her eyes softened when he lay on top of her and nearly kissed her. *Had she and Calder escaped with the dreadmarrow?* Ratcher had revealed nothing. But if his sword fight with her had caused enough of a distraction to allow his friends to get away, then it had been worthwhile. It soothed him to think of his failure like that. There were different ways of winning, and a personal loss might still mean victory for one's allies.

His goals were the same, to free Lance and kill Ratcher, but whereas once he didn't care whether he lived or died at the end of it… now he yearned for life with all his heart. He longed to see Tessa again, to hold her in his arms, and if he found the courage, to confess his love for her.

He still had hope. He just needed to sleep and then he would form a plan.

TESSA

I made mutton stew for supper, cooking it over the fire. The meat was an extravagance, but after all we'd been through—Papa facing death itself—it seemed as if we deserved a reward. Papa made no remark on the expense, which wasn't like him, as he usually questioned every penny spent. His mood had been gloomy and distracted since he revived, and I could only hope a filling meal would soften him, and begin to turn him back to himself.

"Papa, do you feel ready to travel?" We could not expect to remain undetected in Mr. Oliver's home forever. I needed to bring my father to a place of safety.

He stared at the wall as if he hadn't heard me.

"Remember how we talked of leaving Sorrenwood? You wanted to move to Blackgrove."

Papa lifted a bite to his mouth, and chewed on it slowly.

"I'll pack our things tonight. We can set out on foot before dawn, and hire a coach at the Square."

I waited for a response. He reached for the bread and tore off a piece.

"Please, Papa. I need to get you somewhere safe. This has been all my fault, that you died, or nearly died." When I told him what had happened, I stopped short of revealing that he had, truly, been dead.

"I know who I am now, Papa. I understand why you didn't tell me. Mama must have made you promise not to look for her if she ever went away, because your search might have lead Fellstone to me. I know what he is to me, but it doesn't matter. You're my real father."

Papa lowered his fork, perhaps listening now.

"I know what must have happened sixteen years ago. You passed by the graveyard on your way home. A desperate woman, my mother, tore off her wedding ring and threw it in the dirt. She carried a sword—the one you kept hidden in the cabinet—and was obviously with child. When you asked where her husband was, she begged you to hide her from him. The lord's men tore apart the town in their search, but you kept her safe. Because you fell in love with her."

Papa looked at me for the first time since we sat down. "*No*," he said. "*Not her.*" He lowered his voice to a whisper. "*It was for you.*"

"What?" I stared at him in confusion.

"I wanted *you*. A child. To raise as my own."

His words shocked me. "Why had you never married? You could have had children."

He shifted his eyes, but not before I glimpsed the sorrow in them. "Marriage isn't for some," he said wistfully.

#

Later as I helped Papa prepare for bed, his sleeve drew back, exposing a festering boil on his lower arm. The last time I'd seen such a mark was on Lord Fellstone's back. "When did you get this?" I said.

Papa pulled his sleeve to his wrist. "It's nothing."

"We need to fix it. I wonder if it will work without the sun." I fetched the dreadmarrow and brought a lamp to the table by his side.

"What's that?" Papa said.

"It will cure you." I pushed up his sleeve and tried to catch the light from the flame with the dreadmarrow.

"How does it work?" he said.

"It's, um, science," I said, remembering Calder's answer to me about something nearly as miraculous. However, it was not working at all at the moment.

"Where did you get it?"

"It isn't important."

"Tell me!" That angry tone again from Papa.

"What does it matter if it cures you?"

"It seems like magic. Did you get this from Fellstone?"

I didn't want to tell him, nor did I wish to lie. But my silence made no difference; Papa read the answer in my face. He yanked his arm back. "Get rid of it! I won't use anything that belongs to that demon. No wonder I don't feel myself. I've been in a foul mood ever since I woke up."

"You would've died without it."

"You should've let me die."

I lowered my gaze, stung to my core.

He softened his tone. "Some things aren't worth the price that has to be paid for them."

"Your life?" Surely that was worth any price.

"Even that," he said. He took my hand. "Death comes to all of us. You must learn to accept it."

#

After Papa fell asleep, I tucked the blanket around him and brushed my lips against his forehead. I stepped back to gaze at him, my heart swelling with love and concern. A part of me yearned to do nothing more than stay by his side and tend to him for the rest of his natural life. Or must it now be considered an unnatural life?

Another infection had appeared above his ankle. Lord Fellstone had warned me the magic would be too much for him. And now Papa had forbidden me from using the dreadmarrow again. I could do nothing further for him.

But there were others who needed my help. The fates of Mama, Ash and Calder continued to weigh heavily on me. If not for my friends, Papa would be dead. They had acted bravely and selflessly in helping and protecting me, at the same time setting aside their own desires. Now they would never be able to fulfill their goals. I felt certain that if I had been the one to die, they would have carried on, stolen the dreadmarrow, and themselves returned to bring Papa back to life. How could I do any less for them? As the only one left of the three who set out, I needed to pursue their deepest desires as if they were my own.

I had made my decision before Papa drifted off to sleep. I picked up Calder's bag, with the dreadmarrow protruding out of it. "Find Mama. Restore Calder. Free Lance," I whispered to myself. I hoped Ash, if he was somehow watching me, would forgive me for not wishing to kill Ratcher. No matter how depraved she was, the idea of taking a life went against my nature, and in any case, it would've been foolish to imagine I had a chance against her.

I raised the windrider to my lips.

#

I was relieved to find the window of my bedchamber open, just as I'd left it. I flew in and landed on the floor, scraping my claw to change back into myself. My first task required a search through Calder's bag. As I combed through it, I was no longer surprised at how long it took him to find items inside it; rather, it seemed a miracle he could locate anything at all. An enormous number of jars, vials, tins, and things that I could not hope to identify, were jumbled together with no apparent organization. In fact, when I looked back at the overall size and shape of the bag, it didn't seem possible that so many items could have been placed inside it.

Why hadn't Calder labeled anything? A scribbled description on the cap of a jar would have gone a long way towards speeding up my search. I could only assume that he knew by looking what it all was, and he didn't wish to leave clues for anyone—like me—who violated his privacy. At last, after a great deal of searching and some amount of trial and error, I found the canister that held the invisibility powder. I sprinkled the tiny bit that remained over the dreadmarrow. It faded until the wand could no longer be seen, and then I hid it on the floor in the back of the wardrobe. I wanted to be certain the dreadmarrow would not be found and returned to Lord Fellstone while I was busy elsewhere.

Instead of concealing it, I left Calder's bag out on the table, hoping to give the impression it was an article of no importance. I set off from my room and hurried toward the Great Hall. From there I approached the entrance to Lord Fellstone's anteroom. Four sentries stood guard, and blocked my way as I drew near.

"I request an audience with his lordship," I said. The guards hesitated, exchanging glances, but then the one nearest the door knocked and received permission to enter. He returned shortly thereafter and ushered me in. Immediately he went back to his post, closing the door behind him, and leaving me alone inside the lord's receiving room—a setting so lavishly appointed that even the most fastidious of visiting royalty would be hard pressed to find fault with it.

I sat on the edge of a plush chair to wait for him. A moment later he emerged from the inner chamber with Lady Harlan beside him. She kept her chin lifted and threw me a venomous look before she went out, leaving the door to be shut by the sentry behind her.

I paid her no heed, struck by the change in Lord Fellstone's appearance. He looked a decade older than when I'd last seen him. His face was lined, and his posture bent as he turned toward me. He had another small infection on his neck, which I hoped would make him anxious for the return of his dreadmarrow, and therefore more likely to grant me concessions.

"I knew you'd come back," he said. "You can't escape who you are."

"I only came to offer an exchange," I said. "I'll give back what I took if you agree to several small requests of mine."

His eyes went cold at my mention of requests. He showed no curiosity as to what they were; it would not surprise me to learn he'd never conceded anything in his life. Nevertheless, I spilled out my list. "Release Ash's brother Lance from your army of wraiths. Restore Calder, who became a cockroach. Tell me the truth about what happened to my mother, and release her if she's being held here."

"You forget yourself." His words cut like ice. "No one makes demands of the Conjurer Lord Fellstone."

I tried not to squirm under his unsettling gaze. After a moment, his eyes shifted past me.

"You should have heeded my advice to forget your mother," he said. "But since you insist on knowing her fate, I've decided there's no harm in revealing it to you." He led me to a corner of the room, where a covered bird cage hung, and lifted off the cloth to reveal a russet sparrow perched inside. I turned back to him in confusion.

"I believe you're familiar with the sparrow family," he said. "Her name is Faline."

A sensation of dread crept over me. "My mother's name?" I said hoarsely. I moved closer to the cage and tried to catch the sparrow's eye, but like any other bird, it had no interest in meeting my gaze.

"She won't know you," Lord Fellstone said. "She's nothing but a sparrow now."

"This is my mother? It's really her?" I didn't believe him. If she was wearing a windrider, she had only to scrape her claw to change back. How could she not know who she was? I never forgot myself when I became sparrow-me.

"Once her transformation was complete, the windrider dropped from her, and she flew back here like a homing pigeon," he said.

"I don't understand."

Lord Fellstone's eyes went to the windrider dangling from my neck. I had meant to leave it in my room, or at least hide it under my blouse, but somehow I'd forgotten. I did sometimes wonder if the windrider had a mind of its own, and did not wish to separate from me any more than I wanted to be separated from it.

"You've used the windrider," he said. "Have you not sensed its power? Do you feel like a bird sometimes?"

"No!" I said. But my "no" trailed off and ended in a sound that resembled a chirp. I slapped my hand over my mouth. I didn't want to listen to him, and I tried but failed to prevent the sudden realization from flooding my mind. The whistling, the nesting behavior, eating seeds and almost even a beetle… I had to admit he was right, even while I was Tessa I displayed all the traits of being a bird.

"It's remarkable, isn't it?" he went on. "But unless you give it up or learn to control it, the windrider transforms its owner into a bird, permanently." He reached over abruptly, grasped my chain, and yanked it off my neck.

"Give it back!" I cried out.

"You see what a grip it has on you already? You can't bear to part with it. But I won't take the chance of my daughter ending up like her mother." His tone softened. "I can teach you to control spells instead of their controlling you."

I looked at the poor sparrow sitting in her cage. *Mama, is that you?* I leapt forward and unhooked the cage door, pulling it wide open. "Fly, Mama!" I cried out.

She fluttered out of the cage and swooped up to the ceiling, where she settled onto the chandelier.

"She'll return when she's hungry," his lordship said.

"Change her back!"

He gave me a look that sent prickles down my back.

"Please," I said. "My lord, I beg you."

"I cannot change her back." His face was pale as he sank into a chair by the door. "Leave me now. Return what you stole. Only then will I consider requests."

I knew I would gain nothing by pressing him further. Before leaving, I glanced up at Mama. She seemed content resting on the chandelier. But I silently swore I would find a way to restore her, even if it took a lifetime.

ASH

He woke during the night, well after darkness had settled over the room. Gradually he made out the shape of the crib that was meant for Tessa but never held her. A disturbing thought flashed through his head: *what if her mother had never taken her from the castle?* He wondered how the insidious influence of her father might have changed her. It was hard to imagine her any different than she was, but who better than Fellstone to crush every ounce of virtue inside a person?

A stab of pain shot through his side when he shifted in the bed. Worse than that were the feelings of fatigue and weakness that enveloped him. But he knew he must get up and move to another part of the castle. He forced himself into a sitting position and began to contemplate his next steps. The darkness would help conceal him as he moved about, and with some effort, he hoped to keep himself from dwelling on the persistent throb of his wound.

He took out Calder's map from his pocket and looked at it again. Before he'd been so intent on finding Ratcher, he hadn't noticed Tessa's bedchamber. Calder had marked it with a "T", and used the words "DO NOT ENTER" to designate the nursery. The rooms were beside each other.

He wondered if she might be there. For her sake, he fervently hoped she'd made it out of the castle. If so, the room would be empty now. They would have searched for him there earlier; Ratcher would've thought of it, if not the soldiers. Hopefully they would not think to inspect it again. He could hide safely in her chamber a while longer, as he gathered his strength and formed a plan. If, however, she hadn't managed to escape... he might put her in danger by coming to her. He would have to take that risk, because she could already be threatened, might already need his help. The more he thought on it, the more he realized this was not a choice. He *must* go to her room, *must* do everything in his power to learn her fate.

He listened at the crack to confirm all was silent, before opening the door and peering out. He glimpsed no movement or shadows. Holding Scarface's dagger before him, he stole out into the hallway and crept forward until he reached Tessa's room. He let himself in.

Though he knew it was for the best, heavy disappointment filled him when he discovered the place empty. No lamps were lit and the fire had gone cold; it did not appear that she would be returning. He slumped down on a chair by the table, and took a handful of walnuts from the basket. It came to him that the pang he felt at his waist was a result of hunger as much as the effects of his cut. The light scent of roast pork further stirred his appetite, and he looked up for any sign of the meat itself.

That was when he saw it. Calder's bag, left right out on the table beside the fruit basket. It was a wonder he hadn't noticed it immediately, but his mind wasn't working at full force at the moment. His eyes shot around the room. "Calder?" he whispered. No answer came.

It gave him hope. Calder would never be far from his bag, unless it was taken from him, and if that were the case, they would not have left it here. Moreover, if Calder was nearby, perhaps Tessa was also.

They were still a team, and his help would be wanted. He needed to be stronger.

Ash finished the walnuts, and ate a pear, an apple, and two oranges, briefly wondering where Fellstone could have gotten oranges this time of year, particularly ones that tasted so juicy and delicious. The food would hold him for now. He stood and walked toward Tessa's bed, nearly stepping on a beetle on his way there. He sat on the bed, wondering at its softness. If one could float on a cloud, it must feel like this. He glanced once more around the room, feeling the soothing effect of its beautiful furnishings caressed by moonlight. This, then, was how it felt to be rich. It was like falling under the spell of an evil seductress who only wished to steal your soul.

It occurred to him then that Tessa was no longer the daughter of an ordinary locksmith. Her mother was a noblewoman and her father, one of the richest and most powerful men in the land. *How can the son of the local sexton who earns his keep digging graves, ever presume to ask for her hand in marriage?* When word got out regarding her true parentage, the suitors would form a line outside her door. They would come from far and wide to lay their wealth and titles at her feet.

He snorted at himself. How ridiculous he was, letting his mind wander to thoughts of marriage. He was a fugitive inside an enemy castle, a hopeful assassin planning to attack and kill its most formidable occupants. Whether he succeeded or not—and he was painfully aware how small his chances were—there was little likelihood he would leave this place alive.

He noticed the beetle moving across the floor toward the table where Calder's bag rested. On second thought, it wasn't a beetle but a cockroach, which he supposed was some sort of beetle too. But he'd been confused because it ambled in a very un-cockroach-like manner. The ones Ash had seen before had shot past him like oiled lightning.

He watched it curiously and lifted the dagger, thinking of stabbing it, wondering if the flash of movement would get the bug running. He didn't like insects, though a cockroach was better than a spider any day.

The cockroach paused and almost seemed to be looking up at the table. It would be easy—too easy—to kill this slow-witted, slow moving bug, but he had no good reason for it. The cockroach was a poor, miserable creature, which, like Ash, had most likely been hunted and harassed ever since entering this vile fortress. Ash set down the knife and lay back on the bed. He would close his eyes to rest for a few moments. Then he would decide his next move.

TESSA

Two sentries followed me from Lord Fellstone's chamber and made certain I returned to my own. They positioned themselves on opposite sides of the door. "Thank you, I have no further need of your services. You may leave," I said, as if I really were accustomed to having my commands obeyed, as the privileged daughter of their lord and master.

They stared straight ahead and remained fixed to the spot, making it clear they would not be following any commands of mine. I went into my room, shutting and bolting the door behind me. A soft breeze from the window drew me to it. As I gazed out at the sky, I touched the place where my windrider ought to be, before recalling Lord Fellstone had taken it from me. I glanced back at the door, frowning as I pictured the guards standing sentry all night in the corridor.

At last I turned toward the bed and froze at the sight of a man lying on the quilt. A second later, I recognized him as Ash. *Who put his body on my bed?* I approached him with heavy steps, as my chest grew tight.

He opened his eyes and turned to look at me. My jaw dropped… a gasp emerged. This must have amused him, because he smiled and sat up, and then I knew, without a doubt, he was not some ghostly visage, but Ash himself, alive as he ever was. It was Ratcher who had told me he was dead, and I should have known better than to trust anything she uttered.

I didn't pause to think before I ran to him and threw my arms around him. He went rigid at first, probably from shock, but then he returned my embrace. I was so overjoyed to find him living, I just wanted to hold him, to feel his warmth and the life flowing through him.

"Ratcher said you were dead," I whispered into his ear.

He pressed me closer, and again I wished that he would kiss me. I tried to hide my disappointment when he drew back from me a moment later. I understood why; this wasn't the time to indulge our feelings. But for once I yearned for him to be less disciplined, to set aside duty and obligation for a little while.

Ash stood up. "She only—"

"Shhh," I interrupted. "There are guards just outside my door."

"She only wounded me," he whispered. Keeping his voice low, he explained how he and Ratcher had dueled, and how he'd escaped later by killing the boarman.

"Thank the gods you're alive," I said. "How do you feel?" I looked at the cloth wrapped around his waist, with a small circle of dark red where his blood had seeped through.

"Better. I can manage," he said. "Tell me how it went with you and Calder."

With a heavy heart, I spoke of the spell that had transformed our friend. Ash gave an odd look as if there were something he wished to say, but he kept silent. I told him then how I'd used the dreadmarrow to bring Papa back from the dead. I didn't say how different Papa seemed, because that might sound as if I were ungrateful for the gift he'd received of a second chance at life. Lastly, I described my encounter with Lord Fellstone, and the state of my poor mother.

Ash walked to the table and began to look around. "We can't wait," he said. "Fellstone isn't going to bargain with you. Perhaps your mother is safe for now, but Calder runs the risk of getting eaten or stepped on. I don't think he knows how to be a proper cockroach." He looked into Calder's bag. "Here he is," Ash said.

I hurried over to his side. Inside the bag, resting on one of the many vials, was a cockroach. "Calder?" I said. Needless to say, the cockroach didn't respond. "I suppose it must be him. Somehow he was drawn to his own bag."

"I'm sure it is," Ash said. "He didn't run like a normal cockroach."

"Well, good," I said. "This makes things easier. We have one of them. We just need to get my mother."

"We have to kill the lord. According to Ratcher, it's the only way to break his spells."

I wasn't sure how I felt about it. The man was evil, no doubt. And yet he was my father. Even if I'd never known him as such… even if he'd never filled that role for me… there seemed something terrible and unnatural in the thought that I might be the cause of his death. But I had no other ideas for saving Mama and Calder.

"How would we even go about it?" I said.

"The man is flesh and blood, isn't he?" said Ash.

"He has powers that protect him." I hesitated. "But he seemed quite ill when I saw him. I'm not sure why. Perhaps he needs to use the dreadmarrow every day."

"You think he might die without it?"

"I don't know. We have to keep it from him as long as he refuses to help us. We should leave here with it tonight. And we must take Mama and Calder with us, to keep them safe."

Ash looked reluctant. Waiting went against his nature, yet he must've known how little chance he had of killing Fellstone, even in the man's weakened state. After a moment, he nodded.

I felt about on the floor in the wardrobe until I found the invisible dreadmarrow. I brought it to Calder's bag and tucked it on the side, trying not to disturb Calder the cockroach.

"What're you doing?" Ash said, staring with a baffled look.

I remembered that he'd never seen—or rather, never *not* seen—the invisible Calder. "Invisibility powder," I said.

"I get it. One of his magic tricks."

"Not magic," I said. "It's—"

"Alchemy?" Ash said, smiling. He picked up Scarface's thick-handled dagger and stepped toward the door.

"Don't forget the sentries," I said. "And Lord Fellstone took my windrider." I knew what we would have to do, but still I hesitated.

"I'll kill them both," he said, not looking quite as confident as he sounded.

"You might manage one, but not the other. And I wouldn't be much help. In any case, I don't think we can do it quietly, and the castle would be alerted. We'd have no chance after that." My eyes shifted to the tapestry that hung from the wall beside the hearth. Strangely, I dreaded what I'd seen in my vision—myself bound and alone, at the mercy of a demon with a knife—far more than I feared any supernatural beings. Though both might reside beneath the castle, for all I knew. Still, the passage was our only chance for escape.

"I believe there's another way," I said, going to the tapestry. I lifted it from the corner, and found the door behind it. Ash came up behind me.

"It leads underneath the castle. There should be a similar passage to Lord Fellstone's anteroom. But… it may not be safe."

"No route is safe," Ash said.

"I mean… I was told there were monsters," I said.

Ash shrugged. “We faced one before. At least you did. My turn now.”

“Let’s hope it doesn’t come to that.” I turned toward the door.

“Wait,” he said. “Take this.” He handed me the long dagger he’d been using, with symbols carved into its handle. “I took it from Scarface,” he added, seeing my look.

“Don’t you need a weapon?”

He looked around the room. His gaze stopped on the fireplace tools by the hearth. “This will do.” He grabbed the iron shovel.

I tucked the knife into my belt and pushed against the entrance to the passage, which had no knob. It didn’t budge.

“Try again,” said Ash.

I leaned my shoulder into it. Suddenly the door came unstuck and opened inward. I nearly fell into the passage, only just managing to grip the edge of the wall to steady myself. I stepped over the frame and held the door open for Ash.

He handed me a lighted lamp before joining me in the passage. Letting the door close behind us, I had a moment of panic, seeing that there was no knob on this side either. Ash pushed back on it and we found that the door swung both ways. If all were the same, we would have no trouble entering his lordship’s chambers, if we could find the passage that led there.

Before taking a step, I held out the light to look around. We stood in a cramped space between the walls, at the top of a narrow, winding iron staircase, rusted with age. Of course, we would need to go down to end up under the castle. I exchanged a glance with Ash and was about to proceed when he moved in front of me.

“Let me,” he said.

I didn’t argue. This was one time when I was happy to let him play the hero. He tucked the shovel under his arm, held Calder’s bag with his left hand, and gripped the iron rail with his right as he began his descent. I followed his lead, holding the lamp with my free hand.

The place stank of mold and decay. I would have liked to cover my nose, but I didn't dare let go of the rail. Several of the iron stairs wobbled under my weight, and I wasn't sure if they would hold. It might've been my imagination, but I thought I heard a low moan in the distance. It could not have been the wind blowing through the tunnels, because the air was still and hung over us like a stifling blanket.

Ash was halfway to the bottom when the step broke under his foot. He dangled for a moment, clutching the rail and trying to hang onto Calder's bag. He found purchase on the step below, but in the meantime, his shovel fell from under his arm and clattered all the way down to the bottom. He looked up at me in disgust with himself.

"Do you think anyone didn't hear that?" he said.

"We'd better be quick," I said. He lifted me down to where he stood, and from there we moved swiftly to the ground below, where Ash retrieved his shovel. The passage at the bottom went in one direction only, so we were not delayed by the need to make a choice yet. The narrow width forced us to travel single-file, and Ash had to keep his head bowed to avoid scraping the ceiling. He insisted on leading again, and I insisted that the one in front must carry the lamp to light our way. As we moved forward through the cramped space, we also seemed to be moving downward. I struggled to fill my mind with pleasant thoughts to keep from imagining the horrors we might find so far beneath the castle.

Before long, we came to an iron door at the end of the passage. It wasn't locked, but Ash opened it cautiously to check what was on the other side of it, before ushering me through. It appeared we'd entered an enormous cavern. Ash held up the lamp, but we could not see the far side, and its ceiling, bathed in darkness, was high above us. For me it was a welcome change after the confinement of the tunnel. We agreed we must be well below the inner courtyard, and that, perhaps during a siege, weapons and supplies were stored here. Broken and rotting crates were stacked against the wall beside us. This had to be the meeting place if all hope was lost, and the castle was to be evacuated. There must be one passageway—which we would need to find later—that led outside.

"If we go left, the first door we reach should lead to Lord Fellstone's chambers," I said, basing this on how our rooms were laid out above.

Ash nodded and handed me the lamp. He hooked Calder's bag on his shoulder, raised the iron shovel, and gave me a reassuring smile. I held the light in one hand, and the dagger in my other. We stepped forward, keeping close to the wall. Soon we noticed strange wet, white deposits on the ground, which resembled bird droppings. At first they were small, but then we saw a much larger pile ahead of us. Ash and I exchanged puzzled looks.

"Wait here," he said. He moved forward to make a closer inspection of whatever it was.

I knelt and peered at the smaller deposit nearest me. I wasn't sure, but it looked as if there were small bones and maybe even a tooth in the midst of the white goo. Something whooshed above me, making me look up. I let out a shriek when a horrid creature, a snake with wings like a bat, flew down from above and landed a few feet ahead of me. Somehow it balanced with as much as a third of its body sticking straight up. *I hate snakes.* But this was worse—menacing and unnatural—the way it blocked my way, confronting me.

I moved slowly backwards. The creature's neck flared wide, looking like a hood around its head. It hissed at me. I retreated further, but the thing slithered toward me. I held up the lamp... undeterred by the flame, it just kept coming. I thought about using my knife, but the strike of a snake would be faster. Another step and

I was pinned against the cave wall. The creature sprang forward, but before its fangs reached me, Ash came out of nowhere and slammed its head with his shovel, crushing it.

I breathed again.

"It's a slitherbatt," he said. "Have you seen any others?"

I shivered and raised the lamp. We peered toward the roof of the cavern high above us. *Is it undulating?* It was dark and I couldn't quite make anything out, except a vague sense of motion. I glanced at Ash, whose nervous gaze did nothing to reassure me.

As we watched, another slitherbatt dropped from the ceiling, and I realized it had been hanging upside down, as a bat would. What if there were some sort of trellis up there, for them to coil their tails around? If there were two, there could be thousands.

Ash and I turned to each other. "Run!" I said.

We took off side by side. The motion must've attracted the creatures; they began plummeting by the dozens, landing all around us, skidding toward us. One dropped on my arm, and I cried out, shaking it away, losing hold of the lamp. It broke hitting the ground and went out. *I can't see anything.* But I could hear the horrifying swish of their wings, and the crunch of gravel as they wriggled over it.

Ash was ahead of me, swinging the shovel from side to side, whacking slitherbatts out of our path, clearing a way for us. I followed behind him as well as I could, my eyes gradually adjusting to the dark. But suddenly I felt a sharp sting as one of the creatures struck my thigh and punctured my flesh. I stabbed at it with the dagger, tearing its wing, and it let go of me, falling to the side. Its bite had gone through my clothing; maybe that would lessen its effect. I had no doubt its venom was poisonous. *How much did it take to kill a person?* I prayed we would not die today. Not here. Not now. But when I tried to follow Ash, I stumbled, sank down on my knees and fell onto my side. I couldn't move my limbs. I tried to call out, but my mouth hung limp. Only my eyes were still able to dart from side to side. I couldn't see Ash, couldn't even hear him anymore. He must not have seen me fall. Or worse... so much worse... he too had been struck and lay as I did, helpless to save himself or me.

But then, I couldn't believe it, the slitherbatts rose into the air, and flew back toward the roof of the cavern. I said a prayer of thanks inside. I'd thought they might all crowd around and eat me, but that wasn't the way snakes ate, and I was too big for any one of them. Now I wondered if they were only defending their territory. If I could only move... I focused all my thoughts on lifting one hand, but it just lay there. What happened to the power that shattered Lady Nora's glass? I cursed myself for not taking lessons from Lord Fellstone when I could have.

That was when I saw it, descending toward me. Its giant mouth open, exposing sword-like fangs. Its body the width of a tree trunk; its tail trailing far behind. Its wings spread as wide as my house. The blood drained from my face, and the hair lifted from the back of my neck. It lowered itself to the ground along the path that had been cleared, undulated toward me, and opened its mouth wide. I was going to die in the belly of a snake.

Ash dove to the ground beside me and snatched up the dagger from my inert hand. I think the giant slitherbatt would have struck him, but its mouth was unhinged for swallowing. He ran behind its head, leapt on its back, and plunged the dagger into the snake's right eye. The beast howled in agony. Ash clung to its hooded neck while he tried to shift sides. The snake whipped its head, causing Ash to slide down, but still he hung on. He clawed his way back up, using jabs with the knife to hold himself in place. He hung perilously from the beast's neck as he thrust the dagger into the second eye. The viper wailed and snapped its head backwards.

Ash flipped off the creature and landed hard. He looked dazed as he struggled to pull himself back up. He staggered toward me as the slitherbatt reared its upper body, preparing to strike. Ash had only one thing—the dagger—and he threw it at a boulder not far from us. The clatter drew the animal's attention, and it struck where the dagger had landed. Ash wasted no time, but grabbed me up and tossed me over his shoulder. He raced to an open doorway—the next passage—and laid me down inside it, several yards from the entrance. To my horror, he spun around and ran back out to the cavern. In the second it took me to wonder why, I realized the answer. Calder's bag was still out there, with Calder the cockroach inside it.

My head lay facing the opening to the cavern, and I watched as seconds later, Ash came into view again, backing toward the passage, holding Calder's bag in one hand, the iron shovel in the other. The creature slithered toward him, faster than before, driven by rage. Its open mouth shot forward and Ash smashed a fang with his shovel, keeping it from sinking into him. But at the same time, something sprayed out of the creature's mouth, covering him in a fine mist. He turned and dove back into the passage as the slitherbatt sprung at him again. Its yawning maw struck the stone surrounding the entrance to the passage, and it dropped back in pain and misery.

Ash slammed the iron door shut. He turned toward me before dropping onto his knees, clapping his hands over his face, and moaning in agony. I knew then the venom had gotten into his eyes. I felt the most helpless I ever had in my life, lying on the ground, watching him suffer, unable to lift a finger or even utter a word of comfort. He remained like that for some time until at last, mercifully, the pain must have lessened, and he lowered his hands.

"I'm blind," he said. Even at our lowest moments, his voice had held more hope than it did now. I struggled to form a response, but it was futile.

"Tessa?" he said. He reached down and picked up Calder's bag. Feeling the walls of the passage around him, he made his way toward me. His foot found me, gently nudging against me. He knelt beside me, whispered my name again, and lifted my arm, which hung limp in his grasp. As he bent over me, his unseeing gaze stared past me. Red streaks crisscrossed his eyes.

He lowered my arm, threw himself on the ground, and buried his head in his arms. The sounds of weeping arose. *Cruel, cruel irony.* He'd blinded the viper, and the viper had extracted the identical revenge. Not an eye for an eye, but two eyes for two eyes.

It was not long before he stirred again. Even in the direst situations, Ash felt compelled to take action. He lifted his head and whispered the word, "Dreadmarrow." Calder's bag was beside him. He opened it and reached inside, being careful to move his hand slowly, giving Calder the cockroach ample time to move out of his way. At least his loss of sight would not affect his search for the invisible dreadmarrow. After feeling inside the bag for several moments, he pulled the wand out, grasping its imperceptible form with his fingers.

I could tell from his expression, now that he had the dreadmarrow, he did not know what to do with it. After thinking for a minute, he touched me again to feel how I was oriented. Then he leaned forward and held the dreadmarrow above me. "Abracadabra!" he said.

It was not the most inspired start.

He took my hand in his so that he could feel if I might move. Again he lifted the wand, and this time he waved it over me. "Unpoison her!" he said. "Bring her back to life!" He continued with a string of phrases all meaning the same thing, and waited a moment for a reaction from me. When none came, he said, "Read my mind, you stupid dreadmarrow!" He waved the wand up and down, and back and forth, across my body. He touched its tip against my forehead, chest, arms, and legs. But none of it did any good. He leaned back against the wall. "Please gods," he whispered. "Let her live."

I knew now that he believed me to be dead. I'd mourned his false death before, and now he would grieve for mine. Panic shot through me as the thought occurred that he might leave my body here, or worse yet, bury me. If only I could find a way to show him I was alive.

But Ash had a different plan. He stood up suddenly. "Fellstone," he said. "Fellstone can use the dreadmarrow to bring you back to life." He bent and found my waist to lift me over his shoulder. He took Calder's bag with his other hand and set off along the passage.

No! That's what I would've said if my mouth would only work again. *Don't do it.* Because giving me up and returning the dreadmarrow meant giving up on all of us. Ash would be sent back to the dungeon. I would receive better treatment, but my room would be as much a prison as his. There would be no one to save Mama or Calder. I would not have anything of value to bargain for their lives. Was this how our quest would end? We'd managed to save Papa, but for what? He would be miserable living alone without me by his side, and miserable contemplating the magic he owed for his life. What value was life without happiness?

Ash had to hunch over to avoid scraping my body against the roof of the passage, and he had to keep one hand against the wall to steer himself, but still he strode steadily, without hesitation. I knew from before that when he made up his mind to do something, nothing could stop him. He'd decided the only way to save me was to present me and the dreadmarrow to Lord Fellstone, and that was what he would do.

We soon came to the end of the passage, where it opened to the iron staircase that must lead to his lordship's chambers. The way did not stop here, as it did below my room, but continued in another direction. Of course, the lord of the manor would have his own direct route of escape, unlike all others in the castle, who would first need to survive the slitherbatt gauntlet. What hurt most, however, was the realization that our plan would've succeeded if Ash hadn't been struck blind, and me, made helpless by those creatures. We would only have had to fetch Mama before making our escape.

Ash found the stairs with his hands and started up them. They were wider and in far better repair than the ones which led down from Mama's former room. Carrying me made it awkward for him, but he clung to the rail and moved purposefully forward, one deliberate step at a time. When we reached the top, he set down Calder's bag and laid me on the landing.

Muffled voices came from the other side of the wall.

Ratcher said, "...did precisely as you instructed."

Fellstone, though he'd looked so weak when I saw him earlier in the evening, spoke in harsh, angry tones. "Then why didn't the elixir work? Look at me. I'm older, not younger. I would wonder if she's even my daughter, if I didn't feel our connection so strongly."

"If only you had your dreadmarrow—"

"Dreadmarrow be damned! I would not need it if the elixir worked as it ought."

"My lord," said Ratcher, "tell me what you would wish me to do. The blood of Fellstones also runs through me. I would drain my own veins of it, if there were any chance it would return you to your youthful vigor."

The blood of Fellstones runs through her. Is she... is she also his daughter... my sister? I recoiled at the thought. Besides, if she were... Mama would never have left her behind when she ran away. Ratcher and I were nothing alike. She'd shown herself to be wicked and cruel, many times over. *But*—the thought nagged at me—*so is Lord Fellstone, and he's my father.*

"Your blood is tainted," Lord Fellstone said. "It would never do. Your mother came of the sewers of Hardragon."

Of course. Her mother was not, *could not*, be the same as mine. Ratcher must be my half-sister. I wondered at his treatment of her, so different than the distinction he'd shown me. How did she feel to hear herself spurned? *No.* I would not allow myself to consider her feelings. Sister or not, she would never have my sympathy, not after what she did to Ash's brother.

"Fetch me fresh ingredients, and another dram of Teresa's blood," Fellstone continued. "Do not fail me this time. My patience grows thin."

I caught my breath. *My blood?* My face burned as fury welled up inside me. My hand shot forward of its own volition, and gripped Ash's leg. He started, losing his balance, barely managing to grab the rail and stop himself from falling. I saw that his face was ashen when he bent over me seconds later. Whether my sudden movement shocked him, or the knowledge of my father's treachery, I didn't know.

The voices in the chamber went silent. Had they heard the creaking of the rail? It appeared they had not, when a moment later, Ratcher said, "I'll go to her now, my lord."

"Bring it in the morning," Lord Fellstone said. "I will go to my bed."

"Of course, my lord. Good night." There were sounds of footsteps crossing the room, and doors opening and closing. It seemed the anteroom must now be empty.

After waiting a moment longer, Ash whispered into my ear. "I thought you were dead." Relief flowed out of him. "The poison's wearing off. I can see a bit."

He helped me into a sitting position against the wall by the door. "Do you think you can stand?" he said in low tones.

I tried lifting my leg, but although I could shift its position slightly, there was still no strength in it. He turned his ear close to my lips. "No," I managed to whisper.

"Wait here, then," he said. "I'll try to get your mother."

"Wait," I said weakly. "My pouch..."

Ash opened it and found the packet of sunflower seeds I kept in there with my picks and skeleton keys. I hoped if he held them out in his hand, Mama would fly to him. With that thought, a sudden feeling of elation surged through me. *We're going to succeed.* His sight was returning, and so was my movement. He would fetch my mother, and after waiting a little longer till I could walk again, we would escape. Fellstone, lacking the dreadmarrow or my blood, would probably die, and then Calder and Mama would also be free.

Ash straightened, turned to the door, and pushed cautiously against it, trying not to make any noise. When it was sufficiently open for him to slip through, he entered the room, leaving the door ajar behind him.

A light flickered on. "Seize him," Lord Fellstone said.

It was a trap. I heard noises in the room. Knowing Ash, he was putting up a struggle, but there had to be too many for him to fight.

Ratcher peered through the doorway at me, a smug look on her face. "Please," she said, "join us."

"Take him to the dungeon," said the lord.

"No!" I cried.

Two sentries came out to the landing, lifted me up, and carried me inside. Ratcher picked up Calder's bag.

Three more guards surrounded Ash, whose hands were now bound behind his back. Lord Fellstone stood near them.

"Let us go, and Mama too, and a certain cockroach... and you can have your dreadmarrow," I said. My speech came out slurred, my mouth still partly numb from the poison.

"Have you been drinking?" Ratcher said.

"Silence!" Lord Fellstone shouted. "Return my dreadmarrow by tomorrow noon, or he burns at the stake."

"What? No! You can't do zat!" I said, cursing my inability to speak clearly.

"I look forward to it. We haven't had a good roasting in some weeks." He turned to the guards. "Take them away. Her to the tower room."

Ash caught my eye before the three men transported him out. I thought the look was supposed to convey that I shouldn't give up hope, but it could as easily have meant, "Think hard, I have no idea what to do."

The guards who held me pulled me forward, expecting me to walk, but I stumbled on my first step.

"Carry her, you fools," Lord Fellstone said.

The guard with cold eyes lifted me and took me out of the room, while the one whose face was pockmarked followed behind. I thought about asking to take Calder's bag with me, but then dismissed the idea. Best to treat it as if it were of no importance. As they carried me away, I made certain not to glance at it. But I knew it rested by Ratcher's feet, and she would not be one to overlook it.

ASH

They were back where they began, he in his cell, she in her room. Worse, he now knew he would not be able to kill Ratcher, save Lance from being a wraith, or restore Calder to himself. The cockroach was inside the bag which had fallen into Ratcher's hands, and if she didn't kill him, no doubt a kitchen maid soon would. Tessa could not help anymore, without her windrider or the dreadmarrow, though in any case, the latter did not appear to be as valuable as they'd hoped. Lord Fellstone had made it clear he would not bargain for it.

As soon as the soldiers left him in his cell, Ash grabbed the jug of water and poured it into his eyes. It gave him some small relief, though they continued to throb. Still, it was nothing compared to the torturous burning he felt when the creature had sprayed him. Now, his vision had mostly returned, though it remained blurred, as if he was looking out at the world through a thin grey veil. But what had happened to his eyes paled in comparison to his anguish over Tessa dying, as he'd thought. He had been prepared to give up everything and everyone to save her.

He could kick himself now for his carelessness and stupidity. He should've checked her breathing. If he'd been thinking straight, he would've remembered snake bites could cause their victims to lose all motion. The venom must have burned right through his eyes into his brain. At least that excuse was better than none.

He leaned back against the wall and closed his eyes, picturing the one thing that had brought him happiness in all this: Tessa running into his arms. She'd truly been affected by his death, perhaps almost as much as he had been by hers. If he'd given into his feelings, he would've kissed her, would've held her in his arms so tight she might have lost her breath. He still felt he'd done the right thing by breaking away from the embrace. It would've been wrong to exploit her grief and take advantage of the warmth and affection she felt for a friend. He was grateful for the instant of joy she'd given him. It was what he would picture in his mind, tomorrow, on the stake, before he died.

TESSA

The guards switched lifting duties at the bottom of the long, winding staircase leading to the tower room. It was quite undignified to be carried at all, but I was not given a choice about it. When we reached the door, they took away my pouch, full of the tools of my trade, before dropping me unceremoniously on the floor inside the room. I heard the lock click after they shut the door on me. I was not at all concerned about the keys, as I knew I could be through the lock in no time whatsoever with the use of two hairpins, but I could tell from the lack of departing footsteps that the guards had remained by the door.

I looked around and recognized the room as the same one where I had seen Ratcher for the first time, healing Lord Fellstone with the dreadmarrow. There was a bitter irony in my ending up here, the place where it had all begun, after I'd foolishly flown up to the window to see what vile person had given the signal for the boarmen to chase down the pitiful man. I had my answer now. He was a monster without bounds, who would sip the blood of his own child to extend his wicked life.

I'd expected an austere sort of prison room, but instead it was luxuriously furnished just like my mother's bedchamber. The bed was smaller and not as ornate, but appeared no less comfortable. Most likely they had moved her here after her first failed attempt to run away.

I picked myself up off the floor. The effects of the venom had mostly passed—leaving only a sort of tingling in my bones—and I could move about freely again. I opened the window and looked down at the dizzying drop to the ground below. There would be no escape that way.

I checked the room for hidden doors, though I did not expect to find any, nor did I think I could take any more slitherbatt encounters if I did find another secret passage. I did not have to worry; the walls were solid and provided no exit.

I went to the bed and threw myself down on it. The dreadmarrow was in Calder's bag. I couldn't return what I didn't have. Moreover, I had no idea how long the invisibility powder would last, and even if it was still working, Ratcher could by now have felt out the shape of the wand inside the bag. Most likely I would have to make another deal for Ash's life. Lord Fellstone said he wanted to teach me. I could pretend to have a change of heart, make him believe I would cooperate with everything he asked of me. I must act as if I cared to be his daughter.

And then there was the matter of my blood. It explained the bit I found on the sheet when I first arrived. I wondered how much had been taken. At least he would have to keep me alive to guarantee a steady supply, though he might not care if his thirst weakened me. I wasn't certain if I should feel reassured or frightened that his health had deteriorated since I arrived. It might mean he would give up on the elixir and stop draining me, or the opposite: he could decide he needed a much larger amount.

My eyelids grew heavy. I'd barely slept since our quest began. Weariness settled over me, and despite my desire to work out a plan,

I found myself closing my eyes and curling up on the mattress. I was nearly asleep when a gentle sound, the fluttering of a bird's wings, drifted into my consciousness. It brought back the memories of my time as a sparrow, and I felt a deep longing to fly again. I opened my eyes and saw a crow perched on the table. First I thought I was dreaming, especially when the crow turned my way and looked at me as no crow would ever look at a person. But I knew it was real when the bird hopped down to the floor, scraped its claw three times, and transformed into Ratcher.

I sat up, suddenly alert. "Have you come for my blood?" I asked.

She approached the foot of the bed. "Don't tempt me."

"I heard him tell you to get it."

"No need. I have it already. I took it when you lay unconscious after the wraiths attacked you."

"I thought he already used that in his potion," I said.

"He thinks so too. But I took the liberty of exchanging it for something far better. We needn't discuss that. I came for the dreadmarrow."

It made my heart quiver to hear that she hadn't yet found it inside Calder's bag, though it brought me no closer to the dreadmarrow myself. "You may tell his lordship I'll return it in the morning in exchange for Ash's release," I said, trying to project more confidence than I felt.

"Give it to me and you'll get back your mother and cockroach friend as well," she said. "Oh, and that brother who's a wraith will be released."

"You can do that?"

"Those who live by the dreadmarrow, die by the dreadmarrow. If I destroy it, Lord Fellstone dies, and his spells die with him."

Her admission shocked me. "You want to kill him?"

"You can't seriously be surprised," she said. "I've been helping you all along."

"Helping me?"

"First I tried to frighten you into running away. That would've been your best option."

"Outside my house?"

"You insisted on coming anyway, and then I had to change tactics. Who do you think left the sparrow windrider for your invisible friend to give back to you?"

It surprised me that she'd detected Calder. But I needed to remain focused on what was important. "I don't understand why you would turn against Lord Fellstone," I said.

"I have my reasons."

I'd seen him act cruelly towards her. But he'd also trained her as a conjurer, and relied on her as a trusted adviser. Would she betray him with so little motive?

"Tell me how the dreadmarrow can be destroyed, and I'll do it myself," I said.

She laughed. "You can't do it. You're not a conjurer."

"Lord Fellstone said I was born to it."

"Do you really think it's so easy?" she said. "You would need years of training to access that power."

We were at a stalemate. She wanted the dreadmarrow and I would not give it to her. That she had Ash's twin murdered in barbarous fashion before his very eyes, was reason enough.

"If you wish to kill him, you must find a way to do it without the dreadmarrow," I said.

"Foolish girl, do you really think Lord Fellstone will ever allow you or your friend to leave the castle? You know too much and you've shown your willingness to defy him."

She had a point. *You know too much.* This was true. I particularly knew too much about her plans to murder her lord and master. She'd come to me with sword and dagger. As soon as she learned the location of the dreadmarrow, she would kill me. If I didn't tell her, she might torture me to get it out of me. And in the end, she would still kill me.

The crow amulet dangled from her neck. I forced myself not to stare at it, though I had a powerful urge to seize it and become a bird again. I stood up from the bed. "Why do you wear that mask?" I said.

"We were discussing the dreadmarrow," she said.

"Perhaps I'll give it to you if you tell me why you wear the mask."

"My beauty is so devastating it would kill those who would look upon it," she said. "Now tell me where it is."

"I'm not certain I believe that answer. Let me see for myself. I'm willing to take the chance of being struck dead." I took a step nearer and reached up as if I were about to pull off her mask. Her hands went up to hold it in place.

That was when I snatched the windrider, tearing it off her neck. I lifted it to my mouth to blow on it, but she grabbed my arm and clawed at my hand. I shoved her away and wrenched back my arm, still clutching the crow, as she drew out her dagger. I had no hope against her… she was stronger than me and armed with a knife. Only one chance remained. I sprang away from her, dove for the window, and leapt out of it.

Falling is so much faster than you think. I plunged toward the ground, blowing frantically on the windrider. Inches from impact, I became a crow but it was too late to transition into flight. I landed hard on the stone and all went dark.

ASH

He was at the swimming hole with Lance, who was already in the water. Ash grabbed the rope, ready to swing onto it, when Lance suddenly cried out. His head disappeared as if something were pulling him under the surface. Ash leapt and rode the rope out over the water, releasing above the spot where Lance went under. He plunged in and swam downwards, searching for his brother. Everything was perfectly clear, though the lake was usually so murky you couldn't see your own hand in front of your face. He spotted Lance some distance below him. An enormous creature with tentacles had hold of his leg, pulling him further and further into unknown depths. It struck him that the swimming hole had never been so deep. Ash swam down as fast as he could, and grasped Lance's hands. He pulled and pulled, but the creature was stronger, and Lance's fingers slipped from his grip. Ash was forced to watch helplessly while his brother was drawn to his death.

Ash opened his eyes, realizing it was a nightmare, but unable to shake the feelings it evoked. The dreams were always like this, with Lance the same age as Ash, as if he never died before now. The manner of his death changed from nightmare to nightmare, but Ash's failure to save his brother remained constant.

He slept no further after that. It was still dark when he heard the rattle of keys at the door. Two guards entered and released him from his chains but kept his wrists and ankles cuffed. They lifted him to his feet and dragged him between them.

"Where are you taking me?" Ash said.

The guards exchanged a smile. "Not far. But don't worry. You won't be coming back here."

He felt a weakness in his stomach, but he held himself up. He was going to die, that much was clear. The thought that Tessa had not returned the dreadmarrow sent a pang of sorrow through him, but he shook it off. Most likely she did return it, but Fellstone betrayed her. No one could trust the word of such a man. Once he had his precious wand back, nothing could prevent him from killing Ash, smothering a bird, crushing a cockroach. Ash did not think he would harm Tessa, so at least there was that to comfort him as the flames approached and seared his skin.

When they reached the outside, they made him walk, but movement was slow as he shuffled forward with his feet bound together. They had not gone far before he looked up and saw the platform with logs heaped up high upon it, and the stake where he would be tied. A deep shudder took hold of him, and he stumbled. He probably would have fallen on his face, but the guards held him up until he was steady again, and then pushed him forward.

They reached the viewing platform, where Lord Fellstone himself was already seated in the center. He wondered if he should feel honored that the ruler of the realm considered his death of sufficient importance, that he would watch it himself. An aristocratic-looking couple sat to one side of Fellstone, and a very old lady to the other. The lord himself looked older, weaker, and more bent than he had only last night. Three young people around Ash's own age stood to the side looking excited to be allowed to watch his roasting.

"Here's a rare treat for us," the older-looking boy said.

"He's very young, Malcolm. I wonder what he did," said the young lady.

"He attacked Ratcher, but she had no trouble beating him down."

"Defeated by a girl," the other boy said. "No wonder. He's a lowly gravedigger's son."

The young woman giggled. "That's convenient. His father can bury him at no cost."

As the guards pulled Ash onto the stand, Ratcher mounted the viewing platform. He heard her speak to Lord Fellstone: "My lord, has the girl returned your book and dreadmarrow?"

"She has not," Fellstone answered. "Her friend will suffer for it."

Ash wondered what Ratcher was talking about. Tessa hadn't said anything about a book. If there was a stolen book, he would put money on lying Ratcher having taken it herself. Which meant the return of the dreadmarrow might not be sufficient to save his life, even if Tessa were to arrive with it this very minute.

As the guards began to tie him to the stake, he looked around but caught no sight of her. He could not believe she had not even come. *Had she refused to hand over the dreadmarrow?* No, he couldn't doubt her. If she wasn't here, then something had gone wrong, something had happened to her. His feelings changed from fear for himself, to fear for her.

The guards finished tying him to the stake and stepped down from the stand. Ash strained at the rope, but they'd done their work well. There would be no escape for him.

Lord Fellstone gave the signal to start the fire.

TESSA

I woke in complete darkness feeling utterly disoriented. *Where am I? What am I?* Not human, that was certain, but I didn't quite feel like sparrow-me either. And then the memories came flooding back. *Ash.* I had no way of knowing how much time had passed, or if daylight had dawned. It was dark here—wherever here was—but outside it might be midday for all I knew.

I needed to act with urgency in the hope that all was not yet lost. I realized I must have transformed into a crow at the last moment before hitting the ground. I felt my larger size compared to being a sparrow, and moreover, I was infused with feelings of aggression that I'd never experienced as sparrow-me. Under normal circumstances, it might take time to grow accustomed to this strange new form.

But I had no time. I needed to escape from wherever I was and find a way to save Ash. I beat my wings and found myself in a tight space. It felt like scratchy cloth covering me; it seemed she'd put me into a burlap sack. I poked all around me, searching for the opening. Before long I found the place where she had tied a tight knot. I stabbed it with my beak and clawed at it with my foot, but the knot held firm. I wanted to scream with frustration, but I had to hold myself together, for Ash's sake, and I had to be quick about it. I walked the length of the sack again, and this time I noticed a pinprick of light, revealing a tiny hole in the material. Excited, I bit down on a loose thread and yanked it hard. I alternated between jabbing my beak at the hole, and picking at the threads, creating a wider opening until finally it was large enough for me to slip through.

Light seeped in from an open crack. *Let it be no more than the color of dawn.* I was inside a drawer, which would crush me if I tried to transform back into myself. The drawer had not been quite shut, perhaps to allow me air, or more likely by accident. The gap was too narrow to allow me passage, but I thought if I pushed on the drawer, I might widen the opening enough to squeeze through it. I pressed and pressed against the wood, without moving it at all. I tried flinging myself at it, but that was a mistake which only resulted in an aching head. I went back to pushing, though it was futile; I lacked the power to force the drawer open. I hammered at the wood with my beak, as if I were a woodpecker, and made a small notch, but at this rate, it would take hours to create a hole, if that were even possible.

My heart sank with despair. I'd run out of ideas for how to save myself and Ash. Stuck inside this wooden trap, I would not be able to return the dreadmarrow in time. If I were human now, I would have shed a torrent of tears, but instead only a half-hearted croak came out of me.

That was when I remembered I had a voice. So often I forgot that I could "speak" as a bird, even if I didn't understand the language. It was another long shot, but at least it was one more thing to try. I let out a caw, startling myself by how loud it was. Of course, a crow has a much bigger sound than a sparrow. I cawed over and over, an angry, desperate call.... There had to be a kind soul in the castle who would free a crow... *and save Ash's life.*

When I heard the click of a door opening, I crowed faster and louder. A moment later the drawer was pulled open and light flooded in from the room. I flew out instantly, right past the boarman with half an ear—not exactly who I had pictured coming to my rescue, but he served the purpose just as well. He stared at me in confusion, no doubt believing I was Ratcher, and wondering how I'd managed to get myself trapped inside a drawer.

I circled the room looking around. Ratcher had dumped out the contents of Calder's bag on the floor. Where was the dreadmarrow? The boarman was beginning to get curious about my activities, and I knew I must act fast. I landed on the floor to check under the furniture. A moment later, I spotted the dreadmarrow beneath the bed, fully visible once more. It must have rolled away when everything splattered on the floor, and she had not been able to see it. As I flew under and snatched the wand with my beak, I saw Calder cowering next to the wall. I ran to him and gathered him up with one of my claws, hoping I hadn't terrified him. It wouldn't do for his tiny heart to give out. I turned back to find the boarman on his knees, his horrid, tusk-y face staring at me. He reached under the bed to snatch me up, but I backed out the other side, using a one-footed hop to avoid hurting Calder. The dreadmarrow was heavy for me, and I wobbled a bit as I took flight, but once I opened my wings wide there was no stopping me. I flew out the window to the open sky.

Outside, I sniffed the acrid smell of smoke and beat my wings harder. A thick grey plume rose from the courtyard. *Am I already too late?* I flew like lightning to the place above the platform in the inner courtyard and stared down at the pyre. The flames had not yet reached Ash. But there was barely a moment to spare before they would. I swooped down, landed on the edge of the roof nearest the pyre, and set down Calder beside me. I turned back into myself and raised the dreadmarrow.

Ash saw me and called out my name. Rivulets of sweat coursed down his forehead, as the flames worked their way toward him.

Malcolm and Lady Nora were staring at me, open-mouthed. I called out to Lord Fellstone. "Here it is. Put out the fire!" I said.

He stared at me. "Where is the book?" he shouted.

"Book? This is all I have," I said. Ash cried out as the flames licked his feet. "Put out the fire!" I screamed to anyone who would listen.

Lord Fellstone turned his face away from me.

"I didn't take any book!" My gaze shifted to Ratcher, standing behind her master, her expression amused. She had the book. But how could I convince Lord Fellstone of that in time?

I held the dreadmarrow closer to the flames. "Put out the fire or I'll throw your dreadmarrow into it!" Ratcher had told me I didn't have the power to destroy it; I prayed that was another one of her lies.

Lord Fellstone, looking weaker than ever, rose with difficulty. He held a post to steady himself. A minute more and everything would be over for Ash. I pretended that I was about to hurl the dreadmarrow, though I didn't intend to throw it at all. If I did, I would have no further bargaining tool against the tyrant.

"Foolish child! Destroy the dreadmarrow and all its cures will be undone. Your locksmith will die," Lord Fellstone said.

Papa will die. Of course he would. Ratcher told me as much. *Those who live by the dreadmarrow, die by the dreadmarrow.* I hesitated, swaying, perilously close to falling, ripped apart by two appalling choices.

Ash cried out, "Don't do it, Tessa!"

"Lord Fellstone—the greatest conjurer the world has ever known—has opened his generous heart to you," the lord said of himself. "Reject his benevolence, and feel his wrath."

I looked at Ash, my heart breaking.

Lord Fellstone focused his steely eyes on the crow amulet. I had wrapped its chain round my wrist, and as I watched, it came suddenly unraveled and fell to the ground below. Immediately after, my hand jerked open and the dreadmarrow flew out of it, moving steadily toward Lord Fellstone, who extended his own hand to receive it. I felt shock… and then fury beyond anything I'd ever felt before. I glared at the wand and it stopped in mid-air. I glimpsed a look of astonishment on the lord's face, as the anger inside me took control of the dreadmarrow, and propelled it deep into the flames.

Had I actually bested Lord Fellstone in a magical duel?

"PUT THE FIRE OUT," he roared.

Soldiers and boarmen raced to retrieve water from the central fountain. But the first to return tossed the water onto Ash, misunderstanding his lordship's intention.

"Not there! The wand!" Lord Fellstone bellowed. His men ran off to fetch more water. Boils erupted all over Lord Fellstone's face, scalp, and body, and he turned toward me. "Look what you've done, horrid child! I curse the day you were born!" He whirled around to face Ratcher. "Do something!"

She leaned over Lord Fellstone and whispered into his ear. Then she stepped back and smiled as he contorted from the agony of infection, overwhelmed by the rot and corruption inside him. When his hand stretched out to her with clutching fingers, she drew away, leapt down from the platform, and darted toward the castle.

Lord Fellstone plummeted from his lofty position. His head cracked against the stone beneath, and blood sprouted from the wound, flowing over his scalp. He writhed on the ground as more blood seeped from all his pores. With a final spasm, he grew still.

The wand was reduced to ashes. I felt a sudden pain in my arm. The sprain that was healed by the dreadmarrow had returned.

Calder sprung up from the cockroach beside me and nearly toppled from the roof. With my good arm, I grabbed his coat and hung onto him. He settled back, turning to me, and I flung my arms around him, despite the pain in one of them. "Calder!" I said.

"What happened?" he replied, entirely baffled.

"Oh, you were a cockroach and lots of other things," I said.

"I do have a distinct memory of the floor being much closer to my eyes than normal."

He and I turned our attention to what was happening all around us. A knight rolled Lord Fellstone's body over to find his eyes open and unblinking. "The Conjurer Fellstone is dead!" he called out.

With a flash like lightning and a poof of smoke, the boarmen separated into men and boars. The boars sprinted toward the forest, squealing and grunting, while the men sprawled on the ground, dazed. Fiend became a German shepherd, which cavorted happily, and a crocodile that ran for the fountain and climbed into it.

The fire was extinguished, though Ash still hung limp at the stake. A ghostly Lance ascended from the ground, looking like a real thirteen-year-old boy, no longer a wraith. Ash closed his eyes as Lance's body floated through his, seeming to pause there for a moment. Ash's face changed, as if the contact with his brother infused him with new strength and confidence. Lance continued rising and drifting upward, along with other wraiths' transparent forms, until they all disappeared into the smoky mist.

The soldiers returned to their true natures, and the atmosphere became one of celebration and liberation. "The Conjurer Lord Fellstone is dead!" was the joyful refrain that passed from mouth to mouth. Two knights jumped onto the smoldering pyre, cut Ash loose, and removed his bindings. Several others helped Calder and me down from the roof.

Ash and I ran into each other's arms.

"Your father…" Ash began and then paused. He feared naming Papa's fate in front of me.

My eyes filled with tears. "I had to let him go." He'd told me himself, he didn't want any life that came of the magic of Lord Fellstone. What I gave, I had to take away. The death of one, for the lives of three. Who was I to play like a god with life and death? Why had such a decision been thrust on me?

Ash's gaze shifted to the viewing platform. I turned back and saw that Ratcher was gone. "Go," I told him. "Find her before it's too late."

At that very moment, a soldier tossed Ash the sword that had belonged to Papa. It seemed like a sign from the gods. Ash hesitated no longer, and set off toward the castle.

Calder walked up beside me. "Your mother?" he said.

"She was a sparrow," I said. "In my father's anteroom. Can you find her?"

He nodded, and seeing that I had no strength for the task at the moment, he went without me to seek her out.

I dropped down onto a step and buried my face in my hands. I wept for my papa, who I'd restored to life, only to send him back to his death.

ASH

Lance is free. It was all he could think of as he raced toward the castle entrance after Ratcher. When Lance drifted through him, it had been an unbelievable feeling. It was as if all the anger and misery that had filled him since the day Lance died was suddenly converted into strength.

Ratcher came running out carrying a large, ornate book. *The missing book.* She didn't notice him until it was too late. He raised his sword and spoke the words he hoped never to have to repeat to her a third time: "*From ash you came, to Ash you return.*" He blocked her way.

She gave a weary sigh, dropped her book, and drew her sword. "This time I shall kill you," was all she said.

Ash surged into attack without even noticing that his hair hung down. He'd had no time to secure it into a ponytail like Lance's. Ash was on fire, though not in the way Lord Fellstone had intended. He slashed and pivoted and rammed his way forward against Ratcher, who despite her considerable skill, had to back away. He came into his own as a swordsman. With acrobatic strength and grace, he swished and swashed, feinted and parried, cut to the left and cut to the right. Ratcher had no time or breath to torture him with her cruel insinuations this time.

Weakening, she slowed in her responses. He slashed her wrist and the sword fell from her hand. She was defenseless as he struck her once through the side. He was ready to plunge his sword into the putrid thing that passed for her heart, when he remembered how she had humiliated him by cutting the tie that bound his hair. Fair play was fair play. He slipped the tip of his sword under the strap that held her mask to her face, and sliced it through. The mask fell to the ground and he stepped on it, dragging it back with his foot before she could snatch it again.

He didn't know what he'd expected her to look like, but certainly not this. She had thirteen long scars, each one beginning around her eyes, nose, and lips, and continuing in a straight line outward to her scalp. She was like a picture of the sun, with the center of her face forming a circle from which the rays shot out. The scars formed thick lines, as if the cuts had been quite deep, and he suddenly wondered how she could have withstood the pain.

She dropped to her knees and bent her head.

Ash lowered his sword, his revenge played out, drained of any desire to take another's life. He was about to turn away when he saw her crawl toward the book. He whirled around and speared the ground in front of it, blocking her hand, before bending and whisking the book up himself.

She turned and limped away.

TESSA

I Anxious to find Mama, and worried for Ash, I didn't allow myself to indulge my grief for long. I looked up from my tears, ready to follow my friends into the castle. But instead I saw Ratcher, bleeding, crawling away from Ash, her face revealed for the first time. I stared in shock at the marks that distorted her features, and told a tale of suffering and torture.

My vision went dark for an instant, and suddenly, a line on my right cheek burned with agonizing pain. *The monster of my nightmares had cut me.* I wanted to cry out, though I knew there would be no one to help me. When sight returned, I found myself bound to the table inside the vile cavern. This time, I knew I was not at Fellstone Castle, but someplace even darker and more menacing. I licked the moisture on my lips and it tasted of blood. The hooded creature passed in front of the candle and footsteps crossed the floor. His knife shimmered in the dim light, and I knew he had returned to make the second cut.

I heard a terrible scream. Someone shook me, and I realized the cry had come from me. Ash was bent over me, trying to calm me while I trembled uncontrollably.

"It's okay," he said, rubbing my arms. "You're okay."

I whipped my head around, searching for her. *Ratcher.* She was creeping still, but her pace had increased. She seemed to have her eyes on some quarry.

Then I saw it too. The crow amulet, lying on the ground below the roof, where Lord Fellstone had forced me to drop it.

"The windrider!" I called out.

Ash saw what was happening, but he hesitated to leave me in this state.

"Stop her," I said, and that was enough for him to spring to his feet and race after her. She heard him coming and dove for the windrider, somehow finding the strength inside her weakened frame. Before Ash could get to her, she blew three times in rapid succession and became a crow. Despite her injury, she took to the air, flapping her unsteady wings to lift herself beyond Ash's reach. A moment later, she soared round the castle wall.

I prayed to the gods I would never see her, or her terrifying memories, again.

CALDER

As he made his way past the banquet table in the Great Hall, toward the entrance to Fellstone's anteroom, Calder was surprised not to feel any hunger yet. But he decided it was better not to dwell on what he might have eaten as a cockroach, which had satisfied his cravings so completely. He was overjoyed to be a man again, and happy to bury that sad chapter in his life when he lived as a bug.

For perhaps the first time in many a century, the entrance to the conjurer's chambers lay unguarded. His stomach tingling with fear and anticipation, Calder hurried up to the door and let himself in. A feeling of elation rose inside him as he spied Faline sitting in the corner of the room. She looked almost as she had when he last saw her, with hardly a line to indicate her age. But at the same instant he realized, with a sinking heart, that she was not herself.

She'd positioned herself near the bird cage, which he thought was no accident. Most likely she'd found it difficult to separate from her home of the last twelve years. She had gathered pillows and piled them into a sort of nest, which formed her seat. Empty seed shells were scattered around her. She whistled a birdlike tune as her head bobbed to and fro with rapid, jerky movements, while she kept a lookout for potential predators.

She was a sparrow in human form.

"Faline." His voice was gentle.

Her face flashed with panic and she shrank into her nest. He slowed his pace as he approached her.

"It's me, Faline… Calder."

Her whistling changed to a loud, angry birdsong, warning him to keep his distance. She beat her arms like wings and seemed puzzled at their failure to lift her off the ground.

"I won't hurt you," he said, sitting down on one of the pillows near her to show her he was no threat. He held out his hand for her inspection.

She sniffed the air in his direction and looked at his hand. Her whistling softened as she grew accustomed to him, perhaps even sensing that he was familiar to her. He drew a little closer and she did not protest.

Twelve years as a bird. *How long would it take to become human again, if that were even possible?* He knew he should not be greedy. She was alive and healthy in body if not in mind. The outcome could've been far worse. And yet heavy disappointment rocked him, to see her there, and yet not there.

"Come with me," he urged. "Tessa is here. Your daughter." He touched her arm, which launched a spirited round of chirping, but at least she did not recoil from him. Perhaps somewhere deep inside, she recognized the name that must be dearest to her, and for that reason, she allowed him to help her up, to hold his arm around her back, and lead her toward the door.

TESSA

I will never forget the moment I saw my mother again. Ash and I were watching as Ratcher flew away and disappeared from our view, when I noticed the two figures emerging from the castle. My gaze shifted and locked on Mama, who looked exactly as I remembered her, although it was possible my memory was influenced by the portrait in the gallery. For a moment I stood frozen in place, and then abruptly I felt my legs move underneath me with a will of their own. But as I ran toward her, I received the first inkling that all was not as it should be. Instead of opening her arms, she clutched them around herself, and bobbed her head.

I slowed as I reached her, and Calder, touching my hand, said, "Give her time."

She looked at me curiously, and sniffed the air around me. I felt certain she recognized me, but the bird instincts which had taken over kept her skittish and afraid of contact. She let me rub her arm.

"Dear Mama," I said. "It's me, Tessa. You're safe now. Lord Fellstone is dead."

She seemed to brighten, and she whistled a few notes. I would need to have patience, no doubt, but I felt confident she would recall how to be a person soon enough, and her time as a bird would fade into distant memory.

#

It was a clear blue-sky day with a gentle breeze when we buried Papa. Mama and I wore black, naturally, and stood together with our arms linked. She still could not speak, and the level of her understanding was equal to that of a young child. She trusted no one but Calder and me. We'd managed to coax her out of the house for the funeral, but she clung closely to us, and would not make eye contact with anyone else. As I gazed at her anxious face, it seemed to me that although I'd wanted to get back my mother… someone who would protect and cherish and advise me… I had returned with a daughter instead.

Papa's coffin lay beside the freshly dug grave. The chaplain muttered something over it, but I wasn't listening; my thoughts were elsewhere. Papa's death, and my role in it, continued to haunt me. I could not change the choice I'd made, and I knew inside that if I had it to do over, I would choose the same again. Yet I wished with all my heart the choice had never fallen on me.

Mr. Oliver stood apart on the other side of Papa's grave. He blew his nose into his handkerchief several times during the service. I thought he must be the only one whose loss was nearly as great as my own. Perhaps I would be able to entice him into a game of backgammon from time to time. If anyone's company could bring me closer to my absent father, it was his.

Calder and Ash were just behind Mama and me. Ash's parents had also come, along with many other townsfolk. I didn't even recognize some of them, but I was grateful for their presence. It made me proud to know Papa had earned the respect and friendship of so many.

Today was the first time I had seen Ash since our return. We'd been busy preparing for Papa's burial, but I thought he would come by the house, at least in the evening after his work was done. He should have known he would always be welcome in my home, but if he believed he needed an invitation, I would give him one now. I turned his way after the chaplain finished speaking, and workers began to lower the casket into the grave.

"Will you come see us this afternoon?" I said.

He stiffened. "I... I wouldn't want to intrude."

"Don't be silly. I'd like you to be there." *What is wrong with him?* He was acting as if we were strangers.

"Okay. Sure. I'll come by later," he said.

I was about to rebuke him and insist he come right now, because, after all, we'd faced *slitherbatts* together, and nothing could be more intimate than that, but I was interrupted by Ryland, of all people. He called out my name and hurried over to us, stepping directly between Ash and me.

"I'm really sorry about your father," he said.

"Thank you," I said coldly.

He looked at Mama, who was now leaning on Calder's arm.

"Is that your mother?" he said. "Hello, Mrs. Skye." He held out his hand.

She chirped.

Ryland, looking confused, dropped his hand and turned back to me. "I'm sorry I didn't go with you, Tessa. I hope you understand. You could've been killed. I only wanted to protect you."

"Sure. I understand," I said.

He grasped my arm and lowered his voice into my ear. "My feelings haven't changed."

"Well, that's one of us," I said. I pulled my arm back and went to my mother's side. Ryland stared at me a moment longer before turning away. I looked around for Ash, but he was gone.

ASH

He circled the town twice before resolving to go to Tessa's house and get it over with. Enough time had passed that his hair and coat were soaked, though the rain had only fallen in a light drizzle. It didn't matter; he would not be staying long. There was nothing between them and there never could be. Best if they both moved on as soon as possible.

He'd made up his mind during the sleepless nights since they returned from the castle. She was a noblewoman now, which made her as inaccessible to him as if he were the earth and she, a star. Despite that, he knew if he were to offer her his hand right away, she might accept, but it wouldn't be long before she came to regret it. When he married, it must be that he had something of value to offer his wife, but in this case, he could never hope to compete with the rich and powerful suitors that were sure to arrive any day now.

He should have made an excuse when she spoke to him at the funeral and asked him to her house, but he had not been quick-witted enough to come up with one. Now he was stuck having to go, but he would prepare a reason in advance why he could not stay.

As he dragged his feet 'round the corner, he spied an official carriage in front of her house, bearing the Fellstone coat of arms. He thought about turning around immediately, but curiosity got the better of him and he continued to the door.

Calder answered Ash's knock and ushered him inside. "Lord Fellstone's steward, Sir Geoffrey, is here," he said.

Mrs. Skye sat on a pile of straw in the corner, making her birdlike movements. Tessa was seated at the table across from the steward, a thin, balding man with a white beard. Calder led Ash to the fireplace, where they both sat down and listened to Tessa's conversation with the steward, though they pretended not to.

Sir Geoffrey explained that Tessa would inherit all her father's wealth—the castle and everything inside it, his treasury, and his many other land holdings. He went over with tremendous glee just how wealthy Tessa would be, beyond anything she could possibly imagine. He spoke of the suitors who would come from far and wide, and how she must be careful as many would seek to deceive her. Ash thought she purposely avoided looking at him when the word "suitor" came up. The steward told her there were official documents to be drawn up, and later to be signed, before she could move into the castle, and that all this would take some time. They would also need to confirm her identity and that of her mother, and this too would cause a delay in the proceedings. He said her mother's mental incapacity created some difficulty, since she could not speak for herself, but in the end it wouldn't matter because she clearly was Lady Fellstone, as evidenced by the portrait hanging on Lord Fellstone's wall. Sir Geoffrey explained that performing these services was a part of his job as steward of Fellstone Castle, and that he hoped Tessa would do him the honor of keeping him on in that capacity once the transfer of property was complete.

Ash couldn't help but see the pleasure in Tessa's face as the steward spoke to her. He did not begrudge her that. Few could resist the offer of a castle at their disposal, and the riches that came with it.

She would have all the gowns and jewelry she could desire, though when he thought about it, she had not shown any real affinity for those things. Like it or not, she'd have to dress for her new role, spending her days mingling with others of the ruling class, and nights dancing until dawn with young lords and counts and marquis and whatever else they liked to call themselves. There was no place for him there.

Ash waited until Sir Geoffrey presented a document for Tessa's signature, and while she was bent over that task, he slipped away.

TESSA

Who would've thought I would set out for Fellstone Castle as the locksmith's daughter, and return as the heir to the conjurer lord and his massive fortune? I was stunned when Sir Geoffrey came to tell me all that I would inherit. Was it wrong to feel some happiness over this stunning reversal? I couldn't help but love the thought that my family would never want for anything, and that it would be within my power to help the people of Sorrenwood become prosperous again.

It annoyed me when Ash left without a word. He could've waited a little longer; the steward left soon after he did. All of this... *craziness...* had nothing to do with the way I felt about him. He ought to know the money meant nothing to me, except in the power it gave me to perform good works and help others.

After supper I walked to Ash's house. His father came to the door and told me he'd gone out to Krieg's Tavern. I went there next, though I'd never been inside it before in my life. The sounds of music and raucous celebration spilled out from the windows onto the street. I supposed they must be drinking to the death of the tyrant.

Inside, people were closely packed and the floors were sticky with ale. I forced my way through to the counter and looked around as best I could. I spied Ash at a table in the back, and began to make my way toward him, until I saw who his companions were. Anna sat beside him, and her twin Margaret was across the table next to Ryland.

As I stood for a moment staring at them, Ash glanced my way. A strange look flashed in his face… some combination of guilt and shame… but he stubbornly forced away all feeling until his features were blank again. He averted his gaze as if he hadn't seen me.

Later, I couldn't remember how I got out of the tavern. I had a vague recollection of a drunken man stumbling into me and taking the opportunity to grope me as I passed. I gave him a brisk shove that toppled him. The tears began as soon as I reached open air. They mingled well with the hard rain that started to fall as I crossed Higgins Bridge. When I reached home, I found Mama asleep on her nest, but Calder, who was staying in Papa's room, sat by the fire reading "The Trials of Kallos." He gave me a curious look when I told him the wetness on my face was due to the downpour. I closed myself in my room, tore off my clothes, pulled on my nightgown, and got into bed. I wouldn't allow myself to weep anymore, but I could not keep the image of Ash's arms wrapped around me from seeping into my dreams.

#

A week later, Calder and I sat together by the fire in the late afternoon, while Mama swept the floor by the table. She liked to keep busy but could not yet read or go out by herself, and so I'd taught her some simple chores to do inside the house. She particularly liked the broom and would sweep for hours on end.

"How were you able to force the dreadmarrow from Fellstone?" Calder said. We were speaking of events that had taken place at the castle for the first time since returning home.

"Perhaps Ratcher helped me," I said.

"She wanted him to die?"

I nodded. "She was supposed to provide my blood for his elixir... but she told me it came from someone else."

Calder stood and poured himself some whiskey. "At the castle morgue, I learned Ratcher stole blood from a dead man. I suppose if you drank that in a potion, you might feel quite dead yourself."

"Between that and not having his dreadmarrow... it was enough to weaken him."

Mama paused abruptly by the window to look out at a bird that was singing. I couldn't see it from where I sat, but I thought it sounded like a sparrow. She whistled back at it.

I turned to Calder. "It must be very hard for you to see her like this."

"Hard for both of us."

Why did he compare my feelings to his own? Anger rose up inside me, at Calder and others like him—self-righteous men who made decisions based on their stodgy notions of what was honorable.

"You love her, don't you?" I blurted. Without waiting for an answer, I barreled on. "Then why did you let her go to Lord Fellstone? Why didn't you run off and marry her yourself? Did you think she would never love you because you were cook's son? Or because of some other imaginary shortcoming you perceived in yourself?" Perhaps, given his height limitations, it was not the best choice of words. But still I went on. "Why not tell her how you felt?"

"I was going to," he said quietly. "Until she said she was madly in love with somebody else."

His words stopped me short. "Not Fellstone...?"

He shook his head. "A handsome young man of her acquaintance... a fortune-hunter, as it turned out. He disappeared as quickly as Faline's parents could threaten to disinherit her."

My heart went out to Calder. "I'm sorry," was all I could think of to say. Rejected so many years ago, and yet here he was, her loyal servant still, though she could no longer even say his name. We glanced her way as she settled into her nest, arranging some bits of cloth around the center.

"Do you remember I promised to tell your fortune?" Calder said.

"I think I would rather not know it," I said.

"Let me have a look."

I held out my right hand to humor him. "Does it matter which one?"

"If this hand is gloomy, we'll try the other." He traced a line on my palm. "Where it forks," he said, "the line that veers off is stronger than the other. It means you will leave Sorrenwood."

"Will I?"

He concentrated on my hand. "I see you settling far from here. It's a lovely place, with rolling green hillsides and a clear river running through the valley. You live in a beautiful house, full of love and warmth. Your mother is there with you. And your husband." He threw me a sly glance at that.

"And who might that be?" I asked in a nonchalant voice.

"Seeing into the future is not like reading a book. There are no names, only vague images of what is to come. You must figure out for yourself who he might be."

I drew back my hand. "Well, it all sounds very idyllic. But I can't leave here."

"I beg you to consider it." His manner grew somber. "You understand the death of Fellstone will attract other conjurers to our land?"

"The thought has occurred," I said.

"Leave while you can. It's the safest path."

"I have something to ask you." I went to my room and returned with "The Conjurer's Book of Incantations," which Ratcher had been so anxious to take away with her. "What do you think I should do with this?" I said.

"Have you looked inside it?"

I shook my head. "Not for lack of trying," I said, demonstrating the book's refusal to open when I pulled on its cover. "Lord Fellstone must have set a spell to keep it closed."

"Burn it," Calder said. "Conjuring brings nothing but wickedness."

"Is magic wicked, or the conjurers who bend it to their evil purpose?"

"You cannot separate one from the other."

"How will Sorrenwood defend against the conjurers that will come?"

"The town has Fellstone's battalions. It isn't up to you or me. Soldiers are needed." He nodded his head toward the fire. "The book?"

I brought it to the hearth and stood for a moment gazing down.

"A bit closer, I think," said Calder.

I dropped the book into the blaze and watched as the flames rose up around it.

TESSA

Mama was asleep in her nest when I slipped from my bed and tiptoed into the main room. Calder snored with a rumble and a wheeze inside Papa's room. The fire had gone out. I took Papa's heavy garden gloves and approached the hearth. I reached into the embers, and drew out the book from underneath them, blowing away the ashes on top of it.

The book was undamaged, as I knew it would be, since I had tested it with a candle flame the day before. It had to be protected by a spell. I wondered again why the dreadmarrow had no such defense. I could only speculate that either Ratcher had somehow removed it, or I myself did it without understanding how, when my mind seized control of it out from the lord.

I felt a twinge of guilt for deceiving Calder. I was testing him when I asked what I should do with the book. If he'd encouraged me to keep it, I would've opened up to him about my plans. But since he chose the opposite… I knew it would be best not to confide in him. In any case, no one should know that I would be teaching myself magic. The element of surprise could not be overestimated. Naturally Calder wished to protect me. No doubt he saw me as a child. It would take time for him to get to know the person I'd become during our quest, following the dangers I'd faced, and the knowledge I'd gained about my own origins. I didn't feel anything like a child anymore.

My thoughts flashed to the cave where I was helplessly bound, bleeding from the first cut to my face, and filled with terror as the demon returned with his knife to slice me again. I nearly cried out, though I knew now it wasn't me in that vision, but Ratcher. Somehow I'd read her memories. Whether because she'd purposely forced them on me, or due to some bond we had as half-sisters, I had no idea. The one thing I knew was that it was no mere nightmare, but the true image of how Ratcher's face came to be as it was.

Is Lord Slayert that demon? I didn't know, and I prayed never to find out. At the same time, I knew I must be prepared should he march on Sorrenwood. Only a conjurer could beat another conjurer. He would sense me and seek me out, whether or not I had the power to defend against him. And thus I knew, I must develop my skills before it was too late. My father—Lord Fellstone—had told me conjuring was in my blood. I lacked only the knowledge to direct its purpose.

The shadow of movement outside drew me to the window, where the light of the moon set off the trees in a haunting silhouette. It was only a bird—a hawk, in fact—landing on the old oak nearest the house. The hawk settled onto the branch with its profile turned in my direction, but it was too far to tell if its eyes were closed, or fixed on me. I could not have said whether or not this was the same hawk whose attack had driven me to Fellstone Castle and initiated all the events that had followed, but if it was... well, stranger things had happened since then. For now, I took it as a sign of how much I still had to learn.

I believed that knowledge was strength. At the moment, I could not open the conjurer's book, but I was the daughter of a locksmith, and I had not yet found a lock that could keep me out. I would find my way into its secrets soon enough.

The End.

ACKNOWLEDGMENTS

My heartfelt gratitude to these wonderful writers who've kept me motivated throughout the years with their feedback, friendship, advice, and encouragement:
Ilo Orleans, CV Herst, Lisa Mammal, Mike Sundy, Jill Ferguson, Patricia Houden, Vandy Shrader, Kris Newby, Jocelyn Osier, Cathy Thrush, Ken Kuwayti, Ken Sharp, Nada Djordjevich, Alexandra Amarell, Sheila Bonini, Laura Browne, Cindy Cheung, Linda Martin Collery, Vicki de Mey, Quanie Miller, Anton Gill, Harvey Jacobs, Allen Rosenberg, Jerry Sexton, Debbie Steinmetz, and Julie van den Hout.

Thank you to my wine group for being the place where we can talk about anything, no matter how weird. You keep my writing life fueled: Giuliano Carlini, David Cox, Vicki Cox, Laura Draxler, Susan Rendina, John Sadler, Frank Sarnquist, and Lori Trippel.
Truth comes out in wine. -Pliny the Elder

A special thanks to screenwriter Donna Brodsky, whose talent, kindness, and never-say-die attitude continue to inspire me.

Sheri Davenport, I couldn't have made it this far without you. Accomplice and ally, travel buddy and writer/reader/sympathizer. *Thank you* for following this path with me.

Undying gratitude to Maria Jose Fernandez-Sarabia Bischoff, dear friend and fellow crazy person, who, if there were fairness in the world, would've outlived me.

Much love to my American and Turkish families for their patience and support: George & Harriet Benedict, Bill & Kay Liscomb, Jim Benedict, Ahmet & Huriser Kaptanoğlu, and Sabahattin & Mine Günceler. Mom and Kay, I can never thank you enough for the thousands of words you've tirelessly read, and the myriad of ways you've made my writing better.

To the four men at the center of my universe—my husband Sinan and sons Tanner, Alan, and Derek:
A man travels the world over in search of what he needs, and returns home to find it. -George Moore

ABOUT THE AUTHOR

Marjory Kaptanoglu is a screenwriter and novelist. Her scripts have won the Grand Prize in the Cynosure Screenwriting Awards, Slamdance Film Festival, International Horror & Sci-fi Film Festival, and Harlem International Film Festival, and have been recognized by the Academy Nicholl Fellowships in Screenwriting. The indie films produced from her scripts have screened at major international film festivals, winning several awards.

Marjory is the author of two other novels and expects to complete the *Dreadmarrow Thief* sequel in 2019.

Before turning to writing, she worked as a software engineer at Apple Computer, where she designed the text-editing software for early versions of the Macintosh. She graduated from Stanford University with a B.A. in English, and continues to reside in the San Francisco Bay Area with her husband and a massive hound named Samson.

To contact Marjory, join her newsletter, or learn about her upcoming novels, visit marjorykaptanoglu.com or fb.me/marjorykaptanoglu.

Please consider submitting an online review of *Dreadmarrow Thief* wherever you purchased it.

66251580R00152

Made in the USA
Columbia, SC
20 July 2019